The Prada Plan 3: Green-Eyed Monster

The Prada Plan 3:
Green-Eyed Monster

Ashley Antoinette

www.urbanbooks.net

Urban Books, LLC
78 East Industry Court
Deer Park, NY 11729

The Prada Plan 3: Green-Eyed Monster Copyright ©
2013 Ashley Antoinette

ISBN 13: 978-1-60162-537-3
ISBN 10: 1-60162-537-5

First Printing February 2013
Printed in the United States of America

10 9 8 7 6 5 4 3

Distributed by Kensington Publishing Corp.
Submit Wholesale Orders to:
Kensington Publishing Corp.
C/O Penguin Group (USA) Inc.
Attention: Order Processing
405 Murray Hill Parkway
East Rutherford, NJ 07073-2316
Phone: 1-800-526-0275
Fax: 1-800-227-9604

Introduction

Fuck life. That's how this shit feels to me right now—
like death, like I'm living in hell on earth. As a man,
how do I take this shit? Life was good in New Yitty. A
few years ago the only worries I had were getting and
spending bread, while making sure I kept my nose
clean. Now those days seem to be long gone. Life is full
of sleepless nights, bags have formed under my eyes,
and burdens weigh on my shoulders. I'm aging before
my very own eyes. And for what? In the name of love,
right? I used to think so, but now I'm not so sure.

Before YaYa I was cold. Handled women the way
that I handled the streets—calculating and efficient,
but never getting too close to the fire to avoid being
burnt. But when she walked into my world I broke all
of the rules, ignored the signs that she wasn't the one,
just because I wanted to convince myself that she was.
Now, I don't know what the fuck this is. I can't call it.

The day I saw YaYa I knew I had found a bad bitch.
Excuse my language. I mean no disrespect, but I'm giving you that real-nigga shit right now. Green eyes, skin
with the honey tint, wide hips, fat ass, with the slick lip
to match. She was a straight-up East Coast chick, and
I felt the arrow pierce my heart from Cupid's bow as
soon as she flashed her pretty smile. I remember how
my heart stopped beating in my chest at first sight. Despite me playing it cool, I knew she was my equal.

Shit was official when I started ignoring texts from ten others just to be with this one girl. I knew then that she had me. She had no clue what she did to me, but I had never been more sure of anything in my life. There is something about a man when he's chosen his bitch—that one woman, his ride-or-die. He becomes territorial and will go to the end of the earth and back for her. Pop any nigga that disrespects her.

Now, I'm no sucker for love. I know you've seen that type. You ladies probably run all over that type. Spend his paper then ignore his phone calls because he gave you everything too fast. Nah, that's not the kid. I'm the one you look at your phone every half hour to see if I've hit you with a text yet. The one that you diss your home girls for because you would rather cake it than hit the town. I'm the man that will cop you the new whatever—shoes, handbags, cars—just so you can go to the hood and stunt on all the chicks that hated on you during your come-up.

It took a special woman to make me go to that level, however, and before I met Disaya Morgan, I had done these things for no one. I wasn't into cuffing a chick, never had been, but she was different. I fell under her spell almost instantly. We were supposed to have our hood happily ever after. You know how it goes. She was supposed to be my Bonnie. Ride shotgun in the foreign whips. Take trips to exotic spots and fuck under the stars on the beach as the waves washed over our toes. All that good shit. Pop bottles in clubs as we sat on our thrones and the hood kissed the ring of the king. King of New York, king of Houston, king of anyplace I occupy because I boss up everywhere I go. I chose YaYa as my queen. On some G shit, I even forgave her after she crossed me repeatedly, because she was the source of my heartbeat. When she walked into a room, I was proud because every head turned to admire what was mine. We had that real black love once upon a time. Not the corny type, but that real hood love affair. Shit could have been good . . . epic . . . and life would have been grand.

So why couldn't we have all that? Why are we living in a nightmare? How did shit go so far left? I understand every girl from the ghetto has a past, but YaYa's past is more like the present because it never stays in the rearview. It haunts her, haunts us, haunts me.

I've got to be real frank with y'all right now. . . . I don't know how much longer I can hold on. Shit's real different around my way lately. She's different. I'm on hard times. The DEA is breathing down my back, just waiting for me to show them my hand so they can slip a silver bracelet around my wrists and lock me up for life. On top of that, money's low. Money's damn near gone. When you're used to living grand, small money don't go as far as it used to. Then there's YaYa. Her entire essence is different. Since the fire, she's . . . she's . . . not YaYa.

After everything she's been through, I would be wrong to leave. Right? But I don't want to stay out of obligation. I want the connection that we used to share. The one that felt real . . . right . . . I don't know. Something's just off with her. She's not herself . . . but I'm no storyteller or griot in the least, so I'ma pass it to someone who can spin the tale so y'all can feel it. First you heard YaYa's side, then Leah's. I won't call this my story because I'm not a limelight type of nigga. I prefer to play the back, stay low key. Let's just say that there are three sides to every story: YaYa's, Leah's, and the truth.

Now, there's only two people on the planet that can tell it to you with authenticity. They're from where I'm from; they move how me and my lady move. They're the best at what they do. I believe y'all know them: Ashley and JaQuavis. Well, JaQuavis is busy penning his next classic, so he's going to let Ashley take this solo. So without further adieu, I'm handing it over his Mrs.—*New York Times* bestseller, Ashley Antoinette. Do your thing, ma.

Chapter 1

"I don't understand why she hasn't awoken yet. It's been a month. Is she going to make it, Doctor?" Zya asked, watching as her medical staff catered to YaYa's injuries. She stood with her hips cocked and one hand tucked in the silk pocket of her Zac Posen editor pants as she impatiently awaited an answer.

The doctor took his time in replying as he concentrated on taking YaYa's vitals. The buzz of the many machines that she was connected to indicated that she was alive, but she had yet to open her eyes. "Doctor?" Zya pushed insistently. She crossed her eyes and gave him a stern look, demanding a response.

The elderly Indian man removed his stethoscope from his ears, hanging it from his neck, and then turned to his employer. He had been on call for Zya since she graduated to queen pin status. In her line of work she needed someone with his medical expertise on her team, and he had proven very useful to her—until now. Now it seemed that no matter how much he attended to YaYa, she just wasn't getting better.

In a lot of ways, YaYa reminded Zya of herself. They each possessed a heart the size of a lion and a hustler's spirit. Zya hoped that YaYa found the strength to pull through.

"I don't know, Ms. Miller. Every burn has been attended to. My nurse has met all of her physical needs. We just have to wait and hope that she comes out of this coma. I have worked with some patients who never come out of them, and others who recover in no time. Just be patient," the doctor said as he packed up his medical instruments and left the room.

Zya sighed as she stood over YaYa. "It will be such a shame if you don't make it out of this. You don't even know the greatness that lies in your future. All you have to do is wake up," Zya whispered solemnly. YaYa's eyes flinched slightly, and Zya squeezed her hand gently. "I know you hear me, YaYa. Get your strength up, ma, and come back to the land of the living."

The sudden blare of the machine rang out in the room, startling Zya. She gasped in shock and stumbled backward. The numbers on the heart monitor dropped drastically, and alarms summoned the doctor back into the room.

"What happened?" he asked as he rushed to YaYa's bedside and immediately began to attend to his patient.

Zya's mouth fell open, yet no explanation came out as she shook her head frantically. "I . . . I don't know. The machines just . . ." She paused and shrugged her shoulders in confusion as wrinkles creased her forehead in concern. "They just started going off. What's going on?"

"I'm losing her!" the doctor called out. "Start chest compressions," he ordered a nurse who entered the room in haste.

Zya was pushed aside as she watched the doctor try to bring a dead woman back to life. After what YaYa had been through, it would take nothing less than an act of God to stop her from walking through death's door.

***

YaYa stood on the threshold between the living and the dead as she desperately fought the slow, inevitable fate that awaited her. The stench of burning flesh plagued her as her incinerated skin melted away. She could still feel the flames engulfing her. The orange-and-red fire struck her like lightning bolts and nipped at her soul like a rabid dog as the polluted smoke destroyed her lungs. She tried to resist, fought to breathe, but the more she struggled, the worse the pain became.

I'm dying, *she thought.* Please, God . . . help me. *It was a name that she had called upon many times before, one that she wished she had praised more often throughout her life.* If I had more faith in Him, maybe my life would not have turned out this way, *she thought as tears slipped from her eyes.*

Disaya Morgan was in a subconscious state, stuck between darkness and light, yet she felt the pain that she had endured pulsing through her all at once. It all culminated inside of her in this moment. Her life was flashing before her eyes, and all she saw was a string of painful memories: the fire, her child's kidnapping, the loss of Indie, the death of her mother, the silver shackles on her father's wrists, being raped as a child. It all came back to her at once, pouring over her, drowning her in sorrow. Everything turned black as her mind spun. Her heart beat so rapidly it felt as if she had stampeding horses inside of her chest.

"Please, God, help me. For once just save me," she sobbed as she fell to her knees in desperation. She knew that she was dying. She felt life's force leaving her, her energy and will to live abandoning her. It was as if she was being drained, like she had a slow leak and her soul was seeping out.

Her surroundings went completely dark as a voice filled her ears.

"The reason why your precious God never answers your prayers is because you're not his child."

YaYa recognized the voice before she ever looked up to see who was standing before her. Her heart skipped a beat.

"Mommy?" she called out as she raised her head. Her mother, Dynasty, stood before her.

"Hi, baby," Dynasty replied as she knelt before YaYa and stared into her face.

YaYa hadn't seen her face in years, but she remembered every feature as if it were yesterday. Dynasty was striking, and YaYa's heart fluttered anxiously as she looked at the most beautiful woman she had ever had the pleasure of knowing.

"Mommy?" YaYa repeated, her lip trembling. "Am I dead?" YaYa asked as she began to sob.

Dynasty nodded her head as she knelt before her daughter, cupping YaYa's face in her hands. "Yes, baby girl, you are dying," she confirmed.

"Is this heaven?" YaYa asked.

"Do you feel pain?" Dynasty asked.

YaYa nodded her head and held on to her mother's forearms while crying in extreme excruciation. "Yes . . . so much that I can't take it. I feel it all. I remember it all," she grieved.

"You're in hell then, baby. This is it. Dark, lonely, but most of all it's painful. Hell is not the fiery myth that man has made it out to be. It's just pain . . . eternal pain," Dynasty whispered solemnly, knowing all too well that her sins had led not only herself but also her child to this very place.

"Oh God!" YaYa cried. "My daughter . . . she needs me. I can't die, Ma. I don't want to go to hell. I don't deserve to be here! I need more time . . . time to take care of her. Time to make things right." YaYa was

hysterical as she thought of never seeing Skylar's face again. The mere notion of not being there to raise her child was suffocating. It felt as if the devil himself had plunged his hand inside her chest and torn out her heart.

"There are no do-overs, YaYa. Once you're here, you're here. Even if you're sent back for a little while, you'll eventually come back. Forgiveness and retribution are for God's children. Once the devil touches you, you're his offspring, and it's hard to go good once you've already gone bad. It's like a loaf of bread: once it stales, ain't no saving it.

"You're my daughter. If you're anything like me, not even God can save you. We're too hardheaded to live righteous. We want what we want, when we want it, and we'll use what we got to get it," Dynasty said as she smiled. YaYa could see her thinking back on years past to the good old days. Dynasty shook her head and said, "That damn Prada Plan."

YaYa pulled away from Dynasty and looked up at her in confusion. "Why would you teach me that? You're my mother! You're supposed to teach me the right way, guide me the right way!" YaYa yelled.

Dynasty cocked her head to the side and put one hand on her hip. "No, no, baby girl, you got to be accountable for your own actions. I gave you the game, but you applied it your way. I said, 'Use what you got.' You've got a brain to think. Did you use that? You've got a conscience to decipher right and wrong. You use that? You chose to work the sweet spot between your legs to get by. You chose the easy route. You could have been anything. Your Prada Plan could have taken you to the moon and back. You chose—"

"To be like you," YaYa cried. "I am my mother's child, but I won't end up like you."

YaYa closed her eyes and held up her hands to the sky, crying hysterically while on her knees. "God, please forgive me, Father, for I have sinned. I need you right now, Lord. I need you to wrap your arms around me and please take me back to my daughter. Take me back to Indie. God, spare me with your love. I know that I haven't spoken to you like I should. I haven't believed in you like I should, but I'm here now. I'm here, not to ask you why so many bad things have happened in my life, but to ask you for the chance to live so that I may learn the lessons that come with those bad times. Please, God, please! Save me, for I am your child. . . ."

***

"Charge to ten!" the doctor ordered as he waited to shock YaYa's heart for the third time.

"Help her! Do everything that you can!" Zya demanded as she stood in the background, anxiously watching the heart monitor screen. YaYa had been flatlined for more than two minutes, and Zya was losing hope.

"Clear!" the doctor called out as he placed the defibrillator on her chest and sent a charge to YaYa's heart. Her body jerked off of the bed slightly, but her pulse didn't change. The doctor pulled back and looked at Zya sympathetically.

"She's gone, Ms. Miller. I'm sorry. She's been under too long. There's no bringing her back from this. You just have to let go," the doctor said.

Zya shook her head and said, "Again. . . . Do it again."

"Ms. Miller . . ." the doctor protested.

"Do it again! I pay you enough to make miracles happen! Do it again, damn it!" Zya yelled, losing her cool, something that was uncharacteristic for her.

The doctor shook his head, feeling like it was a lost cause, but he followed her orders.

"Charge to twenty!" he instructed. The nurse charged the machine and then the doctor called, "Clear."

YaYa's body jerked violently once more, lifting off of the bed slightly. Zya bit her bottom lip, and the room went silent as everyone stared at the heart monitor.

"Come on, come on," Zya urged. She closed her eyes and dropped her head, but as soon as she was about to give up . . . *Beep* . . . *Beep* . . . *Beep* . . .

YaYa's pulse showed up on the screen, faintly, but it was there. The doctor looked back at Zya in amazement, knowing that the odds of YaYa coming back to life were slim. "There's that miracle you asked for," the doctor remarked as he stabilized YaYa.

Zya sighed in relief, not sure yet why she was so invested in this young girl. "Will she be okay?"

The doctor nodded his head and replied, "We'll monitor her closely to make sure that she doesn't code again, but for now her heart is beating. That's all we can ask for."

Chapter 2

Leah sat perfectly still as the sound of her heartbeat racing echoed in her ears. Her eyes darted from the nurse to the doctor to the medical aid. Back and forth, she looked at them, trying to read them. *Is it bad?* she thought, wondering how her skin would look and trying to gauge their reactions to prepare herself for what she was about to see.

In their faces she saw nothing. The medical team that surrounded her was strictly professional as they removed the bandages from her body. The severe burns had taken an entire month to begin to heal. Days of painful infections had plagued Leah, and excruciating skin grafts had been performed, all in an attempt to save her. The doctors were working around the clock to save as much of her skin as possible, but unbeknownst to them, Leah was welcoming the deformity. The more unrecognizable she was, the better her plans would unfold.

She cringed as the sting of the sterile hospital air hit her face when each bandage was removed. The dirty gauze was filled with pus, blood, and dead skin as they took it off piece by piece.

Leah could not stop her eyes from filling with tears. She could only imagine how gruesome she looked. Her looks had gotten her by when she had nothing, but she would easily exchange that for the chance to step into YaYa's shoes. YaYa had love, an entire world full of people who worshipped the ground she walked on, and if this was the pain that Leah had to go through in order to have that too, then it was worth it.

"Okay, Ms. Morgan. I want to prepare you for what you are about to see. There is severe damage to your face. Healing the burns was only the first step. You have many more steps and face many more challenges on the road to recovery. You have to remember to be thankful to be alive right now. Don't focus on how you look," the doctor said, preparing her for the worst.

Leah nodded her head and reached for the mirror that one of the nurses held in her hands. Her hands shook as she brought it up to her face. Nothing could have prepared her for the sight of her reflection. Her face was completely destroyed. The fire had eaten through her skin like moths on old fabric. She felt like a monster.

"Get out!" Leah whispered.

"It will get better. I've already begun discussing your case with the best plastic surgeon in the city," the doctor explained as he tried to ease her worries.

"Get out," she repeated.

The staff didn't move. They all stood there with their stoic expressions.

"Get out!" Leah screamed as she threw the mirror across the room, causing it to shatter into pieces. Finally the nurses hustled out of the room, fleeing from her outburst, but the doctor remained by her bedside.

"It has only been a month since the fire. You have to give it time to heal. You are physically and emotionally damaged, Disaya. We are only trying to help you."

"I just need a moment to myself," she replied as a tear fell from her eyes. She couldn't even wipe it away because she was afraid to touch her own face.

"I'll do my rounds and be back in half an hour. I know how you feel, Disaya. Please try to stay optimistic."

Dr. Fannigan was her attending physician and had been with her every step of the way through her recovery. He stood tall, six feet two, with handsome all-American boy features and a slim yet athletic build. Surely in his prime he had been the captain of somebody's Lacrosse team. With his Johns Hopkins medical degree and good looks, he was like a superstar amongst the many nurses and female doctors on staff. The slight gray that had begun to appear at his temples gave him a distinguished appearance. It was he who had saved her life. Had it not been for his experience and expertise, she would be lying in a shallow grave.

Leah knew that she should be grateful for all of his efforts, but his calm tone was irritating her. He couldn't possibly know how she felt. He had never been ugly in his entire life. Not even an old childhood scar marred his perfect exterior. The empathy he displayed was fabricated and made her even more insecure.

Yes, she had asked for this, but the old adage of "be careful what you wish for" couldn't be more true. Her skin was so badly seared that all that could be seen was pink flesh. The hair had been burned completely from one side of her head. Leah couldn't help but think that this was God's way of punishing her. She had felt the fires of hell, and He had scarred her for life. Was this His way of paying her back for all of her bad deeds?

The doctor exited the room, leaving her to process her predicament.

Fuck it, she thought as she climbed from the hospital bed. She walked to the attached bathroom and looked at herself in the mirror. She wasn't even recognizable, and her heart pounded furiously as she became overwhelmed with anger. Although her insides were spoiled and rotten, she had always been beautiful on the outside. Now her exterior matched the ugly intent of her heart.

The only thing recognizable about Leah was her eyes, but it was the thing she hated most. They were the only thing left that could keep Leah from playing the role.

Taking over YaYa's identity wouldn't be simple. She was lucky that she had gotten away with it thus far. YaYa's beautiful, bright green eyes set her apart. Upon awakening in the hospital, Leah had been so heavily bandaged that her eyes were slightly hooded by the white gauze that protected her skin. Everyone was worried about her as she clung to her deathbed, and when she finally regained consciousness, they were too overjoyed with excitement to notice that she wasn't who she claimed to be. Elaine and Slim could barely see her eyes, let alone distinguish their color. Her looks were completely destroyed, her voice raspy from the damage to her larynx and smoke inhalation. Everything was in her favor to become the new Disaya Morgan; the only thing in her way was the color of her own eyes.

Because of this, Leah refused to see anyone. The only people who came in and out of her room were doctors and nurses. She had banned Slim, Elaine, and even Indie from stepping foot inside. Indie didn't even get a chance to see her once he got out of jail. By the time he arrived at the hospital, Leah had asked everyone to leave before anyone could put two and two together. Now she was panicking. She had been so delusional before the fire that she had overlooked a critical piece of the puzzle.

Leah had done too much plotting . . . so much scheming and lying to get to this point. She and YaYa had gone from fast friends to lovers to enemies within the blink of an eye. YaYa didn't know that all along

Leah was an unseen enemy from the past. They shared a father, a man who showed unbalanced favor toward YaYa, and Leah would always hate YaYa for his faults. The resentment that Leah harbored had pushed her over the edge. It had turned her into a woman obsessed.

After being trapped in the deadly fire, she saw an opportunity to take YaYa's place and finally live the life that she had always admired from afar. Burnt beyond repair, she knew that she could pass as YaYa . . . if it weren't for those damn green eyes. How she had forgotten such a detail was beyond her, but her lies were too deep to retract them now. As every day passed, her risk of the truth being discovered grew.

Luckily YaYa's medical records hadn't been faxed from New York, so the doctors had no clue that they were treating an imposter. It was just Leah's luck that YaYa's mother had been neglectful and other than her birth, no other doctor's visits had been made. YaYa barely had a medical history. No vaccination records existed, no emergency hospital visits, no broken bones, nothing. It was as if YaYa had disappeared off the map until she gave birth to her daughter. Even still, the over-crowded state of New York was slow in forwarding the files to Texas. It was working in Leah's favor, at least temporarily. Eventually those records would come, blood types would be compared, and faking would no longer be possible. Leah could feel the walls crumbling around her. As soon as those records arrived, her true identity would be discovered. She couldn't let that happen under any circumstance.

A knock on the door took her attention away from the mirror, and she slowly walked back toward her bed.

"You should be in bed. There are nurses that can help you back and forth to the bathroom," Dr. Fanni-gan said.

"I'm fine. I can still piss on my own," she remarked snidely. The mixed emotions she felt overwhelmed her as she meandered solemnly across the room. She didn't know if she should be happy or sad. She finally had the chance to be YaYa, to know what it felt like to be loved like YaYa, to be catered to and doted over like YaYa. That part she was eager to experience, but she also mourned the fact that she would never be Leah Richards again. The knowledge that she would never look in the mirror and see her own beautiful face staring back at her made her chest sag with sadness. She would never be able to recognize herself. Whatever new face they gave her would look nothing like her old one. It was a large sacrifice, but one that she was willing to make.

The fire had been a drastic turning point in her life. That girl had indeed died in the fire, so she had to become YaYa. If she didn't, then she would be no one; she would become a girl with a hideous face and a lonely soul that no one could ever love. If Leah didn't pull this off, things would go bad and life wouldn't be worth living. Everything was riding on this.

She was too far in to turn back. She had to be like a chameleon and adapt to her surroundings. She had to bury her true self if she wanted to move forward as YaYa. The first thing she had to do was change the color of her eyes.

"Your entire family has called numerous times to check on you. You'll be going home soon. They seem very concerned. I know that your face looks bad, but once the burns completely heal we can begin the process of reconstructive and cosmetic surgery. I don't think your family cares how you look. They're just glad that you're making progress. I think seeing them would help with your healing," the doctor said.

"I don't want to see them. I don't want to see anyone until after the surgery," she said firmly. She climbed into bed, wincing as her healing flesh rubbed against the starchy white sheets. "When can I have that done? I need a new face, Dr. Fannigan. I can't stay like this."

"I've already set up a consultation with a colleague of mine. Her name is Dr. Maroni, and she is the best cosmetic surgeon in the state. She will be able to answer all of your questions," Dr. Fannigan said. He checked her vitals and then prepared to leave. "Is there anything else that's bothering you?"

"My eyes," Leah answered. "My vision is kind of blurry. I wore prescription contacts before the fire. I'd like to order more. If I'm going to be stuck in this hospital bed, I at least need to be able to read a book to pass the time." She gave him a friendly smile, showing him that she was in good spirits.

Leah had been a master manipulator her entire life, and the doctor fell victim to her game with ease. "Of course. I'll have one of the nurses take you to the ophthalmologist's office on the eighth floor," he replied. "Until then, try to rest and think about allowing your family to visit."

Leah nodded her head and replied, "I will. I promise I'll think about it."

Chapter 3

"She won't see me," Indie whispered as he sat behind the large executive desk and pinched the bridge of his nose, closing his eyes in deep contemplation. "It's been a month and I haven't seen her face. She barely takes my calls. This shit is eating me alive, Ma. I just want to be there for her."

Elaine sat on the other side of the desk, listening to the pain in her son's voice. His love for YaYa was frustrating. Even when the two of them got it right, it everything around them seemed to go wrong. It was as if the forces of the universe were plotting against them. YaYa and Indie's flame never stayed lit for long.

YaYa's refusal to see Indie tore him apart, and his turmoil could be felt by everyone around him. His patience was nonexistent nowadays, and there was always a heavy tension whenever he entered the room. No one knew how to approach him; everyone was on pins and needles because his stress level was at an all-time high. Indie had always been cool under pressure, but when the love of his life was facing the biggest battle of all, he felt useless. She was shutting him out, and it felt as if he was losing her, as if she somehow blamed him for her life falling apart. They had found and lost each other too many times before. He knew what it felt like to be without her. Life without her in it was one that was half fulfilled. He wanted nothing more than to be by her bedside as she healed, but she wouldn't allow it. The separation was torture.

"She has been through a lot, Indie. She will come around. Give this time. That girl loves you and she loves Skylar. When she is ready she will call you," Elaine said.

Skylar's cries broke through the air and Elaine stood to her feet. "I'll go check on her," she said as she hurried from the room.

Indie stood to his feet and sighed heavily. He had the weight of the world resting on his shoulders. Everything was up in the air. His business in the streets was at a standstill. The dismissal of his case had been a bad look for the DEA, Agent Norris in particular, and ever since the day he walked out of prison a free man he had been under tight scrutiny. Norris had a personal score to settle with Indie after he was downgraded in rank because of the botched case. Indie could feel eyes on him every time he left the house. He could practically hear the cameras flicking as the feds snapped pictures of everyone coming and going from his residence.

They were trying to build a case around him, which meant Indie had to keep his nose clean. Hustling wasn't an option. He was hot, and he knew that although he had a crazy connect with Zya, she wouldn't dare deal with him as long as the *federales* were lurking in his back yard. He wouldn't even put her at risk in such a way. She had reached out to him numerous times since his release, but Indie always rejected the call. If he were a fish on the federal scale, than Zya would be a whale. She was a prize catch, and he refused to lead Norris to her front door. He was too noble to contribute to Zya's downfall. He only hoped that she got the hint and stopped calling.

Until things cooled off, Indie would have to go legit, and with the limited funds he had left that would be a daunting task. Nobody wanted to deal with a businessman with large plans, yet small pockets. He had to have something to bring to the table. His case, YaYa's medical bills, and repaying his debt to Zya after Khi-P had tried to back door him, had left his finances in a delicate state. Not to mention the extra security he had hired since bringing his daughter home. He paid goons around the clock to keep his home and his family secure. If he had taken that precaution when he first brought YaYa to Houston, then Leah would have never been able to get close enough to touch his queen. Skylar's kidnapping would never have happened. If he had been more cautious, YaYa would never have gotten caught up in a game of cat and mouse. None of the chaos would have occurred.

He was an intelligent man and never made the same mistake twice. There was money left but not much; a quarter-million dollars would only last him so long. He had to play his cards right and flip his funds before they ran dry. He needed the attention off of him so that he could get back to doing what he did best: moving weight. He had never been a little nigga and he never would be. As long as there was air in his lungs he would be a boss.

***

YaYa opened her eyes and was immediately blinded by the sunlight that streamed into the room through the open terrace. A month was a long time to be cloaked in darkness. She hadn't seen the sun in quite some time, and its brightness caused her to squint.

The sheer curtains blew lightly as a cool breeze spread throughout the room. *Where am I?* she thought as she looked around in confusion. The immaculate room was a far cry from the white walls of a hospital. The beautiful travertine floor and expensive furnishings were too exquisite for the place to be any type of medical facility. She looked at her arm at the IV that had been placed into her veins. Undoubtedly she was in someone's home and they had taken care of her, but whose?

YaYa attempted to speak but quickly found that her throat was raw and scratchy. She couldn't speak beyond a whisper as she tried to call for help. She felt weak, extremely weak, as she sat up in the bed. Her head spun as dizziness overcame her.

She gripped the sheets that covered her legs and closed her eyes as she inhaled deeply, trying to stop the room from spinning. Her hands felt raw, and when she looked at them she noticed her injuries for the first time. Burns covered her hands. A gruesome pattern of brown skin and pink flesh made her stomach turn. Tears filled her eyes and she gasped as she held her hands out in front of her. She was so shocked that she didn't even hear anyone enter the room.

"You're awake," Zya exclaimed in surprise. "I know you have a lot of questions and I'll answer them all, but first let's get the doctor in here to make sure that you are okay."

YaYa's mouth hung wide open as she nodded her head obediently. She didn't know what to say. Zya was the last face that she had expected to see. *Why did she bring me here? Where is Indie? My daughter?* she thought. Images of the fire popped into her mind as everything came rushing back to her. *I almost died! Where is my daughter?*

The thought of Skylar caused YaYa to rise out of the bed. She pulled the IV from her arm in a panic, ignoring the pain and the slight blood as she ripped it out improperly. She climbed from the bed, legs wobbly from being immobile for so long. She took one step, her bones creaking, aching as her knees shook like fragile limbs on a tree. Before she could fall she gripped the bed and leaned her weight on it, breathing heavily as exhaustion plagued her.

Zya and the doctor entered the room.

"YaYa!" she yelled as they both rushed to her side. They steadied her and helped her sit on the bed.

"Where is my daughter?" she asked. "She was in that house with me. Is she—"

"No . . . no, she's not dead, YaYa," Zya said calmly. "Your daughter is fine. She is with Indie."

"Why am I not with Indie? What is going on?" she asked. "Where the fuck am I?" YaYa was hysterical as she thought of her family. "Why am I here with you?"

"I'll explain everything, YaYa. The doctor is going to make sure everything is okay and then we'll talk," Zya said. "First you need to rest." Zya nodded to the doctor. They seemed to have an understanding of what YaYa needed without even asking her.

The last thing on YaYa's mind was sleep. She wanted answers, she wanted her daughter, she wanted to avoid the darkness . . . the hell that she had just awoken from.

YaYa watched Zya step back as the doctor stuck her with a needle. Within moments she felt a calm wash over her. Everything in the room seemed to slow down. She gripped the doctor's forearm as he guided her gently back onto the pillow. Her eyelids felt as if they weighed a ton. She tried to stay alert, but the sandman pulled them down slowly.

She fought the slumber as long as she could. YaYa had already missed too much. She knew too little. The last thing she wanted to do was sleep, but as the drug took its course through her veins, she slowly slipped back into the darkness and said a temporary good-bye to the world.

***

YaYa awoke at dusk. With a heavy heart and a mind full of questions, she sat up. The shot the doctor had given her had mellowed her out, and she groaned as she looked around the room. She found Zya standing near the bay window with a glass of wine in one hand as she peered out at her vast estate.

"Welcome back to the living," Zya spoke without looking. "Have you ever seen the sunset over a Tuscan village?"

YaYa didn't respond as Zya turned toward her.

"It's one of the most beautiful things you will ever see. I know you have a lot of questions. Join me on the veranda and I'll tell you everything," Zya said. She snapped her fingers and out of nowhere a large Italian man entered the room.

"Please place Ms. Morgan in the wheelchair by the door. You are her personal guard. Whatever she needs you see to it that she gets it. Until she regains her strength you are to escort her wherever she needs to go," Zya ordered.

"Yes, ma'am," the man replied. He went to YaYa and scooped her into his large arms, then placed her into the chair. They followed Zya out to the veranda, where a beautiful vintage table was set up with two chairs and an umbrella.

YaYa was immediately taken aback by the scenery. All she saw was miles and miles of beautiful, lush mountainside with little towns tucked in between. The ocean bordered it and the sound of waves crashing could be heard as they broke against the bottom of the hilly terrain.

"Where are we?" she asked.

"Italy," Zya replied.

"This is where you live?" YaYa asked. She was clearly out of her league. She looked around at the large villa that surrounded her. "This is *your* house?"

Zya chuckled as she recalled a time when her own mentor had introduced her to another world, a world of power, luxury, and prestige. She had been just as easily impressed as YaYa was today.

"This is my house. One of many," she confirmed.

"Why am I here?" YaYa questioned.

Sympathy filled Zya as she looked at YaYa. Her injuries were extensive. The scars from the burns covered the right side of her face, her ears, her neck. They were gruesome, hideous, and made YaYa feel like a monster as he heart fell into her stomach. Amazingly the left side was untouched and a hint of her beauty was still visible. She looked like two different people from two different angles. It was as if both God and the devil had a hold of her, in a battle over one lost soul.

"I was impressed by the way you came up with the money that Indie owed me. I don't know anyone who could have flipped a profit so quickly and so efficiently. I mean, it was genius really. Instead of targeting the hustlers, you went after their women. You wooed them first and showed them what you had for sale. They became your middlemen and relayed the message back to their boyfriends, husbands, brothers . . ." Zya paused, shaking her head as she recalled how smoothly YaYa had organized her dope sales. She moved bricks better than most niggas moved ounces.

"It was so well executed that I wondered why I had never thought of it. You moved like a pro, YaYa. So I became curious. I wanted to know who you were. Where you came from. I had you followed.

"Then the fire happened. Afterward I pulled you from the rubble. I tried to get to your daughter as well, but the firemen recovered her first."

"Was she hurt? How is she?" YaYa asked eagerly with all of the tenderness that only a mother could express.

"She's well. God must have covered your little girl, YaYa, because she walked away from that fire with minor injuries. Burns that won't leave scars. You, on the other hand, weren't so lucky," Zya said.

YaYa's eyes went to her scarred hands. Zya's followed.

"Your hands were burnt the worst because you had gasoline on them. The fire consumed them quickly and then spread slowly. Your face is damaged—not beyond repair, but it is different than you remember. You were covered in black ash after the fire. My people could barely recognize you under the rubble, but most of the burns on your face have healed. The scar tissue just needs to be addressed," Zya informed. There was sympathy in her stare as YaYa touched her face. "It's bad, but not as bad as you might think. Would you like to see yourself?" Zya asked.

YaYa nodded and Zya gestured for the guard to retrieve a mirror. The man disappeared and seconds later came back holding a mirror in his hands. He handed it to YaYa.

She took it into her hands, terrified of what she might see. Her chest heaved up and down in anticipation. When she turned it around, her heart sank and her eyes widened slightly in horror.

"I have assembled a team of the finest plastic surgeons in the world. They can help you, YaYa," Zya assured.

YaYa was speechless as she placed the mirror face down on the table. She was ugly, damaged, and although it was superficial, it hurt to see herself that way. One side of her face was fine; only a few scars were present and would undoubtedly disappear with time. The other half, however, was marred with deep burns. Her cheekbone and ear were pink in color and covered with scabs as her body struggled to repair itself.

"Leah. Is she dead? If she is, then these burns are worth it," YaYa said as tears of rage pooled behind her lids.

Zya didn't respond.

"Is . . . she . . . dead?" YaYa asked, this time more insistently, raising her voice slightly.

"No," Zya replied with reluctance. "She is hospitalized in Houston with severe injuries. Indie has been footing the bill for her care. I'm sorry to be the one to tell you that."

YaYa's heart felt as if it stopped beating as a sharp pain ripped through her chest. Her lips quivered. "What?"

"I can't imagine how hard that must be to hear, YaYa. Considering your beef with this girl, I am confused as to why he is taking care of her. His loyalty is questionable, and I wasn't sure if you even wanted him to know that you were alive. I have tried to reach out to him, to find out what is going on, but he doesn't accept my calls.

"I'm wanted in the States, so my visits there are few and far between. Under normal circumstances it would be simple for me to reach out to Indie, but since his federal case was dismissed, the Feds have been watching his every move. He has been under heavy scrutiny. They have him covered like he is John Gotti or something. I haven't found the opportunity to get the message to him that you are here with me. I have to be careful with this. I can't take the risk of being associated with him right now," Zya finished.

YaYa's blood boiled at the thought of Indie taking care of Leah. After all that she had been through, all that they had lost at Leah's hands, she didn't understand it.

He wouldn't. How could he? she thought. Her good sense told her that there was more to the story, and she knew that she had to get home as quickly as possible.

"I need to get back to him . . . to my daughter," YaYa said.

"I understand, but I do want to offer you a proposition before you go. I'm unable to keep up with the market in the States. I'm not there, so I can't keep my finger on the pulse of the drug game. It is expensive and difficult to keep things in order from halfway across the world. I need eyes in the US. I need a partner that can do what you did for Indie. Move weight, stay under the radar, and make money discreetly. I was going to shut down my dealings in the States completely until I met you."

YaYa's head felt crowded as so many different things raced through her mind at once. The last thing she was thinking about was entering the dope game. She wanted to see Skylar; she wanted to confront Indie; she wanted to murder Leah. She had a thirst for revenge that wouldn't go away until she was standing over Leah's grave.

"I know that you have a lot of unfinished business concerning this girl Leah. I can end that for you. With one phone call, a nurse can put a shot in her veins that will put her down like a rabid dog. No mess, no questions asked," Zya said.

YaYa's heartbeat sped up at the thought of Leah being taken care of. She closed her eyes as tears leaked from her eyes. It would be so easy, so quick, if she let Zya handle things. YaYa could finally feel safe. She would finally be able to live without looking over her shoulder, wondering when her past would come back for another torturous rematch.

Leah had taken so much from YaYa. She had damaged so many parts of YaYa's soul. It should have been easy to give Zya the green light, but she couldn't. She wanted to beat Leah, but she wanted it to count as her own win, no matter how hard it was for her to attain. Leah's demise wouldn't be satisfying unless she did it herself, unless she was the one who orchestrated it. Leah versus Zya was unfairly matched, but Leah against YaYa was as equal as it came. YaYa wanted to prove to herself that she could come out on top, that she could personally deliver Leah's fate. She wanted to taste the sweetness of revenge.

Her lip quivered as she opened her mouth to respond. "As much as I want to say yes, I can't." She opened her eyes, which were now red and clouded with the tears that she struggled to stop. She gasped emotionally, choked up from the thought of the strife that Leah had caused. "This is something that I need to do myself. A peaceful death is too generous for her," YaYa admitted. "I want her to feel what I feel. I want her to hurt."

Zya leaned back in her chair and crossed her lean legs. She was slightly surprised at how cold-blooded YaYa was. YaYa wanted to handle her problem herself in her own way, and Zya had to respect it. There were very few women who had the courage to stand up to those who had wronged them, yet YaYa seemed determined to.

Zya flipped her hair in the wind and stared YaYa directly in the eyes. "You know what distinguishes me from you, YaYa?" she asked. She didn't pause long enough to receive an answer as she continued to speak. "Power. You've been chasing this girl, seeking revenge against this one girl for years. She is hard for you to touch. Damn near impossible for you to destroy without destroying yourself. And do you want to know why?"

A lone tear escaped YaYa's eyes. "Why is that?" she asked.

"Because you don't have enough pull. No muscle, no respect, no legend behind your name. You're just a girl from the hood beefing with a bitch that wants what you have," Zya said. "If you take me up on my offer, you'll be so much more. You'll be able to touch this Leah and anyone else who crosses you. You'll have access to the button, YaYa."

"Button?" YaYa asked.

"One push is all it takes to make a woman like Leah disappear," Zya said. "No scars, no back and forth, no risk to your family. Just a problem solved."

Zya could tell that she had YaYa's ear. What she was offering was a once-in-a-lifetime opportunity. Most men would risk their lives to find a plug like the one Zya was offering to YaYa. All YaYa had to do was say yes.

"You have time to think about it. You can't fly until my doctors clear you anyway. Before you leave we will talk about it once more. If you say yes, this will be the beginning of a new life for you, YaYa. If you say no, I trust that you'll walk away with no memory of who I am or what we have discussed."

YaYa nodded, still distracted by her proposition and all that she had learned. "I can't sit here knowing that Leah is so close to my daughter. If something happens to her, I will never forgive myself," YaYa said.

"You can try to contact Indie yourself if you like. It is my understanding that Leah's injuries from the fire were even worse than yours, so she will be hospital-ized for a while. She is nowhere near your daughter at the moment," Zya confirmed, easing YaYa's fears only slightly. "I'll stay up to date on her status. The moment she is released I will let you know," Zya assured.

"I'll leave you here with your own staff to take care of you. You'll have a butler, a chef, doctors, nurses, and a driver. They are at your disposal for as long as you need them. If you need me, the butler knows how to reach me. I have a family, so I can't stay around the clock, but I'll come anytime you call."

YaYa nodded gratefully as the guard wheeled her back into her room. Once she was alone, YaYa broke down. She sobbed like a baby as she hugged herself tightly. She had been through so much, endured great pain. The physical burns on her body were nothing compared to the blows that her heart had absorbed. She was damaged in so many ways. YaYa needed re-demption. She needed it the way that her lungs needed air, but her thirst for revenge was too strong. She couldn't walk a straight path until she handled Leah. She was determined to settle that beef . . . even if it meant that she would self-destruct in the process .

Chapter 4

Indie knelt down in front of Skylar and saw nothing but purity in her innocent face. Even after being kidnapped and kept from her parents, her smile still radiated brightly like the morning sun. He loved his child more than his own life, and he was so grateful for her presence. She was the bond that linked him and YaYa—walking, talking proof of their connection. She symbolized everything that Indie and YaYa represented. He hoped that Skylar could be the glue that kept them together when the stresses of life tried so hard to tear them apart. He knew it was selfish. Putting that responsibility on Skylar's shoulders wasn't fair, but it was all he had at the moment.

As he kissed her cheeks, he saw YaYa clear as day. She was a perfect blend of the two. Every day Indie showed her pictures of her mother, to keep the image of YaYa fresh in Skylar's mind, but enough was enough. He knew that she wanted no visitors, but maybe baby Sky would be just what YaYa needed to snap out of her secluded depression.

Indie picked up the toddler and then turned to Elaine.

"Are you sure YaYa is ready for this?" Elaine asked. "She made it clear that she didn't want to see anyone."

"I need to see her, Ma. Sky needs her mother. We just want to be there for her," Indie confessed. "She wouldn't turn her own daughter away. I know she misses Sky."

Indie stepped out of his town home and secured Skylar in the back seat of his car. The Dolce tailored pants he wore were accented well with a smoky-gray collared shirt and Italian made shoes. Indie cleaned up nicely. He was in tune with the streets and saved his 501s, fitted caps, and Gucci kicks for his days of block spinning. He was on his grown man shit, rocking his big boy fits and exuding nothing but strength and authority as he ducked into his Range and pulled away from his home.

As soon as the black rims on his car started spinning he checked his rearview. Sure enough, an unmarked federal vehicle was tailing him. "These predictable mu'fuckas," Indie mumbled. He hit the OnStar button in his car and waited as his call was connected.

"What up, doe?"

The voice of his young soldier Chase filled his speakers.

"Yo, baby boy, where you at?" Indie asked, his cool baritone level and in control.

"At the wash waiting to get my shit detailed. What's the move?" Chase responded.

"I can't do much right now. The spotlight is shining too bright on me, nah mean?" Indie replied.

"Uh-huh. Let's get 'em off you then, big homie. Swing through. I'll be here," Chase answered.

Indie disconnected the call and headed Chase's way. The sorry pigs behind him bent every corner right along with him, all the way to the fifth ward. The closer Indie got to the notorious neighborhood, the more the scenery scrolling by outside his window changed. Suburban turned to the hood before his very eyes. He hated to even bring his daughter to this part of the city, but he knew that where he was headed he had love. Indie had quickly established respect in the South, and no intentional harm would come his way.

He pulled up to the detail shop and into one of the bays. The workers quickly closed the garage door as if his car was being serviced. He saw Chase waiting, sitting in his matching Range Rover with a genuine smile on his face.

His young lieutenant was extremely loyal, and Indie appreciated that fact. Through it all, Chase had remained true to form. He didn't switch teams just because Indie had fallen off. Despite the fact that Indie had not been in touch in weeks, Chase was still ready to jump to action whenever Indie called. Indie knew he couldn't pay for that type of loyalty. Real niggas were born not bred, and there was a shortage nowadays. Indie appreciated that he had such a thorough soldier on his team.

"Let me take it from here. Let's switch the plates and I'll take these coppers for a personal tour around the hood," Chase said with a smirk. "These niggas around here don't give a fuck about no badge, bro. It's only two of them too. They can smell pork around here from a mile away. They'll be lucky if they leave out of this mu'fucka," Chase said seriously.

"Good looking out, fam," Indie replied.

"How's wifey?" Chase asked.

"Not good. I'm headed that way now. Meet me back at my spot in a couple hours. Pull straight into the garage. Moms is there. She'll let you in," Indie instructed. "We've got to talk about some things."

Chase nodded. After they switched the plates, he threw up two fingers then honked his horn to let the workers know to lift his gate. He pulled out, and sure enough the feds were there waiting. They couldn't see the driver behind the dark tint, but they took the bait and were led away by Chase.

Minutes later, Indie rolled out inconspicuously and headed in the opposite direction, eager to get to YaYa.

The hospital was bustling with action as he carried Skylar down its halls, bobbing and weaving to avoid being run down by the scrambling people in doctors' coats and scrubs. When he arrived at YaYa's room, he peeked inside the glass square at the top of the door. The room was extremely dim, and only the light from the bathroom created a small glow. He saw that her bandages had been removed, and he didn't flinch at the sight of her. To him, she was the epitome of beauty. He didn't care how disfigured she was. His heart yearned for her in more than a physical way. He opened the door and stepped inside the room.

"Hey, YaYa, we're here. It's only Skylar and me, baby girl. We miss you. We just want to see you," Indie said. "You're never going to feel better sitting in here in the dark. You need the light, ma, to remind you that you're alive. The curtains are closed, the lights off . . ."

His voice caused Leah's breath to catch in her throat as fear overwhelmed her. Grateful for the darkness in the room, she immediately turned her back to him as he came closer to the bed. He sat in the chair next to the bed. "I prefer the dark," she said, her voice quivering nervously.

Leah closed her eyes and inhaled deeply to try to calm her racing heart. She felt as if she would go insane. It was like the walls were closing in on her. Living on the edge of a lie so huge was a balancing act, and Leah wasn't agile enough to avoid the fall. She could see her own demise, and she was trying to postpone it as long as possible.

"I told you not to come," she said. "Why would you bring her here?"

Her anger threw Indie off guard as he responded, "She's your daughter. She needs you."

"I don't want to see her! I don't want to see you! Just get the fuck out!" she screamed irately. "Get out! Get out!"

"Disaya . . . you've got to tell me something. Where is this coming from? We just want to help you through this. Everybody. Me, my moms, Slim. We don't want you to go through this alone. We're trying—"

"I don't want you to help me through anything, Indie. I don't want you to see me like this. Please just leave. Give me time. After the surgery you can come, but I can barely look at myself. I don't need you and everybody else gawking at me," she reasoned, lowering her voice and softening her tone. She had to remember that YaYa wouldn't blow up at him in that way. Where Leah was hard, YaYa was soft. She had to keep that in mind if she didn't want to be discovered.

"Turn around, baby girl. Just look at me. Let me see you," Indie said. This was so unlike him. He was never the type to stay when he was unwanted, but after almost losing the love of his life, he was no longer ashamed to love. He didn't want his pride to keep him from his soul mate. He just knew that he could make her feel better.

"Hold your daughter." Skylar began to cry as he tried to hand their daughter off to YaYa. She squirmed and contorted her body as she wailed loudly in protest. Indie thought that Skylar was reacting to the tension in the room, but Skylar knew that she was in the presence of evil. Her natural intuition told her that Leah was not her mother, and the baby wanted no parts of this evil woman.

"I don't want to hold her! Get out of my room with the fucking crying!" Leah demanded, losing patience.

Indie stood to his feet and sighed in frustration as he took Skylar and rocked her gently to calm her cries. "It's okay, baby girl. Mommy's not feeling well. Everything is going to be fine," he whispered, but even he didn't believe the words. Seeing his daughter so cruelly rejected angered him, and at that moment he didn't even want to try to remedy things.

He retreated from the room in confusion. His internal alarm was sounding off, blaring loudly. There was nothing reminiscent of YaYa. He couldn't put his finger on it, but he knew that something was amiss.

"What the fuck is wrong with her?" he asked the doctor that he bumped into on his way out of the room. "She doesn't want to see her own child. This is the little girl that she was trapped in that house trying to save and all of a sudden she don't want to see her?" Indie asked. "That make sense to you?"

"What she has been through is very traumatic. I've scheduled a consultation with a plastic surgeon tomorrow. Once her face is reconstructed, then we will urge her to see a therapist that can help with the emotional things she's going through. She rejected therapy when she was first admitted, and we thought it was best to give her some time before we forced the issue again. It is definitely time for her to start expressing her feelings to someone professional. It will help her cope with the changes in her appearance. It is all a healing process. You just have to be patient," Dr. Fannigan answered.

Indie nodded and walked away in defeat. He had never felt so disconnected from YaYa. In all the time that he had known her, they could always feel one another. Now he just felt cold resentment taking her place in his heart. It seemed as though life was tearing them apart, putting them at odds once again.

He cradled Skylar in his arms, knowing that if it weren't for her, he would have let go of YaYa a long time ago. He was trying to be a man, a good man, and hold her down. With the resistance from his other half, it was no easy job.

***

Chase chuckled to himself when he saw the shocked faces of the federal agents when he finally stepped out of the car. Indie had instructed him to pull into the garage, but Chase had to add insult to injury by parking on the curb. As soon as his feet hit the pavement, they rolled down their windows and anger was evident all over their faces. Outsmarted, they had been taken on a wild goose chase. Indie had given them the slip, and Chase arrogantly flaunted it in their faces as he walked up the walkway headed to Indie's front door. He stuck up his middle finger and scoffed as he turned his back on them to ring the doorbell.

Indie opened the door. "You wild'n, li'l homie," he said with a laugh as he stepped to the side to allow Chase entry inside his house.

"Fuck 'em. They ain't got shit on me. I keep my shit clean. All they can do is watch with they lookin' ass," Chase said. "Where's Sky and Mom dukes?"

"I decided to send them back to New York. After visiting YaYa in the hospital I realized I can't focus on her recovery and their safety at the same time. That's what I want to talk to you about," Indie said. "Shit is dead down here, fam. I can't do shit down here. I've drawn too much attention to myself. . . . Agents at my door every day. I can't move the way I need to. I can get lost in New York. I can't do that down here. I'm a big fish in Houston; in New York there's too many people for them to focus on one. My shit will die down a lot quicker there. After YaYa has this surgery, we're gone."

"I don't like what I'm hearing, duke, but what can I say? It's your call. I hate to see a good thing end though, my nigga. I know we at a standstill right now, but I was hoping we would pick up where we left off. The streets is ours for the taking," Chase said.

Indie shook his head. "That's a young man's game, Chase. I'm not that no more. I'm headed for thirty. It's time for me to diversify. I've got a man back home that can help me go legit. Invest and flip my money legally. Play the stock market, all that. I can't put my family at risk no more. If it was just me, things would be different, but YaYa . . ." Indie shook his head at the thought of her and took a seat on the large leather sectional that occupied his living room. "This game is eating her alive, yo. It's not for her."

"She's fucked up, huh?" Chase asked. "Trina and the girls tried to go see her, but she just turned 'em away."

"She's turning everybody away. She wouldn't even hold her own kid, yo. Barked on me and ran us out of her room like we were strangers. She's not the same," Indie said. "She's a New Yitty chick, though. Fifth Avenue shopping, Harlem doobie-wearing type of girl. I just need to get her back there . . . get her in good spirits, nah mean?" Indie took a deep breath. "I would never leave you hanging though, Chase. You've been nothing but loyal to me. I'll introduce you to the connect, put you on before I break out. How that sound?"

"Sound like a nigga getting an invitation to eat at the table, big homie. That's love," Chase responded as they slapped hands. Indie stood, signaling that the short meeting had met its conclusion.

Indie wished that he could pick up and leave without looking back, but he couldn't leave YaYa behind, not yet. He would do his all to make it work with her, and he hoped that she would meet him halfway. It was easy to love a person when all they showed you was the best of them. Now he was witnessing the worst. He had no idea that the devil was trying to take YaYa's place. His guard was down, and he was falling victim to Leah's twisted manipulation.

***

"Can you read the top line for me, please?" the doctor asked.

Leah placed her face in the eye examination machine and recited the first line. She had 20/20 vision and could see perfectly fine, but that didn't stop her from sounding off the letters incorrectly.

"Is that *T* or *I*?" she feigned innocently.

Leah switched personalities as easily as she switched shoes. It was all a con to her, one big game, and she played different roles to get her way. She was in a hospital full of professional people with white coats and MDs after their names, but she was outsmarting them all with ease. Leah was borderline brilliant, but her intelligence flirted with the edge of insanity. She had never taken a con as far as the one she was now trapped in. The things that she was willing to do to become an entirely different person were beyond any sane person's imagination.

"I'm having a really hard time seeing these letters," she said.

"Has your vision always been an issue, or is this something that has happened since the fire?" the doctor asked.

"It seems to have gotten worse since the fire," Leah added for sympathy. She watched as the doctor scribbled in her chart, and then her eyes scanned the room.

A knock at the door interrupted them, and they both turned their attention toward the door as a nurse entered the room.

"I apologize for interrupting. I have a patient on the phone who needs to speak with you. She says it is urgent," the nurse said.

The doctor sighed and gave Leah a smile. "I'll be right back. Hold tight for a while," the doctor said.

She nodded and watched him walk out of the door in haste.

As soon as he left the room, Leah hopped down off the exam table. She placed a chair against the door and then rushed to the cabinets as she urgently pulled them open, rifling through them frantically.

"Hurry up . . . hurry up," she whispered to herself as she searched through shelves and drawers. Finally she came upon a small cardboard box and she smiled. Samples of contacts spilled out as she nervously tried to filter through the different brands and shades, looking for the color she needed.

She heard the doctor's voice nearing, and she looked over her shoulder in paranoia. "Fuck!" she whispered harshly. She grabbed a plastic glove and began stuffing the contacts inside. She didn't have time to go through them now, so she took them all. She filled it to the top and tied it as if it were a balloon, and then grabbed a small sampler bottle of solution. The cabinets and drawers looked as if a hurricane had hit them, but she didn't have time to restore their order. She closed them frantically, removed the chair from the door, and hopped back onto the examination table with only seconds to spare.

Flustered, she steadied her breathing as the doctor returned. She hid her stolen necessities under the thin fabric of the hospital gown as she gave him a reassuring smile. She held her hands over her stomach to keep the glove in place.

"I'm writing you a prescription lens that will help with the vision," the doctor assessed.

"Thank you," Leah responded. She couldn't care less about a pair of glasses. She had gotten what she had come there for.

When she was finally inside the privacy of her own room, she pulled out the glove and quickly found all of the green contact lenses that were inside. She held four pair in her hand. It was more than enough to last her until she was discharged and could access them without trouble.

Leah went to the bathroom to insert them into her eyes. The slight sting that irritated her pupils was a small price to pay. When she lifted her head and set her sights upon the light green image reflected in the mirror, her lips turned up in a devilish grin. Her transformation was almost complete. A sigh of relief escaped her lips as she gripped the edges of the sink.

I can't believe they're falling for it. All I've got to do is make it out of this hospital with a new identity and my life can start over, she thought.

A light tap on the door interrupted her, and Leah quickly hid her stolen goods in the shower, ensuring that she closed the curtain so no one could see inside.

"Just a minute," she called out.

Leah emerged from the bathroom.

A woman introduced herself. "Hello, Disaya, my name is Dr. Maroni, head of reconstructive surgery."

Dr. Maroni, a beautiful older woman of Italian descent, stood confidently before Leah with an entourage of medical residents behind her. Most people who saw Leah's burns flinched, but this woman seemed unfazed by the horrendous damage that the fire had caused. In her profession, she had seen worse.

"I wanted to stop by and introduce myself and my team. I know that the fire caused a lot of damage to your face, but I want to assure you that I can help. I have seen many cases like yours before and treated them successfully," she informed. She held Leah's face gently and began to touch and inspect the burns. "You seem to be healing well. There are no signs of infection. I think we can proceed with the next step. We can start the cosmetic procedures. We can do the first procedure tomorrow morning. Sound good to you?"

Leah walked back to her bed and crawled under the covers before she answered, "Yes. As soon as possible. I'm just ready to get out of here and start a new life. "

Dr. Maroni reached out and grabbed Leah's hand. "Don't worry. I am very good at what I do. I'll get you on the board for tomorrow. I'm going to give you a beautiful new face."

Chapter 5

YaYa felt like a spectacle as Zya and the nurses stood back while the surgeon removed the bandages from her face. Every part of her hurt, and as the air blew gently against her new skin, she winced in pain. It felt as if razor blades were being sliced across her tender face. "Aghh," she groaned as she gritted her teeth, trying to remain strong as the man in front of her worked.

"You will have some pain. A lot of pain, actually, until you are completely healed. I can prescribe Vicodin for that, and it should subside over time."

The pain was so intense that YaYa closed her eyes and breathed in a rhythm. *Deep breath in, slowly exhale out . . . Deep breath in, slowly exhale out,* she thought.

The gawking sets of eyes that glared at her as the doctors and nurses stood around her made the moment even more nerve-racking.

"Is it bad? What does it look like?" she asked anxiously as she looked up at the doctor. It felt like hell, but she silently hoped that the pain was worth it.

His face was serious. Wrinkles creased his brow, and he had broken out into a slight sweat as he cautiously removed each bandage. His hand was steady as he operated with precision, tugging ever so gently until her entire face was free.

A look of shock crossed Zya's face, causing YaYa to panic. Her hands shot up to her face in fear.

"What? Is it horrible? Please just let me see my face," she said urgently. YaYa rushed from the bed toward the full-length antique mirror that sat in a corner of the room.

"It's better. You look like yourself again. It's not perfect, but it's getting there," Zya said optimistically as she came up behind YaYa and placed her hands on her shoulders to show support. "You're still healing, but I can see *you*," Zya said.

YaYa touched her face, causing it to erupt as every nerve on her face was set on fire. Excruciation took her over, and it was agonizing as her hands explored her new face, but she couldn't stop. She was in disbelief as the doctors and nurses stood back, admiring their work from afar. She was speechless. Her hands and arms were still badly burnt, and she would always bear the marks of the fire in those places. Her face, however, was drastically improved. No, it wasn't perfect, and it never would be, but at least she didn't feel as though she had been destroyed by the fire.

She was extremely red and swollen. The doctor had taken skin grafts from her back and applied them to her face. She felt like Frankenstein as she looked at the results. She could still see the dark bruises from where the skin had been stitched into place. It was ugly and it hurt like hell, especially around her eye where the skin was pulled tightly, but it wasn't burnt, and that was all she could ask for.

Her back ached, and she winced as she bent her arm back awkwardly to touch the gauze-covered spots. Her skin was tender to the touch, and she sucked her teeth in pain.

"It will only take a few weeks to heal completely. Your face and your back will begin to look better as each day passes. The swelling will go away, the pain, the incisions will disappear. The markings that are left behind can be worked on more in the future if you insist, but for the most part you are very lucky. After the type of burns you sustained, you were not supposed to survive, but you did, and this surgery is only the first step in healing. Considering the amount of damage your face had, I would say that this is a drastic improvement. It may not feel like it to you, but the surgery was a success," the doctor explained.

YaYa couldn't expect to be the beauty queen she once was. Realistically, she never would be. She had her life, and right now that would have to be enough. She was grateful for Zya's help. In her condition she couldn't expect much, but despite this fact, she had been given everything. She was recognizable, and although there would be scars, it was nothing compared to the ugliness that she had expected to live the rest of her life with. In a way she even felt beautiful because her scars were symbolic of the fact that she had survived. It would take some getting used to, it would take a strong heart to make up for the flawed appearance, but YaYa was up to the task.

Her eyes pooled with emotion. She was so grateful for everything that Zya had done for her. Never in a million years had she expected to recover from something so drastic. She had underestimated how valuable life was. To look at her reflection and feel whole again was a blessing. The last thing she needed was for the pains of her life to be written all over her face.

One of the nurses walked up behind her and handed her two large pills along with a cup of water. "These will help with the pain. Take two every six to eight hours. It won't take away the pain, but it will dull it," she said.

YaYa nodded as she accepted the pills, grateful for the slightest bit of relief. She turned to Zya.

"You have no idea how much you have done for me," YaYa said. "Thank you, Zya."

"Thank me with your loyalty, YaYa. Reconsider my offer," Zya replied.

"I have, and I'm in," YaYa answered.

After all that she had been gifted, her allegiance to the game was a small price to pay. Zya had not only saved her life, but made it worth living again. YaYa felt forever indebted. She only hoped that she could carry the weight that Zya was placing on her shoulders. She was a far cry from a hustler. Moving product had been Indie's forte, but she was about to step into the big leagues, and she was diving headfirst.

She was about to walk through the door to the streets knowing full well that it would lock behind her. Yes, Zya was trying to sell her on the money and the power, but YaYa knew that she was leaving out the ills of the trade. Zya neglected to mention that playing the game at such an elite level trapped you. There were only two ways out—prison or death. YaYa had witnessed this with her own eyes. Every day that she was with Indie she could see that he had surpassed the point of thinking hustling was cool. He wanted out. He wanted true freedom, freedom to spend his money without scrutiny, freedom to exist without the guilt from knowing that he fed poison to his own people. He wanted to exit the game, but he had been initiated, and there was no easy way to quit when so many people relied on you.

YaYa knew that she was stepping into a game that may swallow her whole, but she didn't see an alternative. She was going all in regardless. YaYa felt as if she had no choice. Retirement didn't exist for a woman of Zya's stature, and soon YaYa was about to be her equal.

"If I'm going to do this, I need my own people around me . . . people that I trust. I need Indie and my daughter. I need my own circle," YaYa said.

"Understood. I will give you all the time you need to continue to heal and to get yourself together, and when you're ready, I will present you to *my* people. My soldiers will be at your disposal. Whatever and whoever you need brought to you, they'll take care of it," Zya said.

***

Leah lay on the operating table, her head covered in a cloth cap and her hands clasped over her stomach as she nervously wrung her fingers together. The surgical team surrounded her, dressed in blue scrubs and facemasks, waiting for the procedure to begin. Her reconstruction would take eight hours, and everyone was ready to begin the long, grueling process.

Dr. Maroni entered the sterile room, holding her gloved hands in the air, palms out, as she slipped into a paper operating apron.

"The big day has finally arrived. Are you ready?" she asked, overly confident as she looked down at Leah.

"Yes. I just want to look like YaYa," she whispered.

Dr. Maroni frowned and paused. "Excuse me?"

Leah shook her head and smiled uncomfortably, realizing that she had slipped up. "I just want to look like myself again is all," she corrected.

Dr. Maroni nodded unsurely and glanced at the anesthesiologist that was present.

"YaYa, I want you to say your ABCs for me, okay?"

Leah nodded.

"Begin," Dr. Maroni said. She looked at the anesthesiologist. "Put her under," she instructed.

The drug that was slipped into her IV was potent enough to put out a horse, and Leah fell into unconsciousness before she could get to G.

"Place the picture directly in front of me. Hold it up at all times," she said to an intern. A picture of YaYa was removed from the chart and held up, and Dr. Maroni stared at it. She memorized every feature, every unique quirk about YaYa's face, to ensure that she did her best to recreate it.

"Ten blade," she requested.

The surgical tool was placed in her open palm, and she turned her focus to Leah. She frowned then glanced back at the picture.

"Her bone structure shouldn't be different," she whispered.

Dr. Maroni studied Leah intently. To the average eye, it was quite simple for Leah to change her identity, but Dr. Maroni was far from average. She studied faces every day, knew bone structure, was an expert at identifying and creating specific facial characteristics. She hesitated, and the other doctors in the room looked at her with concern.

"Is there something wrong?" Dr. Fannigan asked.

"The girl lying on this table is not the same girl in this picture," Dr. Maroni said.

"What?" Dr. Fannigan answered, flabbergasted.

Dr. Maroni put down her blade and nodded for Fannigan to follow her out of the room. Once they were out of earshot of the residents and interns, she snatched off her mask.

"Open her file. Are there any distinguishing birthmarks, scars, anything that can prove that we are operating on Disaya Morgan?" Dr. Maroni asked.

"Of course we are. I've been treating this patient for over a month! I think I'd know," Dr. Fannigan answered.

"Would you?" Dr. Maroni asked. "Her medical history hasn't been reviewed. That over-fucking-crowded state of New York hasn't sent it yet. All we have to go off of is her word. She's a victim of a fire. She's unrecognizable, but she claims to be Disaya Morgan." She held up the picture of YaYa. "We know for a fact that this is a picture of Ms. Morgan. Why are the cheekbones different, the distance between the eyes wider, the ear size different? I would put my career on the line and say that girl in there is lying about who she is. How could you have missed this?"

Dr. Fannigan looked bewildered as he stared through the glass and looked on to the surgical floor.

"I will not give her someone else's face!" Dr. Maroni protested. "If she's not Disaya Morgan, then who the hell is she?"

Dr. Fannigan pinched the bridge of his nose and stepped closer to Dr. Maroni. "Are you sure?" he asked.

Dr. Fannigan looked perplexed as he went over the time he had spent with his patient. In all his years of experience, he had never missed such an important detail.

"I'm positive, Fannigan," she barked. "How did this get past you, and why is she pretending to be someone she's not?" Dr. Maroni shook her head and snatched off the sterilizing cap that covered her hair. "I'm calling the police. You can explain this to the family that's waiting out there for *Disaya Morgan* to come out of surgery."

***

Indie sat in cargo shorts and a white fitted V-neck shirt, waiting, worrying, and praying for everything to go as planned with YaYa's surgery. He hadn't even been able to speak to her before she went in. All he could do was hope that everything went according to plan.

He came alone. He didn't want company. This was something that he had to deal with by himself.

It hadn't even been an hour yet, and he was already going crazy. *How will she look afterward?* he thought.

When he saw Dr. Fannigan approach him, he stood up eagerly. He checked his watch.

"I have something to tell you," Dr. Fannigan said. "Please have a seat."

Indie's heart sank. "Is she alive?"

"Please, Mr. Perkins, sit down," the doctor said.

Indie took a seat and leaned over so that his elbows rested on his knees and his hands were in a steeple beneath his chin.

"Just tell me straight up," Indie said as he bit his inner jaw to stop his tears from forming. "Just say it."

"The woman in the operating room. We have reason to believe that she is not your Disaya," Dr. Fannigan informed.

Indie frowned in utter confusion. "What do you mean that's not my Disaya? Don't talk in circles, Doc. Tell me what it is you have to say," he said seriously as his heart thundered in his chest and his stomach went hollow. He could feel the impending news before the doctor even revealed it. He had felt it all along.

"It's not Disaya Morgan. We don't know who she is, but we are certain that it's not Ms. Morgan," Dr. Fannigan revealed.

The words set a blaze inside of Indie that could be seen through his smoky eyes. "What the fuck you just say to me?" he asked.

"I'm sorry, Mr. Perkins," Dr. Fannigan said sincerely.

"It's Leah," Indie whispered. "It's been Leah the whole time." It was then that Indie realized just how twisted and demented Leah truly was. At first he had marked her as jealous, as out of control, but to keep up a charade this large Indie knew that she had to be out of her mind.

Indie stood to his feet as rage surged through him. The pieces to the puzzle suddenly began to fit together as he contemplated how different he had thought YaYa was being. He couldn't feel her, couldn't love her, because it wasn't her.

"How could I not know?" he asked himself as guilt plagued him.

"None of us knew, Mr. Perkins," Dr. Fannigan replied. "The records had not yet come from New York. We had no blood type, no medical history to compare her to. We only had her word to go by."

Indie was so irate that he couldn't contain himself as he punched the wall with his bare hand repeatedly. His hand erupted in pain as his knuckles busted open and he slid down the wall, overwhelmed by it all. He beat his chest with his fist as if he were trying to knock out the pain.

He went through the moments that he had spent trying to break through to the person lying in that bed. *I talked to her, I loved her, I looked into her—*

Indie's thoughts stopped instantly as his anger overwhelmed him. He buried his face in his hands as he realized, *I never saw her eyes. She never let me look into her eyes. Those eyes would have told me the truth.*

"Oh no," he whispered. "No, no," he said.

Dr. Fannigan stood over him and knelt down beside him. Indie looked up at him with red, grieving eyes.

"She's dead, isn't she?" he asked, already knowing the answer. "If Leah's inside that operating room, then YaYa is the one that the coroner took away."

Dr. Fannigan nodded grimly. "I'm afraid so."

This revelation cut through him like a thousand knives as he lowered his head. His anger melted into grief as he thought of the love of his life buried somewhere, coldly forgotten. No one had acknowledged her passing. There had been no flowers, no choir singing. No loved ones to say their good-byes. His beloved YaYa had just been forgotten, and the fact that he had let it happen would eat away at his soul. Guilt sank into his heart as he thought of how badly he had failed YaYa.

"Where is her body?" Indie asked.

"I'm not sure. You can check with the city morgue. Any unclaimed corpses—"

"Don't call her that," Indie snapped. He stood slowly to his feet, pinching the bridge of his nose as he tried to regain his composure.

Dr. Fannigan shifted uncomfortably, realizing that he was being inconsiderate with his choice of words. "Any unclaimed loved ones are either buried or cremated by the city morgue."

Tears burned his eyes as he thought of the love of his life lying stiff and cold on some metal slab. He had to turn away from the doctor to gather himself. He didn't know what to feel. Sadness, anger, guilt, remorse—all of these things consumed him.

Indie squared his shoulders, turning back to face the doctor. Indie stood toe to toe with him as he leaned into the white man slightly. What he was about to say didn't need to be overheard.

"I've got fifty grand that says you'll make sure she doesn't get up from that table," he proposed.

Dr. Fannigan's eyes opened wide and he looked around nervously as if Indie had shouted his offer from the rooftop. He cleared his throat. "As tempting as that sounds, I cannot do that. My colleague has already contacted the authorities. They will be here shortly. The patient is under sedation, and we will leave her that way until they get here. I'm sorry," Dr. Fannigan expressed. He couldn't imagine Indie's grief.

Indie stormed out of the hospital. His chest was so constricted he could barely breathe. He had missed all the signs . . . ignored all the clues that the woman lying in the hospital wasn't who she said she was.

That's why I couldn't feel her, he thought. Things hadn't been the same. Their connection had been lost ever since the fire, and now he knew why.

His heart yearned for Disaya in the worst way. In that moment, all he wanted was to go to home to a woman, his woman, and feel her soft hands rubbing his tensions away. Their relationship had been tumultuous, but when they were good, they were so good. They were imperfectly perfect together. He would do anything to see YaYa's face again.

What would he tell their child when she asked for her mother? Indie wasn't prepared for this. The game had thrown a lot of harsh realities his way, but this blow was the hardest yet. YaYa had been his everything, and now without her he had nothing. Indie felt empty. He was a man who had lost a woman, and he would never be the same.

He was never one to lose his cool, but he could feel himself coming undone. His jaw twitched as he ground the back of his teeth. There was no way that he could allow Leah to leave that hospital alive. She had taken a life that was dear to Indie, so now it was time for her life to be taken in return.

The hospital would be crawling with federal agents in no time, so he knew that he wouldn't be able to touch her as long as she was under their watch. He would wait. He would stalk her situation until he found the perfect opportunity to deliver her karma.

***

Beep . . . Beep . . . Beep.

The steady tone of the heart monitor echoed throughout the room as Leah opened her eyes. Everything around her was covered in a powder white fog as her mind tried to shake the effects of the drug. She was groggy and weak as her head rolled to the side.

"Hmmm," she moaned. She shivered uncontrollably, a side effect of being put under in extensive surgery.

It doesn't hurt. I don't feel any pain, she thought in surprise as she wondered if the surgery was a success. She lifted her left arm to feel her face, but when she met the resistance of the handcuffs, she froze. She pulled her arm up again, only to have it stop as the handcuffs restrained her movement. She looked down and finally saw the shiny bracelet that bound her wrist. She pulled on it, yanked it roughly as she gritted her teeth in fury.

The door to the recovery room opened, and Federal Agent Norris entered.

"Who are you? Where is my doctor?" she asked. The question was pointless because she already knew the answer. She had been caught.

"Leah Richards, you are under arrest for the kidnapping of Skylar Perkins, the murder of Nanzi—"

It was all she heard before she erupted. Like a volcano, her anger bubbled over. "No! No! You've made a mistake! My name is Disaya Morgan! Where is my doctor? No!" she cried.

The sincerity in her voice made Agent Norris cringe. It was clear that Leah was disturbed. No sane person would ever do the things that she had done. The crimes that she had committed and the extent to which she carried her lies were nothing short of evil. She didn't care about anyone or anything. No one was exempt from her tyranny.

He Mirandized her, and then leaned over to whisper in her ear. "I'm going to make sure the judge puts you under the jail for what you did," he threatened.

A uniformed officer stepped inside the room, and Norris stood. "Keep her under close surveillance. Do not remove those cuffs under any circumstance. As soon as she is coherent and the anesthetic wears off, we're transporting her to county."

Leah was irate as she lay chained like an animal. She reached up to touch her face with her free hand. "You muthafuckas fix my face! I can't stay like this! I can't be like this! Fix my fucking face! My name is Disaya Morgan!" she sobbed. "I just want to be Disaya Morgan!"

Chapter 6

Dark clouds covered the gray sky as Indie rode alone in the black stretch limousine. A small caravan of cars followed as they headed to YaYa's memorial service. It was small with no fanfare. No ghetto pomp and circumstance. Indie had no body to bury, but he wanted to bury her memory and show respect for his lost love. The driver stopped in front of the small church house, and Indie waited for his door to be opened before he stepped out. He buttoned his Armani suit jacket and headed inside.

Chase, Trina, Miesha, and Sydney attended. His parents, Elaine and Bill, were also there along with his daughter, Skylar. Buchanan Slim was on parole and had to rush back to New York before his parole officer realized that he had left the state, so his presence was nonexistent. Despite his absence, there was enough love in the room to fill the entire church.

A large picture of YaYa sat at the front of the church, surrounded by many floral arrangements. His stomach was an empty pit as he solemnly took his seat in the front row. He took his daughter into his arms.

"I'm sorry, son," Bill said. He was the first one to speak to Indie all day. Everyone knew how much Indie had loved YaYa, and no one knew exactly what to say to make things right. Tension was at an all-time high, and everyone held their tongues. This was a heavy burden to bear, and no one could help him. He had to come to terms with YaYa's death on his own.

"Me too, Pops, me too," he responded. The tone of his voice was distant as he stared into the eyes of the photo. He had always been the epitome of strength, but this event had changed the course of his life. It had broken him down. He had so many regrets, but life had no do-overs. This loss couldn't be erased. There was no rewind button, and he was just trying his best to deal.

The pastor of the church kept it short at Indie's request and prayed for YaYa's soul. They each rose and spoke about their fond memories of her before they departed, going their separate ways.

"You sure you want to be by yourself right now, homie? You looked real fucked up over this. I'm no good on the mushy shit, but I can pour some Louis with you and kick back to get your mind off of everything," Chase offered.

Indie shook his head and patted Chase on the back. "Go home, fam. Sky is going back to New York with her grandparents. I need some time alone to get my head together. I'm good," he assured.

Chase only half believed him as he watched Indie get back into the Town Car and pull away.

Indie didn't let his tears fall until he was alone, and only one tear was able to sneak from his eyes before he hardened himself to the point of nothingness. If he opened the flood gates and allowed the dam to break, there would be no stopping his emotions . . . no space between zero and ten. If he drowned in his own sadness, then he would also open himself to the rage that he felt, and the streets would bleed.

Indie hadn't put his murder game down in quite some time. He had trained Chase to be his pit bull when he had needed someone in the streets of Houston touched. If he ordered it, then Chase bit. That was how he solved his problems. Unfortunately for Indie, this wasn't the remedy for his current predicament. Even if he were able to reach out to touch Leah, her demise wouldn't fill the vacancy in his heart. There was no replacing what she had taken away. He would feel YaYa's absence for the rest of his life. She was his one-in-a-lifetime love. Her light had been snuffed way too soon, and although he didn't let outsiders witness his self-destruction, he was rotting slowly from the inside out. His heart barely functioned anymore. Not even the sight of his daughter could brighten this gloomy day.

Indie rested his head against the leather seat and closed his eyes, seeking a moment of solace. He had to remain mentally strong. There were people who still needed him, mainly Skylar, and that left him no room to fall apart.

"Hmm-hmm." The driver cleared his throat. "I'm sorry, sir. I believe we have company."

Indie turned and saw a black sedan with red and whites flashing on the dashboard from the inside.

"Pull over," Indie said. He came off his hip with the banger and slid it to the driver. Without words, the driver took the illegal weapon, pressed a button on the radio console, and a secret compartment slid out. He quickly hid the gun inside, and Indie sighed as he stepped out of the car.

It wasn't much of a surprise when Agent Norris emerged from the vehicle. He flipped his cheap suit jacket back to display the weapon and badge that were on his hip.

"Am I under arrest?" Indie asked.

"No," Norris said as he looked around in paranoia. "I'm here to offer my condolences. If the bureau had handled your daughter's case more efficiently, maybe it would not have come to this point."

Indie flicked his nose in irritation. "Let's not mince words, Agent Norris. You were focused on arresting me instead of finding my daughter, so YaYa had to find her alone. My daughter is alive thanks to her mother, but YaYa is dead thanks to you," Indie said. "You underestimated how powerful I am. Your case against me, your surveillance details outside my house, it slows me down, but it doesn't stop me. My reach is far. If I were you I would be worried every time I turned my ignition over in the morning," Indie said as he stood toe to toe with Norris. A glint of fear flickered in Agent Norris's eyes.

"Is that a threat?" Norris countered. "Are you threatening a federal agent?"

Indie chuckled as a smirk crossed his face. He didn't respond verbally. The look in his eyes revealed that it was not a threat, but indeed a promise that he would have no problem carrying out. "Now, I just said goodbye to someone very dear to me. If I'm not under arrest, then—"

"Look, I'm not here to make it hard for you today. I understand the role I played in this . . ."

Indie was losing patience for the conversation, and he put his hands in his pockets and squared his shoulders as he stared Norris down with pure hatred in his heart. "Let me ask you something, Agent Norris. How did you miss this? Huh? How did you not know Leah Richards had taken my daughter, that she had stalked my family, taken YaYa's identity? If you had put half the focus on finding my kid as you did on locking me up, then none of this would have ever happened. I just buried a memory. Do you understand that? I couldn't even truly say good-bye because you, or none of the other pig mu'fuckas like you, know where her body is."

Norris took the insults because he knew that they were true. He had had a hard-on for Indie from day one and it had distracted him from doing his job. "I'm here to make you a proposition," Norris said quickly.

Indie seemed uninterested and scoffed as he shook his head and turned to get back into the car. Norris's next statement halted him.

"Put me on your payroll and I'll call off the dogs. You'll know when you're under surveillance, you'll have a heads-up on any raids, and most importantly you will have eyes and ears inside the bureau," Norris said.

"I don't know what you're talking about. What payroll?" Indie said, playing dumb. He didn't trust Norris as far as he could throw him. This was the same man who had tried to take away his freedom. This entire proposal smelled like a setup, and he wasn't falling for the okie doke.

"Damn it, Indie, when you walked, my pay went down by thirty percent. The dismissal of your case fell on my shoulders. I'm back to my rookie pay. I have a family. I can't support them on that. I'm offering you a good deal. Put me on payroll. Ten grand per month to have the feds in your pocket is a small price to pay for a man in your *business*," Norris said.

Indie placed one foot inside of the car and turned his back to Norris. Agent Norris watched in frustration as Indie closed the door.

"Just think about it!" he yelled through the tinted glass as the driver pulled off.

Indie pondered Agent Norris's offer and knew that it could prove valuable. What Agent Norris didn't know was that at the moment, Indie couldn't afford to put anyone on payroll. Dodging a federal bullet had practically crippled his street operations in Houston, and his stash was running low. On top of this, Indie didn't trust Norris. If he did have a mole on the inside, it wouldn't be him.

Chapter 7

Dawn in Italy was one of the most picturesque things that YaYa had ever witnessed, and as she walked in her bare feet along the grassy countryside of Zya's land she felt free. Her long silk dress blew as the wind laid gentle kisses on her skin. YaYa felt rejuvenated, alive, and she was grateful. Healing halfway across the world had been like therapy for her soul. She had needed to step away from it all to bring purity back into her life.

She sat on the hilltop and admired the towns miles below Zya's private estate. If this wasn't heaven, it was the closest thing to it. A part of YaYa wouldn't have minded staying there forever. She had already been erased off the map. No one even knew that she was still breathing. It would be simple to start over and never look back.

The idea was tempting, but it was impossible. The one thing that kept her linked to her old life was her child. Tears filled her eyes as she thought of the possibilities, of the life she could lead if she just moved on without looking back. She could see security, safety, but she couldn't see motherhood in that life. If she made that choice, her child would be lost to her forever, and as much as she wanted to start anew, she could never do it without Skylar.

"I have to go back," she whispered as she wiped the tears from her face. She inhaled deeply and closed her eyes. Life had given her a brutal beating, but YaYa was resilient. She had bounced back. Somehow she had survived, but Leah had too. Leah had left a bitter imprint on her life all because of jealousy. YaYa didn't have the luxury to run away because of her child, but she would not let Leah terrorize another moment of her life. Leah had to pay for the things that she had done. YaYa would never be at peace until Leah was out of it for good.

"I have to go back," she repeated, this time with more determination. She stood and dusted her off backside. She took one final look at the gorgeous view before she turned around and returned to the villa.

The personal butler that Zya had left her with met her at the back door. "Ms. Miller is here for you. I've set breakfast up on the terrace for the two of you."

YaYa nodded. "Thank you."

She made her way to the master bedroom. It had become her place of refuge. It no longer resembled a hospital room. No machines, no mechanical bed, no instruments filled the space. It had been restored to its original state with plush, king-sized furniture and silk bedding. She had become so used to the villa that she wished it belonged to her.

She sat on the edge of the bed and reached for the prescription bottles that her doctor had prescribed for her. She was on a combination of Vicodin and Oxycodone. Depending on her level of pain, all she had to do was pop a tiny pill and it took all of it away. She poured two of the pills out into her palm and swallowed them with the room temperature water that she always kept at her bedside. She settled her nerves and then stood to her feet, ready to face her past.

She found Zya sitting on the back terrace. She was always so stunning. Every time YaYa saw her she was taken aback by how beautiful she was. She wore a black

Valentino bandage dress and five-inch Jimmy Choos. Her hair was pulled high into a large bun on the top of her head, and her eyes were covered in limited-edition designer shades. There was something about Zya that screamed money, and it had nothing to do with her wardrobe. Despite the fashionista that she was, it was the way that she carried herself that demanded respect. YaYa found herself intimidated every time she was around her.

"Good morning, Zya," YaYa greeted as she approached the table.

The butler had laid out a feast of every breakfast dish imaginable. Zya sat sipping a mimosa. She flashed a warm smile at YaYa.

"Good morning," she replied. "You look well."

"I don't feel it," YaYa said only half jokingly. She took a seat across from Zya.

"But you look it, and that's what counts. Healing the inside will take more work, more time, and only you can do that, YaYa. All of the money in the world can't buy you peace of mind. But the world doesn't have to see how broken you are. I always keep my shit together because I never know who's watching. You can't allow yourself to unravel. On my worst day, I'll still appear to be at my best," Zya schooled. "Otherwise people think you're weak, emotional, unstable. I'll never give anyone the satisfaction."

"How do you keep it all together without going crazy?" YaYa asked.

"I have someone at home. Let's just say he's my Indie," Zya said, revealing a smile so genuine that it warmed YaYa's heart. She recognized the sign of love, and Indie's face flashed in her mind. "He keeps me sane. I have a child who keeps me sane."

"Maybe that's why I'm going crazy here," YaYa said. "I need to see Indie. I'm too far away from him. There are things I need to say to him, to ask him. . . . These damn doctors won't clear me to fly yet, so I can't go to him."

"I don't think you understand your new position," Zya said. "If you want something, it happens. There aren't any no's at this level of the game, YaYa. If you can't go to Indie, then you bring Indie to you. Go get dressed. I think that when you think of entering the game, you only think of the downfalls. I'm going to show you the upside. We're going for a ride."

YaYa quickly showered and dressed in borrowed clothes. When she emerged, Zya was waiting in front of a shiny red Porsche Cayenne.

"Wow, you may as well keep that dress," Zya said. "After you, I will do it absolutely no justice."

YaYa, who was once used to receiving compliments, felt insecure in her own skin. She ran her hands down the front of the peplum-style dress that hugged her hips.

"Relax," Zya said. "You look amazing."

"I don't feel the same," YaYa whispered.

"You're not the same. You'll never be the same, so we have to make sure that you're better," Zya answered. She held both of YaYa's hands and squeezed them reassuringly. "I've dismissed the drivers. We're rolling solo." She pointed to the Chanel headscarf that covered YaYa's hair. "This doesn't compliment the dress, however. The first stop will be the salon."

YaYa smiled and the two women entered the car. Zya pulled away at full speed and they flew through the Italian countryside.

"I'm going to boss you up by the time this day is over. By sunset you'll feel like a new woman, YaYa," Zya said.

YaYa smiled and Zya continued. "I need you to relax around me, YaYa. Trust me. The business that we are about to enter into together, I will need your trust, your friendship. I don't want you to feel inferior to me, YaYa. You don't need to fear me. Your respect is all I ask."

"After what you have done for me, you will always have that," YaYa replied.

The ride along the countryside was beautiful. They rode for miles along the coast. Finally the scenery changed from hills and ocean views to city life as they entered Milan, the shopping capital of the world. For the first time since being pulled from the fire, YaYa smiled brightly as all of her favorite designers lay sprawled out in front of her.

"We're going shopping?" YaYa asked.

"I'm giving you a complete makeover. A total transformation should make you more comfortable. Women like us wear nothing but the best, eat nothing but the best, surround ourselves with nothing but the best. The best clothes, the best shoes, the best homes, the best schools for our children, the best shooters for our protection," Zya said. "But before we do anything, we're going to get that head together."

YaYa laughed as they emerged from the car. They entered a five-star salon, where her every need was catered to. YaYa's hair, face, and body were revived, and by the time she walked out with her short new cut, she felt beautiful again. She wasn't perfect. Her face still showed damage, scars from the fire and traces of the doctor's incisions were still evident, but she was changed. She felt beautiful, and it was her scars and imperfections that made her feel special. She had survived what would have destroyed most. That was something to be proud of.

As she climbed out of the stylist's chair, she fingered her short hair cut in the mirror, trying to get used to the new look.

"Do you like it?" Zya asked.

YaYa turned her head to look at the side of her face that had been operated on. She inhaled deeply. This was as good as it got. She wasn't exquisite, but she wasn't hideous either. It was acceptable, and she would have to get used to not being the center of attention that she once had been.

"I like it," she said skeptically.

Zya took a seat in the stylist's chair, and YaYa smiled in an attempt to keep her spirits high. "I'm going to take a walk while he styles you. I need some air."

Zya nodded and YaYa turned to leave. The warm air hit her as soon as she left the comfort of the salon, but it seemed to melt the ice block that had been building around her heart.

YaYa just needed a moment to herself with no doctors, no pressure from Zya, no mirrors revealing her new reflection. She just wanted to walk the streets and see how people who didn't know her reacted to her new appearance. She waited for the stares and the whispers, but to her surprise they didn't come. Everyone seemed to bypass her as if she was normal, although YaYa felt anything but.

YaYa bypassed all of the designer shops until she came across a little unnamed shop amongst the bunch. The most beautiful shoes were displayed in the window, and they drew YaYa inside like a magnet. An older gentleman sat behind the counter, working diligently as he removed the platform from a chic pair of shoes. The man looked up over his wire frame glasses, giving her a once over before returning to his work.

"Have a look around. Let me know if you need help with anything," he gruffed. His voice was rough and unwelcoming, despite the fact that it was meant to be a greeting.

She looked around the shop curiously, and out of nowhere the man spoke again. "Been running this shoe shop for forty years, and in all that time, not one man has ever bought a broken shoe inside. It's the women . . . women like you who keep me in business. Broken heel, I fix it. Scuff mark, I buff it out. I work with everybody—the actresses, the models, the designers. They all come to me." As he spoke, he never looked up from the shoe that was in his hand. "All those models come here, have me remove the inside of the shoe, hollow it all out so that it's lighter. They can walk better if the shoe weighs less."

YaYa looked at the shoe in his hand and noticed that the hollow space within the shoe was just the right size to conceal something inside. The wheels inside her head began turning. Instinctively, she could already see cocaine being transported within the hollow space of the shoes.

No one would even think to check these shoes, she thought.

"Now, out of all the years I've been doing this, I've never seen someone as lovely as you, dear," he said.

YaYa laughed because he had only glanced at her for two seconds. Surely he was just being nice. "I think you might tell all the ladies that," she replied with an insecure smile as she picked up a pair of shoes.

The man looked up, and she saw his expression change when he took her in.

"I was burned in a fire," she whispered as she lowered her eyes.

"I see. Well, I never meant those words more, sweet-heart. You're a gem. One of a kind. Come . . . let me package those up for you. They're on the house," the Italian man said.

"Oh no, I can pay you for them," YaYa replied. "The compliment you gave me is more than enough." She smiled as she placed the shoes on the counter and he gave her hand a gentle pat. She glanced at the hollow shoe once more. "Besides, I have a feeling that I'll be back."

"Well, ask for Bruno. We have another location in the countryside as well. He's my son, and we will take good care of you, lovely lady," the man said.

YaYa paid for the shoes and walked out of the shop, headed back to Zya.

The two women ripped through Milan like a storm as they shopped without limit. Zya was generous with YaYa. There was no need to look at price tags. She needed Yaya at her best. She was breathing life back into a lifeless soul by reminding YaYa of her worth.

They had too many bags to carry home themselves, and everything was shipped so that they could mean-der around the town's squares freely.

"I wish I could stay here forever," YaYa said as the day wound down and they sat over dinner.

"Running from your past won't make it go away," Zya said. "What is it about this one girl that terrifies you so much?" Zya had never seen anyone as scared as YaYa. A part of the reason why she was so beaten by Leah was because Leah had gotten to her head.

"She's made my life a living hell since the day I met her," YaYa replied. "I just need her dead."

"You say you want to do it personally," Zya said. "I can respect that, but everything in due time. I'm giv-ing you a chance to build an empire. You build your empire, you gain power, then you ruin her," Zya said. She folded her linen napkin and placed it on top of the table, signaling that the dinner was over. YaYa followed suit and looked around the restaurant, noticing that they were being watched.

"I think someone is following us," YaYa said.

Zya nodded. "Of course they are," she replied. "I never go anywhere without two sets of eyes on me at all times. If you want to be a boss, you have to behave like one. Let this be an easy lesson for you to learn. Take note, YaYa."

"I need Indie here. I need to talk to him. I need answers. I just need him," YaYa admitted.

"Then you call for him," Zya said. "Let's go."

By the time they arrived back at the villa, Zya had assembled some of the most lethal members of her team. Five men, all with ties to the Italian mafia, sat at a round table in the dining room.

YaYa walked in unsurely. There were a million thoughts racing through her mind, but outwardly she appeared cool and collected as she took a seat next to Zya.

"Gentlemen, this is Ms. Morgan. She is my guest here in Italy and will be partnering with me in business. Her word is like my word. If she requests something, you do not hesitate to make it happen. She needs a gentleman brought here from the States. His name is Indie Perkins. His information is inside that manila folder," Zya instructed as she nodded to the paperwork that sat in the center of the table.

One of the gentlemen spoke up. An olive-toned man with dark hair and mysterious eyes reached for the folder. His handsome features stuck out to YaYa immediately. He was younger than the rest of the men and wore a Gucci suit that had been custom fitted just for him.

"Do you want him brought back standing or lying down?" he asked, a charming accent revealing that English was a second language.

Zya turned to YaYa, handing her the floor, and she took a deep breath before she spoke. This was her moment, her time to take the reins and step into her own. "Please, I want him unharmed. I just need him brought to me as soon as possible," she said. Her voice trembled slightly, causing the man to smile.

"No need to be nervous. You're the boss," the guy said. "I'll give you whatever you need."

She blushed at his forwardness and replied, "That's all I need from you."

"My name is Marco A'diamo," he said. "If you think of anything else you need, you let me know."

The men stood and exited the villa. When they were out of sight, Zya turned to YaYa with a look of surprise on her face. "He's fond of you. Marco is fond of no one," she said with laughter in her voice.

YaYa laughed slightly and replied, "Thank you, Zya. You have been a great friend to me."

"I need your head in the right place, YaYa. There is a lot riding on you. If you can establish business for me back home, we both have a lot of money to make," Zya said.

Zya departed and YaYa went up to her room. She exhaled deeply and collapsed against the door as she let the weight of her body slide to the floor. Overwhelmed by life, she felt completely cornered. YaYa's back was against the wall. On top of stepping into a deadly new business venture with Zya, she was separated from her child and Indie. They gave her strength—strength to keep living and strength to face her mental demons as well. Her fear of Leah was almost crippling. With an entire ocean between them, Leah was still too close for comfort. No time or distance was great enough. Only death would suffice, but each time Leah and YaYa faced off, Leah always came out on top. Somehow Leah always found a way to defeat YaYa . . . mind, body, and spirit.

I just need to get rid of her once and for all. She deserves a slow death for what she did to me, for taking my daughter from me, YaYa thought.

She rested her head against the door, and her eyes landed on the orange prescription bottle on the nightstand. She crawled over to it and opened it, her hands shaking. Three large pills fell into her hand as she tipped the bottle into her palm. Her heart sped up from guilt. YaYa knew that she was taking the pills more out of want than an actual need. She had no pain; she just wanted to be taken on a high where none of the stresses of her life could touch her.

***

"How the fuck could I have been so blind?" Indie asked as he sat at his desk with the half-empty bottle of Louis in front of him. He had been sipping slowly for hours, taking himself to a place of intoxication where nothing hurt . . . a place where pain didn't exist. YaYa was lost to him. No one knew exactly where her body had been taken, and the fact that he hadn't given her a proper burial tortured him. He wanted nothing more than to be at her side at that moment. He had failed to protect her, failed to protect Sky. Both of them had fallen victim to Leah, while he had fallen for her charm, her lies, her deceit.

He had always prided himself on being savvy. It was how he had lasted so long in the game. How had this one woman caused him to slip so easily? Had he wanted to see the truth? Maybe he wanted to believe that she was YaYa. Was loving her replacement easier than letting the real thing go? Where was her body?

His 9 mm Ruger rested atop his desk. Beside it sat a picture of YaYa and Sky. A choice was being presented before his very eyes. He picked up the gun knowing that with one pull of the trigger, he could end it all. The overwhelming guilt that he felt would cease to exist, but his heart wouldn't allow him to die so selfishly. His eyes kept drifting to the picture of his daughter, YaYa's daughter, and he knew that he couldn't do it. To leave his child alone in a world so cruel would surely be enough to send him to hell.

He put the cork in the bottle of expensive cognac and swayed to his feet, gathering his bearings. The hollow space in his chest would forever remain empty, because he was sure that he would never find another person to call his equal. The passion that he felt for YaYa was still very much alive, and no woman would ever compare. He placed two fingers to his lips then delivered the gentle kiss to her picture before walking out of the room.

He gathered himself, grabbed his keys, and looked around the house that he had shared with her briefly. He didn't want it; he couldn't stand to be inside of it. Nothing but misery had come to him since the very first night he had brought her here. It was definitely time to leave Houston behind. Life for him in that city was over. He didn't take any of his possessions. Indie simply walked away from it all.

Darkness enveloped him as he stepped out of his house. It was 3:00 A.M. and surprisingly, Agent Norris had called off his dogs, leaving him to mourn in peace. By the time they arrived back for their morning shift, he would be long gone.

Indie entered his car and put his key in the ignition. He was sluggish from the liquor that he had consumed, and where he would have normally seen a setup coming, he didn't suspect a thing. By the time Indie came back up to place his car in drive, he was caught slipping. The eyes of the intruder in his backseat stared into his own briefly as a black pillowcase was slipped over his face. Indie bucked backward as his world went black and he protested against the strength of his attacker.

"Aghh!" he growled. He pressed his foot into the gas pedal and reached until his hands found the gearshift. He pulled it backward, and the car jerked violently in reverse.

"Stop fighting!" the goon ordered in his ear as he put Indie in a chokehold.

Indie kept pressing the gas until his car collided with a tree, causing the goon to let go momentarily. The split second was all Indie needed to unload. He snatched his pistol off his holster and pointed it backward.

Boom!

He fired, and the loud blast caused him to go temporarily deaf. His ears rang, and he grabbed the sides of his head as his mouth fell open in an *O* of excruciation.

He opened the door and stumbled from the vehicle. Two black SUVs pulled up on him, and four men with semi-automatics drew on him. Indie raised his gun and fired with precision.

The men took cover until they heard Indie pause to reload; then they moved on him. Indie was easily outnumbered as two of the men ran up. He was knocked out cold before he could ever react.

***

"Jesus! She said she wanted him brought here gently," Zya said as she frowned at Indie's bound hands and beaten up appearance.

"He resisted, hard. Killed two of my men. Gently didn't work, so I had to put him down hard," Marco replied.

"Cut his hands loose," she ordered.

Marco's face was turned up in a menacing sneer as he cut the ropes from Indie's wrists. He gave Indie a harsh stare, causing Indie's ego to flare. "Little nigga better lower your eyes," he said.

Marco stood toe to toe with Indie, but conceded defeat when Zya's order broke up the show of testosterone. "Enough, Marco. He is a friend," Zya said.

Indie rubbed his wrists and didn't take his eyes off of Marco until he had exited the room. He looked at Zya, enraged. "We've done square business for years, ma. This how you want to end it?" he asked. "Do you know the measures I've taken just to protect you . . . to keep your name out of the dockets of my federal case?" he barked. He thought they had developed a cordial and even pleasant relationship over their years of getting money together. Her ambush came as a complete surprise to him.

"I'm not the one that brought you here, Indie. I apologize for their force, but I assure you that once you find out the reason why you are here, your tone will change," Zya replied apologetically.

"Where exactly is here?" Indie asked as he rubbed his sore wrists and followed the sway of Zya's hips into the sitting room. He looked around the giant home and immediately knew that he had not underestimated Zya's status. She was bossed up in every way. She wasn't a chick who hustled for handbags and Red Bottoms. Zya was heavy in the underworld, affiliated with Supreme Clientele. He only wondered what she wanted with him.

"I've known you for a long time, Indie. You do good business. You're one of the good guys. You found yourself wrapped up in a jam, and my name remains a mystery to the feds. I respect you, and I would like to call you a friend. I usually don't get involved with any beef, especially anything stateside, but for you I intervened when I felt I was needed."

"You're losing me, Zya. I don't understand what you're talking about," he said.

"Let's just say you owe me big," Zya replied with a wink. She nodded her head to the back of the room, and Indie turned, following her gaze.

"YaYa," he whispered when he saw her face. Like magnets they connected, crossing the room swiftly as she fell into his arms. "I thought you were dead, ma. I thought you were gone. On my soul I thought you were dead," he whispered as his hands touched her face, cupping it between his hands as he planted a kiss on her forehead.

Despite all of the confusion, the anger, the resentment that she felt toward him, his presence still melted her heart, and for a moment she allowed herself to linger in love. For a few seconds life was perfect.

"Sssss," YaYa hissed as she cringed from his touch.

"Be gentle, Indie. She still has a long way to go on the road to recovery," Zya said.

He released her face and turned to Zya. He had never been so grateful for anything in his life. "Thank you," he said with so much emotion it brought tears to Zya's eyes. She knew what love looked like, and she was witnessing it in its truest form. There was no doubt that Indie was head over heels for YaYa.

"You're welcome," she answered. "I'll give you two some privacy. YaYa knows how to reach me." She left the villa, knowing that the two had some reuniting to do. Indie turned around, picking YaYa up off her feet, his arms wrapped around her waist.

"I love the shit out of you, YaYa. I'm so sorry, ma. I should have been there," he said.

"You weren't, though. It seems like every time I need you, you're never there," she whispered sadly.

Indie placed her on her feet. Her words wounded him like a man on a battlefield. In her eyes he saw doubt, doubt in his love for her, and he took one step back to make sure that he was seeing things clearly.

"Please, let's sit down. We need to talk," YaYa whispered. She had mixed emotions regarding Indie. Every time she came to a pivotal point in her life, she never knew exactly where Indie stood. Leah was always able to get under his skin. The bitch stayed lurking in the shadows because Indie allowed her to. Although it was YaYa who Leah obsessed over, Indie was the bridge between the two. He gave Leah access to touch YaYa, and because of that, her trust in him was fading. Why was he so vulnerable to Leah? YaYa had to know. Before she gave her heart to him ever again, she needed to be sure that he deserved it and that he knew whose team he was on.

She led him to the custom Venetian furniture and sat beside him.

"You paid Leah's medical bills. Why?" she asked. She tried to keep her voice stern, steady, but her feelings were crushed, and Indie knew her too well to not be able to sense her hurt.

"No. No, ma. I thought she was you. I thought I was taking care of *you*. She pretended to be you. I would still be there with her if the doctors hadn't figured it out," he admitted.

"It shouldn't take a doctor to figure it out, Indie. You're my man. You should know me. My scent, my mannerisms, my heartbeat. My eyes! Why didn't you figure it out? How could you not know that the woman lying in that bed wasn't me?"

"I wasn't by her side, YaYa. She wouldn't let me be. She was too afraid that she would be caught. Her eyes . . . your eyes can't be duplicated, ma. She knew that the moment I looked into her face I would know she was a phony."

"I've been through so much," YaYa said, choking up. "My face feels different, and although I know it's not as bad as it could be, I feel damaged. My heart hurts, Indie. My hands." She choked up as he held her hands up and kissed them softly as he noticed for the first time how scarred they were. "My hair . . ."

Indie's hands traced her jaw line, then moved up her neck to her newly cut hairstyle. Much of her hair had been seared in the blaze. She was left with a short Nia cut. Indie could tell that she was uncomfortable in her own skin, but what she didn't quite get was that she could be bald and still be one of the most beautiful women in the world.

"Don't do that, baby girl. You're beautiful. Your face, your hands, your hair . . . you, YaYa. Every part of you is beautiful, baby. You're a fighter," he whispered as he pulled her near. "Don't ever doubt me, YaYa. I know shit with me hasn't been perfect, but I love you."

"How can you love me like this? I feel like I've been put back together. Like it's all fake. My nose, my skin . . . they pieced me together like a puzzle," YaYa said while crying.

"Look at me, YaYa," he said. She matched his gaze insecurely as he held her hands gently. "You are loved. It wouldn't matter if you had never fixed your face, ma. I would have loved you anyway. I see past the surface. I love you as you are. I love what's in here." He pointed to her chest. "Sky loves you. So many people love you."

YaYa nodded and smiled at the thought of her precious child. "Is she okay?" She sniffed and wiped her nose with the back of her hand.

"She is. You saved her life. There is no telling if we would have ever gotten her back if you had not gone after Leah. You did that," he said. He cupped her chin between his thumb and pointer finger as he kissed her lips.

She took his hand and led him up the steps to the room she occupied.

"You've been here all this time?" he asked as he stepped inside.

She nodded then released his hand as she walked over to the nightstand and opened up a prescription bottle. She poured three large pills into her hand then grabbed the water that she kept at her bedside. She swallowed them down with one gulp.

"What do they have you on?" he asked.

"Vicodin, Percocet, Oxy, you name it," she responded.

"Is it that bad? That's a lot of pills," Indie said in concern.

"Yeah, well, right now the pills are my new best friends," she replied with a meek smile.

Indie could not imagine how she felt, but he could see the strife in her eyes. They had once sparkled with happiness, but he noticed that now they were dulled with misery. She was trying to put up a good front for his sake, but he could tell that so many burdens troubled her.

"I'm sorry you're in so much pain," he said with sympathetic eyes as he grabbed both of her hands in support.

"I'm better now that you're here. Why don't you get cleaned up? I'll be right here when you get out," she said.

Seeing him again was bittersweet. Her love for him was so great, and she instantly reconnected with him, but she knew that Indie's expectations of her were always so big. He thought the world of her, and at this moment she simply wanted to be weak, to be vulnerable, to admit that she was flawed. She could no longer be his perfect Disaya. Everything about her had changed.

Indie never wanted to leave her side, but he could see that she was silently begging him for space. She needed a moment to herself, and he knew her so well that he recognized that. He kissed her cheek and then disappeared as he closed the en-suite bathroom door.

She quickly walked back over to the nightstand. She opened it and took one more pill, closing her eyes as she swallowed it. She sighed and then quickly swiped away the single tear that had escaped from her eyes. The medicine dulled the physical pain indeed, but what she told no one was that it settled her emotions. It made her numb to all of the inner turmoil that had plagued her life ever since she was a little girl.

Chapter 8

The next morning YaYa awoke to the sight of Indie staring at her as he stroked her face. He had held her all night, keeping her close to him in hopes that when they awoke she would still be there. YaYa had slipped through the cracks of his life so many times that he now feared losing her. It was as if they shared a forbidden love, one that the universe couldn't appreciate and continuously tried to pull apart, but he wouldn't let it. YaYa was his solace. She was his better half. This was their third shot at love, and he was determined to make this one last until the end of time. To bury someone only to have them rise from the dead made Indie appreciate her so much more. He just wanted to protect her. He wanted his family complete.

"Good morning, ma," he greeted.

She inhaled his scent and gave him a smile as she snuggled closer, getting tangled in his strong embrace while her head rested on his shoulder.

"Good morning," she replied.

It felt so good to be in his presence again. Indie had a soothing spirit, and being wrapped up in his rapture was the sweetest thing on earth. Loving a man made a woman complete, but loving Indie made YaYa feel as if she had been divinely favored. No other woman knew what it was like to feel the type of connection that she shared with this man. Theirs was a unique love, and she had lost it so many times before that she cherished every second that she was with him.

"I'm ready to take you home. I know Sky misses you," Indie said. "I'm ready to settle down, ma, stop taking so many risks. This game is for the young at heart, especially the way that we play it. I have a plan to expand, to grow into something bigger than selling drugs can ever get us. I'm going to take my last and go legit. It'll be different. Life will be . . . regular, but we'll have everything we need. I promise you, ma, I'm going to crawl up out of this hole. I just need you to ride with me while I'm on the bottom the same way you did when I was on top. I used to give you fifty racks to go shopping. Blow that in a night at the craps table. Those days have temporarily passed us by. I've got a couple dollars left to my name, but I'm not trying to touch the streets. I can't deal with the risks of that life anymore. I just want to be a man and provide safety and security for you . . . for Skylar."

Indie was saying all the right things, making plans to do all the right things, but it was all at the wrong time. YaYa didn't know how to break the news of Zya's proposition to him. She should have been jumping for joy at Indie's progress. He had grown before her very eyes. A man who once would have never given up the game was now willing to walk away for his family. She couldn't ask for a more noble man, but now she was about to throw their plan off course once again.

"What's a couple dollars?" she asked.

"Two hundred thousand dollars," he said.

"It has never been about the money for me, Indie. I love you for everything but the money, but I also know that the lifestyle that you lead, that we are used to leading, we can't maintain with that. Zya wants to plug me," she blurted out.

Indie sat up in the bed and looked at her, unsure if he had heard her correctly. "Since when you speak that language?" he asked, confused.

"She saved my life. She needs a partner in the States. I agreed because I feel like I owe her," YaYa said.

"You owe her?" Indie scoffed with a firm grimace as he sat up. "Did she tell you that? I can speak to her, YaYa. You don't owe anybody anything. I've done enough square business with Zya in the past for her to understand that this isn't for you. Do you know what you're getting yourself into, ma? 'Cause you couldn't handle one grimy bitch that was gunning for your head. What happens when you've got fifty snake-ass niggas coming at you? Because they gonna test you. You're going to look like a fish in a shark tank."

"That's why I need you. I can be the brain; I can't be the muscle," she answered. "I need you to say yes to this. If you don't want me to do it, then I'll walk away. I'll come home. I'll play wifey, but I know you though, Indie. Two hundred thousand dollars to a man like you is like chump change. You'll eventually go back to the game anyway. Zya's putting us back on, babe, and it gives me the power to touch the bitch that ruined my life once and for all. With money comes—"

"Power," Indie finished. He scoffed and shook his head. "I can tell you've been taking lessons at the school of Zya," he remarked. He wiped both hands over his face then rested his back against the headboard.

"Zya's a different breed, YaYa. She makes the game look easy. It's not, especially for a woman," he said.

"I know that. I'm not naïve. I know what I'm saying sounds crazy, but it's something I have to do," YaYa replied.

"It sounds like you have your mind made up, but I can't step into this with you though, YaYa. After embarrassing the feds, they would just love to catch me up in some shit like this. They already have the noose around my neck. They're just waiting for the opportunity to kick the chair from beneath my feet. I'd just put a spotlight on you."

"So what do we do?" she asked.

"You tell Zya no," Indie said. "You come home with me and walk away from her offer."

"I don't want to lie to you, Indie, so I'm just going to be honest. I don't want to tell Zya no," YaYa replied. "You're right. I'm weak, but with an alliance with Zya I become strong. I become powerful—powerful enough to touch anyone who has ever wronged me—and I've got an itch to scratch with Leah."

Indie sighed because no matter how much he tried to protect YaYa, she always seemed to weave a complicated web. At the end of the day, she was going to do what she wanted to. It was clear that she was only running it by him out of respect. She wasn't seeking his approval.

"If you're going to do this then you have to do it my way. There are certain measures you have to take to ensure your safety. You need soldiers—a team of young, loyal, hungry mu'fuckas that will shoot at your command. If you nod your head at a mu'fucka, your shooters should be on point, trigger finger itching and ready whenever, wherever. Then you need a lieutenant to keep everything running smoothly. Yours will be Chase. He's the only person I would trust you with," Indie said.

He continued, "I've learned from my past mistakes, so this time you won't make them. I've got an accountant set up in New York that's waiting to wash my paper. He'll be getting a lot more money from me than expected. Whatever comes in will be washed and legitimized before we ever spend a dime. I'll make sure you're covered on that end.

"Everyone thinks you're dead, YaYa. You'll be safe.
You won't even come under suspicion because tech-
nically you no longer exist. You'll move through the
streets like a ghost. Only those who know will know,
you understand?"

"What would I do without you?" she asked as she
smiled.

"You would be a regular girl in a regular world," he
replied. *And you would have never gotten tangled up
in this mess. You without me is what's best for you. I'm
just too selfish to let you go,* he thought.

***

Swish.
Swish.
Swish.

YaYa watched in amazement as men weighed and
packaged the powder cocaine in the secret caves of Sic-
ily. It was dark, and the tiny makeshift lighting system
that hung from the ceiling of the caverns did little to il-
luminate the place. She had heard stories of miners and
hikers being trapped beneath caves that collapsed on
top of them, and her paranoia was at an all-time high.
Zya seemed at ease, however, as they maneuvered their
way through each system, and YaYa followed her lead,
despite her growing apprehension.

An entire factory existed underground, an illegal
enterprise. She saw the powder-white cocaine sitting
in cellophane packages as they were moved down conveyor belts. Zya had a real-life operation going on, and
YaYa had definitely stepped into an intelligent network
of the world's best drug kingpins or, in Zya's case,
queen pin.

"YaYa, the distribution business is simple. You have
a product that niggas put in their rap songs. It's ex-
clusive, it's expensive, and very lucrative. You will be

my only distributor in the US. Before I dealt with a couple different people that I trusted, Indie being one of them, but when Indie caught his case, I realized that dealing with so many people is risky. I was lucky that it was Indie who got jammed up and not some of the others. Indie stood tall. He's a real man. Some of the other characters that I dealt with would have sung and danced for the feds just to get out of there.

"When I saw how good you were at moving weight, I was immediately interested in working with you. Now you will be my only endeavor in the US. You will be the only one with my product. That's not to say you won't have competition. You'll have competition from the Mexicans, the Colombians, the Cubans, but none of them will have a product that is as pure as mine. This is un-stepped on, YaYa, so it will fly as soon as you take it across the border," Zya said.

"Have you thought of how you're going to get it into the States?" Zya asked. "That burden is your responsibility, and of course, if you get caught it's your consequence to carry. I want us to be clear."

"We are," YaYa replied. "That goes without saying. I want to hire a few girls that I can trust to move the product on international flights."

Zya stopped walking and turned to YaYa in shock. "That's risky," she commented.

"Not the way I plan to do it. There is a shoemaker in town, makes custom shoes, designs for the major designers too. I noticed him working the other day when we went shopping. He hollowed out platform high heels. Wouldn't it be convenient if I filled that hollow space with cocaine? Someone could walk right through security and the X-rays wouldn't detect a thing," YaYa answered.

Zya raised an eyebow and folded her arms over her chest. The game was full of mules who had tried every technique imaginable, but this was a new method that she had never heard of before. Sometimes it took fresh eyes to come up with new ideas. "And you're sure?"

"No, but I'm confident enough to do the test run my-self," YaYa said. The thought of taking such a risk made her stomach do somersaults, but she couldn't expect someone else to do what she wasn't willing to do her-self. She had to do it at least once so that she could see for herself what her team of mules would be up against.

Zya smiled. "That's why I like you. We are on the same page. You're sharp. Our split is sixty-five/thirty-five," Zya said.

"Our split is fifty-five/forty-five," YaYa countered. As soon as the words left her mouth, she wished she could chase them down and swallow them. A lump formed in her throat as she saw Zya stop walking abruptly. *What the fuck am I doing? You don't negotiate with a woman like Zya,* she thought nervously.

Zya turned toward YaYa. No one had ever chal-lenged her before. Most people took what they could get. It wasn't often that Zya didn't get her way, and she couldn't remember a time when she had lost a negotia-tion.

"I'm taking the risk, so I need my percentage to be higher," YaYa stressed, knowing that she would have to split her profits up among her crew, once it was estab-lished. Her back began to sweat and the silk material of her shirt began to stick to her skin. She was aware of the risk that she was taking by standing up to Zya and demanding a larger percentage. She was overstepping her boundaries. Zya could pull the deal from beneath her feet for the disrespect. YaYa was on pins and nee-dles on the inside, but her poker face had always been A-1. Zya couldn't read her.

"It's my product. I'm the connect. Without me you wouldn't even be here," Zya answered. "I could get any hustler in the world to fill your shoes."

"And you just may have to if my needs aren't met," YaYa said, playing hardball. She cleared her throat to stop her voice from quivering. "You have loyalty from me. You know that my lips don't move if I get jammed up. If this thing goes badly, I won't even remember your name. You can't say the same for anyone else that you deal with. You said so yourself. Let's do good business, Zya. The way that I move the product, you will be happy to pay me that percentage."

Zya's eyes narrowed as she pondered YaYa's words. She analyzed the streetwise girl, looking her up and down.

"Okay, YaYa. I'll play your game. Sixty/forty, and that's my best offer. Consider this a first and a last. I never negotiate with anybody," Zya said with a smirk. "It seems I created a monster."

"I guess you have." YaYa nodded in agreement, sealing the deal. She sighed in relief as a smile slowly graced her face. Zya turned and continued to walk. As YaYa followed behind her, she felt her confidence grow. She was coming into her own and a new, valuable friendship had just been established.

Chapter 9

"Are you sure this is where Chase said to meet him?" Miesha said as she looked around the old power plant. The factory, which had been closed for twenty years, was located thirty miles outside of the inner city. It was like a ghost town as Miesha, Trina, and Sydney rode in silence, peering out of the window.

"Call him. This shit is freaking me out," Sydney urged. "There's nobody out here. I didn't think anyone ever came out here."

Trina pulled out her phone to attempt to call Chase, but to no avail. "No service," she commented. "Pull up over there."

Miesha took Trina's instructions and parked between the two large industrial buildings. They got out of the car. Headlights in the distance announced Chase's arrival, and they waited until he pulled up directly next to them.

"Fuck is this? Why we meeting all the way out here?" Trina asked as soon as he emerged from the car.

"I'm following instructions just like you. Indie didn't tell me anything. He just told me where to be and what time to be here," Chase said nonchalantly as he leaned against the hood of his Range.

Two black Lincoln Navigator trucks appeared in the distance, causing the group to focus their attention on the vehicles as they came closer.

"That's not Indie's car," Trina observed. "And if it is him, who is in the second one?"

Chase stepped to the forefront and hooked his fingers through his belt loops. He had the .45 holstered at his waist, so no worries rested on his shoulders. "Whoever it is, they don't want no smoke," he said calmly.

The first car approached and cut its lights as it stopped a few yards away from them. Chase didn't know what to expect when he saw the two Italian men exit and fall into position at the entrances of the buildings.

"Fuck is this?" he asked as he turned to look at the girls, who were equally puzzled. The mystery was revealed when Indie emerged from the car.

"Yo, big homie, I was about to set off fireworks in this bitch," Chase said with a chuckle as he greeted Indie with a handshake and a warm embrace.

"Next time, you shoot first and ask questions later," he schooled. "A real nigga got to respect it. Teach a nigga how to announce his arrival. Nobody's an exception, even me."

Chase nodded as he absorbed the knowledge his mentor was kicking.

"So why we all the way out here, Indie?" Trina asked curiously.

"And who is that?" Miesha asked as she nodded to the second car.

"I called you all together out here because I needed to be sure that this was a conversation that was overheard by no one outside of this circle. Conversations in cars, in houses, on cell phones . . . they have a way of turning up in fed transcripts, nah mean? From now on we don't talk business on the phone or anywhere in a confined space. If you're at home, run a dishwasher, a washing machine, a garbage disposal. Never talk in a car, and if you dealing with someone you don't know, shake 'em down before you open your mouth. Once something is said over the wire, it can't be taken back. Make sure you're cautious and skeptical of everybody that's not a part of this team."

"I feel you on all of this, Indie, but you talking like we major out here. Since you got locked up everything has been slow," Trina said.

"Let's just say things are about to pick back up," he replied. "Before I say too much, I have to know that everybody wants to be here. We don't need any weak links in this chain. Either you're in or out. If you decide to stay, you'll see more money than you ever imagined, but with that comes a price. Once you are affiliated, there are no outs. If you get caught up, you will be expected to ride out your sentence, and in return the people you leave on the outside will be taken care of. This isn't Houston block-hugging anymore. This is major, so I need you to be absolutely sure that this is something you want to be a part of."

Indie looked around at the faces of the young ones that he had put on. He had met them all upon relocating to Houston, but they had been some of the most loyal workers he had ever encountered. They were young and easily influenced, but he had molded them well. They were vicious, tenacious, and eager to get their feet wet in the game. They were like predators. They had developed an acquired taste for the fast life. Fast money wasn't always good money, but they didn't care. They would rather live enormous and sit at the royal table for a few good years, than be the peasants who fought over the scraps forever. A speech from Indie hadn't been necessary. They were convinced . . . all except for one.

"Nothing else needs to be said, duke. If you in it, I'm in it," Chase answered.

"If he in it, I'm in it," Trina said, nodding to Chase.

Miesha nodded her head. "What she said."

All eyes turned to Sydney, who looked like a deer in headlights. "I . . . I . . ." she stammered as if the cat had her tongue. "I don't know. I just got accepted to college in Atlanta. I was all for making some money on the side, but I'm not cool with this," she admitted.

Indie nodded his head. "My driver will take you home," he said. He opened his hand and motioned her to the car. Little did she know that she was a long way from home. Indie couldn't allow anyone to jeopardize the setup. He had mistakenly marked her as thorough. If he had known she wouldn't accept his terms, then he would have never brought her into the fold by inviting her to the meeting.

"I don't know him. Can one of you take me?" she asked unsurely, feeling as though she had done something wrong.

"He'll take you," Indie confirmed.

Tears filled Sydney's eyes as she looked to her friends. All of them seemed to sense the presence of the Grim Reaper, and no one could look at her directly as she was ushered into the car.

As she was driven away, Chase lowered his voice and stepped close to Indie. "I take it she isn't going home," he said.

"Unfortunately not," Indie confirmed. He looked Chase square in the eyes. "It's that serious for all of us, fam. No weak links."

He buried his conscience, forcing himself not to think of the young girl's life that he had snuffed out before it even began.

***

YaYa sat behind the tint of the second truck, her identity protected as she looked at Indie speaking to their crew. She would need more than three soldiers to command, but she knew that she had to keep her inner circle petite. They knew her. They had love for her. She trusted them, and that was something that couldn't be bought. She was saddened to see Sydney choose to leave, but she knew that she had to develop a thick skin. In this game she would lose a lot of people she held dear. It was all a part of it; it all came with the territory.

YaYa's hands shook as she thought of what she had taken on. Zya had no idea exactly how much of an amateur YaYa was. She had moved those bricks before because her back was against the wall. She only hoped that she could pull it off again and again without being caught.

She reached into her clutch for the pill bottle. The prescription drugs had become her crutch. It was like a miracle drug that took away all her worries. She felt nothing when she took it, and although the pain of her surgeries was minimal now, she still took it. YaYa needed it to get by day to day. She popped three of the potent pills into her mouth and grabbed the bottled water that sat in the cup holder. She washed them down quickly and closed her eyes. When she stepped out of that truck, she had to exude power. No one wanted to follow a leader that was lost, and everything was at stake. If she was going to do this, she would have to bury "vulnerable YaYa" and step into her own.

***

Indie walked over to the truck and opened the back door. A pair of Armani stilettos appeared beneath the open door, revealing a perfect pedicure.

"Who is that?" Trina asked as she and Miesha stepped forward, trying to get a better view.

"That's the connect," Chase whispered knowingly, more to himself than to the girls. He looked on curiously as Indie closed the door and revealed the mystery woman that had been sitting behind the tinted windows of the SUV.

"YaYa?" Trina called out in shock as her mouth fell open in an O of surprise.

Miesha was speechless, and Chase chose to keep his questions to himself as his mind spun.

"Hello, guys. It's nice to see you too," she said with a confident yet brief smile. No one would have ever suspected that she had just doubted herself five minutes before. She was calm, collected, in control as she addressed her crew.

"How?" Miesha asked. "We thought you were—"

"It doesn't matter," YaYa interrupted. "Details are irrelevant at this point. All you need to know is what we've already told you. Anything else would put you in a compromising position. You can't tell a story that you haven't heard before," she said, knowing that they couldn't snitch or implicate Zya if they knew nothing about her.

"We'll be moving two hundred fifty kilos per month from overseas. Once it gets here, we'll disperse it throughout the States, starting in the South. Once everybody finds their footing, we'll move east and eventually west. We're going to corner every market and build a team along the way.

"The DEA has cracked down on the main seaports in the country. Everything coming through Miami, L.A., even Houston is being seized. If it's on a ship, the feds are taking it . . . so we're not doing that. We're moving it through the airports, and we're never taking our eyes off the product, because we'll be wearing it," she said.

"What?" Chase blurted out. He looked at YaYa like she was insane. "With all that high-tech security shit at the checkpoints, there is no way we'll get on a plane with that."

"I just did it," YaYa confirmed.

She stepped out of her expensive shoes and held them up for everyone to see. "There is a brick of cocaine in the platform of these shoes. A little old man in Italy ensured that they were taken apart, the product was tucked safely inside, and then welded back."

"A pair of shoes moves what? One, two keys at the most," Trina said. "It'll take us forever to get any real weight across the border."

"So I'll need more women, but these women won't even know what they're involved in. I'm starting a modeling agency. They will go on international shoots and casting calls, come back with the shoes on their feet. They won't even know. They'll be paid for their services and we'll get rich.

"Trina and Miesha, I will need you to help find the ladies. Chase, I'll need you to put together a crew to help you distribute the work once it gets here. We're not breaking anything down. We're moving weight, not pieces. All wholesale," YaYa said.

Indie played the back, watching YaYa as she broke down her plan. He had to admit that it was genius. He didn't even know YaYa was capable of orchestrating something so elaborate. *Where the fuck this shit come from?* he thought, finding this new side to her incredibly sexy.

The first trip would be the hardest to make because they would have to work out all the kinks, but once they found their rhythm and knew the ins and outs of TSA, not even the sky would be the limit. She was about to ready her troops to make sure that they could handle anything they encountered. YaYa stepped back as Indie stepped forward.

"No one knows that YaYa is alive. Let's keep it that way. The feds can't arrest a ghost, and the streets can't touch who they can't see," Indie said. "We'll set up shop at this plant, put shooters on the rooftops, at every entrance. Keep this location to yourselves as well. Everybody has a position to play. Play it correctly and everybody gets rich."

Chapter 10

Leah sat in the courtroom, and she could feel the stares as she sat with her back to the crowd, facing the judge. It was as if everyone's eyes were burning a hole through her gray two-piece jail suit. Bitterness filled her as she kept her eyes glued to the wooden table that she sat behind. Her obsession with YaYa had led her to this moment of judgment, and she felt trapped. Her body was in a terrible state, and she was disgusted with the way that she looked. With no surgery in her future, Leah was forced to live in her current skin. Her life was ruined. She couldn't manipulate anyone looking the way that she did. A part of her appeal had always been her beauty; without that, her gift of gab had disappeared.

The bailiff entered the room. "All rise."

She stood to her feet, next to her court-appointed representation. The sight of his poorly pressed, cheap polyester suit caused her to sneer. There was no way she could win her case with an inexperienced joker sitting next to her. She needed a shark to get out of the web that she was stuck in.

"The Fifty-ninth US District Court is now in session. Honorable Judge Meredith Peaks presiding. All having business before this honorable court draw near, give attention, and you shall be heard. You may be seated."

A white middle-aged woman entered the room, cloaked in a black robe. She sat down and looked out over the attendees. "Leah Richards, please approach the podium with your representation," she ordered. "You are hereby charged with kidnapping, first-degree murder, and conspiracy to commit murder. How do you plead?"

Leah leaned into the microphone and replied, "Not guilty."

"Let the record note that the defendant has entered a plea of not guilty," the judge told the transcriptionist. "Bail is set at two hundred thousand dollars." She banged her gavel. "Let's move on."

Leah had waited all morning for a five-minute arraignment.

"What happens now?" she asked.

"Well, I think you should consider a plea," the young attorney said.

"I'm not considering shit. I need to get out of this, and I need you to help me do it," she said. An officer came behind her and grabbed her handcuffed arms. "Get me off!" she yelled as she snatched away from the officer. "Get me off!" she screamed at her lawyer. "Or find me someone who can!" She was dragged away kicking and screaming.

***

YaYa sat in the courtroom with her large Fendi hat tilted over her eyes. Leah didn't even notice that she had walked right past her. There was no way that YaYa could forget to cook that beef. Her hatred for Leah had done nothing but grown. Her anger was out of control, and YaYa knew that she would have to settle things in order to take back her own life. A better woman would have wanted to move on and never look back. She would let Leah's karma catch up to her, but YaYa wasn't that woman. She wanted Leah to feel her pain. YaYa was out for blood, and it was only a matter of time before her wish came true.

She stood and tucked her crocodile-skin clutch bag under her armpit. Her five-inch heels played a sexy rhythm on the tiled floor as she made her exit. She walked right past a shackled Leah on the way out, bumping her hard as she made her way out the door.

With Leah in custody, YaYa wasn't able to exact the type of revenge that she wanted to. YaYa would pay anything to be put in a room with Leah with nothing but space and opportunity, but that wouldn't happen anytime soon. Just because Leah was behind bars, however, didn't mean that she couldn't be touched. Prison time wouldn't be a cakewalk for Leah; YaYa would make sure of it. She had a vendetta against Leah, and no amount of time would make her ill will dissolve. She would never let bygones be bygones. YaYa wanted Leah's head on a silver platter, and she would go through anything and pay any amount to get it. Get the money . . . get the power . . . get the woman.

***

As soon as Leah was thrown back on the cellblock, the hecklers began. The other inmates were just waiting for the perfect opportunity to get their hands on Leah. Her burns made her seem vulnerable, and on top of being the new girl on lock, she was fresh meat. The other women saw her as weak, and it was only a matter of time before she encountered problems on the inside. Leah needed out of there as soon as possible, or she would lose what little sanity she had left.

Her vendetta against YaYa had made her lose her grip on reality, and for the first time she realized that she had taken it too far. Leah had pushed it to the point of no return. In order to hurt YaYa, she didn't care that she had hurt herself as well.

Her head spun as she entered her cell. She was grateful for the solitude that it provided. Because her case had been such a high profile one, she had walked into the jail with a target on her back. The news had reported Skylar's kidnapping every day for weeks, gaining sympathy from everyone in the city. The D.A. wanted justice for the little girl, not street revenge. He arranged to keep her as safe as possible while inside by assigning her to a single cell.

Leah was one of the few inmates without a bunk-mate, which was exactly the way that she preferred it. It gave her time alone with her thoughts. All she had ever wanted was to be loved like YaYa. She couldn't understand why God would choose to give so much to YaYa while she sat in need of so many things. Jealousy had branded her heart for so long that even now as she was locked up, she felt that YaYa had gotten the better deal. She had no clue that YaYa was very much alive, and she figured that death had to be better than living through hell.

Leah couldn't spend the rest of her days caged like a dog, but what she didn't realize was that she was rabid. Her uncontrollable rage toward YaYa had pushed her to do the most unthinkable things. She knew that she should feel some type of remorse, but it wasn't an emotion that she had come equipped with. She couldn't even portray it on the stand to save her own behind, because she had no idea what the words "I'm sorry" truly meant.

In the back of her mind she still found the sweetest satisfaction in the fact that she had ruined YaYa. She had come into her life like a wrecking ball, knocking down every support system that YaYa had ever relied on. Her actions had come with a price to pay, but if she had to do it all over again, she wouldn't change a thing.

Leah had no clue that she was the only one who had suffered. YaYa was alive, and with Zya's affiliation, she held more pull than Leah would ever possess. Soon she would pay for the things that she had done. She had no wins against YaYa, because she couldn't even see her enemy coming. She was fighting a ghost, and now her own actions were about to come back to haunt her.

Chapter 11

Bang! Bang! Bang! Bang!

The sound of the semi-automatic pistols firing was dulled by the earmuffs that protected Chase's ears. He sat back, watching Trina and Miesha as they became acquainted with their guns. They were amateurs when it came to street beefs, but in their new positions they had to move as if they were seasoned and expected the unexpected at all times. Their aim game had to be on point.

When their clips were empty, they turned to him in excitement. "Look at that. Tell me my aim not nice," Trina said as she hit the button that moved her target toward her. She pulled down the paper and smiled slyly as Chase saw that she had hit it dead in the middle repeatedly.

"Bitch, bye. You aiming at a target that don't move. It's a lot different hitting a nigga with legs," Miesha said, raining on Trina's parade.

Chase nodded. "She's right. Shooting through flesh and shooting through paper is two different things. I need your aim to be on point, but you've got to be able to pop a nigga without thinking twice about it. Trust me when I say that they won't think twice about putting something hot in either of you," Chase schooled.

"Leave that feminine shit at home. Y'all wanna ball like bosses, then you have to behave like bosses. You draw on a nigga then you had better be Picasso," Chase said.

"The best at the draw," Miesha said as she finished reloading her clip and popped it back into the gun. She refocused on the target and popped off. Trina followed suit.

There was no way that Chase was going to send them into battle with no weapons. They had to be nice with it. Their gun game had to be official. Even though YaYa was putting a team of certified goons around them, Chase had learned long ago that when it counted, the only hired hand he could count on was his own. So he trained Miesha and Trina the way that Indie had trained him. That way they would be prepared for anything.

**

"Next!" Trina yelled loudly as she dismissed the model that had just strutted onto the club's stage. They were at Oasis, Houston's most popular strip club, scouting for talent. YaYa had told them to recruit fifty models that she would use for the overseas "shoots."

"Damn, T, you hard on a bitch, ain't you?" Miesha joked as she pulled out more dollar bills.

Chase shook his head and sat back, silently enjoying the show as the girls had their fun.

"That bitch had hella stretch marks. Don't nobody want to look at her ass. Ho got three kids," Trina cracked.

Chase shook his head. Trina and Miesha were having too much fun. They forgot that they were there on business. The task at hand required them to remain focused. Although the agency was fake, the girls still had to look the part. YaYa wanted real models so that to the outside eye, her operation would appear legit.

"Hey, let's get serious. This is cool and all, but let's pick 'em and get out of here. Time is money," Chase said.

***

YaYa sat behind her glass and steel desk as she personally interrogated every girl that had been chosen. Her new business, Mona Modeling Inc., had been named in memory of her late best friend. There was no doubt in her mind that she would have been riding shotgun with YaYa to the top if she were still alive. So she honored her in death.

The prospective models were from all walks of life. There were hood chicks, college students, white girls, black girls, Asian broads. YaYa's team had gone all out to get her the diverse group of "models" that she needed to get the job done. She sat back and took notes on each one she encountered. YaYa wanted to know it all. Legal name, social security numbers, addresses, number of children, names of the baby daddies . . . She was thorough. If she had to reach out and touch one of the girls, they would have nowhere to hide. They had already given her total access to their lives. They didn't know that if things went south, YaYa would send people to their doorsteps. The girls were eager to be signed to her "agency," so they divulged whatever she needed them to without question.

YaYa weeded through them strategically until she had a solid stable. If she wasn't Buchanan Slim's daughter, she had definitely seen him work his magic enough to have the gift of persuasion run through her blood. Her tongue was reminiscent of the slickest pimp. The only difference was that YaYa wasn't selling ass. She was selling dreams.

YaYa was smart. She wasn't running a sorority. No friendships would be established under her watch. The girls didn't know one another. They would simply be strangers in an airport. No nerves were involved, so each girl would travel with confidence and without suspicion. What they didn't know couldn't hurt them.

Each girl received a roundtrip ticket to Milan, where a dummy shoot was set up. They would receive a package to carry back to YaYa. A gift from the photographer, a package from the designer, and without even knowing it, they would carry enough cocaine into the US to get them buried under the prison. Surely the girls would open the box, and inside they would find a pair of shoes. The shoes would go inside a suitcase and become checked baggage until they were hand delivered back to YaYa. It was the perfect plan.

YaYa was moving like the wind, felt, but unseen. There was no way that any bureau could come for her head. She was aligning every stone up to perfection so that there was no crack in her foundation. Any D.A. coming for her head would undoubtedly lose because YaYa was leaving nothing to chance. She wouldn't give anyone leverage to build a case against her. YaYa was untouchable.

YaYa would pay each girl $5,000 upon their return to the States and then schedule another "shoot" in two weeks. Two shoots for each girl per month, carrying two keys back in the platforms of their shoes, fifty girls . . . It all totaled out to 200 kilos per month. YaYa was about to get it.

***

Trina and Miesha pulled up to the Za Za Hotel. It had become YaYa's temporary residence. They pulled up to the valet and handed the older man their keys. The opulent hotel was highly favored by every superstar that visited the city. Anybody who was somebody had stayed there. They hardly even let regulars occupy a suite, so Trina and Miesha were surprised when YaYa summoned them there.

Trina pulled out her cell phone and sent a text to YaYa to let her know that they had arrived. They had been around YaYa often in the past, but as they stood in the lobby, for some reason this one particular time they both had butterflies dancing in their stomachs. Something about her had changed. She seemed withdrawn, as if the power of her new position had sucked the life out of her.

Trina remembered the first time they met, YaYa's smile had been contagious; the light in her eye blindingly bright . . . her soul pure. YaYa had been one of the good people—one of the people that God had placed purity inside, good intentions, a kind heart. When she loved, she loved wholeheartedly and recklessly. The downside to that was when she was let down, her entire heart broke.

Trina and Miesha had witnessed YaYa's heartbreak the day Skylar had been taken, and ever since then she had never been quite the same. They had literally buried her memory, thinking she was gone, only to have her resurrect herself into their lives. That had done something to her. Whether YaYa would ever admit it or not, she had transformed into someone new. Some would say a boss, others a queen pin, but whatever had happened, there was a darkness that now hung over her head. She intimidated Trina and Miesha, but they were loyal to her regardless. They trusted her because Indie vouched for her. They were family, all of them knew.

The concierge came over to them with a friendly smile. "Right this way, ladies," he said.

They followed him onto the elevator and watched as he pressed *PH*, signaling that they were going to the penthouse. Miesha and Trina glanced at each other out of the corners of their eyes as they wondered exactly what they were being called for.

When the elevator opened up, they stood in a small hallway space before a wooden door with silver numbers. Trina felt as if she were standing on the threshold to hell. The suspense was too much. Just the fact that YaYa had asked them not to tell anyone that they were coming to meet with her made Trina wary. She trusted YaYa, but knew that with so much at stake, any little misstep could change the tides of their friendship. After seeing how Sydney had been handled, they both knew that anyone could get got. If you were a threat to the operation, then you became a liability. Liabilities weren't tolerated. All loose ends got clipped.

Did we do something wrong? she thought.

Finally the door opened and YaYa stood before them. Her haircut softly complemented her green eyes, and her presence stunned both girls into silence. YaYa had always been beautiful, but it seemed as though since the fire she was even more so. Her imperfections, the scars from the surgery, the lace gloves she wore to cover the burns on her hands . . . it all seemed to enhance her beauty because they signified that she was a woman who had been through some shit. She was a woman who had endured so much and still come out on top. She was a woman . . . resilient, strong. Like a cat, no matter how many times she had been knocked down, she had always managed to land on her feet.

"Hi, ladies," she said. "Come in."

The BCBG leggings she wore displayed her amazing physique, hugging her curves. It was complemented by a matching blazer with a ruffle shoulder and black diamonds that glistened with every step that her red-bottomed feet took.

"You ladies know the deal. Let's go on the balcony," she said. She poured herself a glass of white wine and poured out four pills from a prescription bottle. She tossed the pills into her mouth and rinsed it down with the wine.

Miesha raised an eyebrow, knowing that drugs and alcohol weren't a great mix, but she kept quiet and followed YaYa as she led them outside. They seemed to be on top of the world as they peered out over the city. From fifty-one stories in the air, the city lights were amazing.

"Reminds me of New York from this high up," YaYa said as she sipped from her wine glass.

Miesha shifted unsurely in her stance. "YaYa, are we in trouble? Like, should I be worried right now?"

YaYa turned and looked at her in surprise. *Are they afraid of me?* she thought. She had no idea how her change of status would change the way those around her reacted. Fear was the last thing that she wanted those close to her to feel. She wanted love. That's all she craved. She would rather be loved than to be feared. It wasn't the way of men, but it was her way . . . the only way, in her opinion, to retain loyalty from her team. The niggas that feared you were the same ones who would pop you if given the opportunity. With love, niggas felt obligated to protect you, to warn you, to pull your coattail if negativity was headed your way. Ego made kingpins rule with fear. She was a woman. She would do it a new way to avoid the pitfalls of the game.

"No, Miesha, you don't have to worry, hon. I called you both here because tomorrow it's go time. I needed to be sure that you're ready," YaYa said.

"We're good," Trina said. "Passports are already on deck, tickets are purchased. I just hope that it's as easy as you say to get past the body scanners."

YaYa pointed at Trina. "See. It's that right there . . . that skepticism that I just heard in your voice. You can't have that tomorrow. That doubt will get you caught. It is all about the art of deceit. You can't walk into the airport feeling guilty. Your confidence has to be at an all-time high. You can't be nervous. You can't be fidgety. You have more control over the situation than you think," YaYa said. "You are the only one who actually knows what you will be bringing back with you, so you are the one that I am worried about. The other girls have the advantage because they are clueless. You have the burden of knowledge."

"Well, Miesha will be there, so—"

"Miesha won't be there," YaYa interjected.

Miesha's eyes widened as she immediately looked around. "I thought we both were going," Miesha said.

"I have another job in mind for you," YaYa said. "Now, both of you can back out and say no at any time. I give you my word that what happened to Sydney will not happen to you."

Trina and Miesha only half believed YaYa as they nodded their heads in understanding.

YaYa continued. "You turned eighteen a few weeks ago, which is the reason why I am asking you to do this instead of Trina."

The lost expression on Miesha's face urged YaYa to continue. "I can't move into the future without first clearing up the past. The federal detention center in Houston is overcrowded, so Leah is locked up at Harris County Jail. I need her touched, and I need her touched by someone I trust. I wish that I could be the one to do it personally, but that isn't possible," YaYa explained.

"Are you sure you don't want to leave that alone, YaYa? She is going to rot underneath the jail for what she did to Sky. Her own karma will take care of her. After everything that you've been through, are you sure you can handle this?" Trina asked.

"I can't handle not doing this, if that makes sense," YaYa replied honestly.

"Does Indie know about this?" Miesha asked.

"No," YaYa admitted. "And I would like to keep it that way."

"What do you want me to do?" Miesha asked.

"I want you to go to jail," YaYa answered bluntly.

Miesha looked as if the air had been sucked out of her lungs. YaYa had anticipated this reaction, but she needed someone young, with no records, and with something to prove to take care of this. For Miesha, this was the turning point. If she pulled this off, she would be in good with YaYa. There would be no dismissing her loyalty to the team.

"I have an attorney on retainer already. You'll commit a petty crime. My guy will make sure that you get placed on the same cell block as Leah. You'll be arraigned, but plead not guilty, and a trial date will be set. While you're waiting for your trial, you'll have nothing but space and opportunity to hit Leah. I don't care how you do it, but I need her taken care of," YaYa said. As she spoke she seemed to zone out. Even the thought of revenge was sweet, and YaYa relished in the moment as she imagined Leah's face in her mind. "I'll pay you well. If you do this, you will never have to worry about money a day in your life," YaYa said.

Miesha stood deep in thought as her eyes shifted to the floor.

"Your son will be taken care of every day of his life," YaYa said.

"Son?" Trina said in surprise as she looked at Miesha. They had been thick as thieves for over a year, and Miesha had never mentioned a child. "She doesn't have a son. I've never even seen you with a kid besides your little brother."

Miesha nodded her head, silently wondering how YaYa knew about the secret child that her mother had helped her to hide. "He's not my brother, Trina. He's really my son," she admitted. She had never spoken those words aloud. After getting pregnant at fourteen, she decided to let her mother raise her child, so that being a young mom wouldn't ruin her life. They had relocated from Dallas to Houston once she gave birth so that Miesha could live a regular life as a teenager without being judged. Hiding her child had killed her soul, and watching her mother struggle to feed another mouth always intensified her guilt.

"You do this, and I will personally make sure that both you and your son are set," YaYa promised.

Miesha knew that there was nothing left to think about. She would do anything to take the burden off of her mother's shoulders. For so long, she just wanted to admit to the world that she was a mother. She loved her son and wanted to claim him, to reclaim her life. She was eighteen, and four years ago she had made a mistake. To be able to take care of her child and repay her mother for all that she had done would right all of her wrongs.

But what if something goes wrong? What if I get caught? What if I can't do it? she thought. Miesha wasn't a killer. She wasn't cold-hearted. She was just an around the way girl that was in love with the street life. She had a thrill for money and was willing to do most things to get it, but could she do this? Even if she did pull it off, would she ever be the same after it was done? Would the guilt eat her alive? These things flashed through her mind as she stood in front of YaYa with her mouth hanging open as she urged herself to speak.

She desperately wanted to be down with YaYa's operation, but was she willing to take things this far? There were certain actions that couldn't be taken back, and this was one of them. It wouldn't be able to be undone. If she failed, would YaYa punish her? More importantly, if she said no, would she end up the way that Sydney had?

Miesha shifted unsurely in her stance. "Can I think about it?" she asked.

YaYa felt horrible for even placing a large burden on such small shoulders, but she had nowhere else to go. Outsourcing the job had proved disastrous. She had to build her own team, make them strong, push them to their limits until they became treacherous the way she needed them to be. The only one who was ready was Chase. He was thorough because Indie had trained him to be. The girls had to catch up, and this was Miesha's chance to prove her value to the team.

"Don't take too long. If I don't hear from you by tomorrow evening, we can forget this conversation ever happened," YaYa replied. She downed the rest of her drink. She turned around and leaned on the ledge as she peered out at the parking lot below.

Leah Richards always put her in a somber mood. A part of her was afraid to start living her life again because she always felt that Leah would come through like a wrecking ball and tear it all apart again. She didn't feel safe. She feared for her daughter's wellbeing. She always would as long as there was still air in Leah's lungs. This had to be done. Once and for all, she needed her enemy to be lying in a cold grave. It was time to put an end to all of the chaos that Leah had caused. What had started out as friendship had turned into an obsession that had spanned across decades. She knew that the only thing to make this end was death, either hers or Leah's.

Now that she was in a position to fight, she was going to get at Leah before Leah got at her. Whoever hit first usually hit the hardest, and YaYa was going for the knockout.

"See yourselves out."

***

"Was she high?" Trina asked as they waited for the valet to bring their car around.

"She took enough pills. I don't think she's supposed to take that many," Miesha said. She shrugged her shoulders. "Maybe she's still in a lot of pain."

Trina folded her arms across her chest and frowned. "Yeah, maybe. Why didn't you tell me you had a son?"

"I was young. It's not something that I'm proud of," Miesha said. The car came around and the girls entered. "YaYa's offer sounds real good right now, though."

"Do you realize what she's asking you to do?" Trina asked. She didn't know why she was whispering. After the eerie meeting they had just had, she was afraid to speak the words too loudly.

The fact that Miesha didn't respond told Trina that Miesha was more than considering the job.

"You're going to tell her no, right?" Trina insisted.

"I don't know," Miesha admitted. "The type of money she's offering can change my life . . . my son's life."

Trina looked at Miesha as if she were crazy. "And getting caught up in that can change your life. This is crazy. We're not killers! You're not a killer. How can you even be thinking about this? Do you really think you can pull that off?" Trina asked.

"For the right price . . . yeah," Miesha said as stared at her best friend directly in the eyes.

Trina sucked her teeth and shook her head. "She ain't right for coming to you for this. Getting money was one thing, but this . . ."

"Just stop, T! Damn, you're not making the decision any easier. What did you think came along with the game? We're selling drugs, moving kilos of cocaine. You think all that target practice Chase had us doing was for fun?" Miesha asked. "Don't be naïve! We're in this shit knee deep. Leah will be the first, but she probably won't be the last. It comes with this territory." Miesha was so passionate as she spoke that her eyes watered.

Reading her as if she were a book, Trina snapped, "Who you trying to persuade? Me or yourself?"

The girls rode in awkward silence until they arrived at Miesha's house. Before Miesha got out of the car, Trina said, "Just make sure you think this all the way through before you say yes. I don't know if I'm about this life. Cooking up product for Indie for extra pocket money was one thing, but this new thing YaYa is running, this is on a different level. How long can it really last?"

Miesha didn't answer immediately as she let Trina's words sink into her brain. "I'll holla at you later, Trina. Love you, girl."

Miesha exited the car, thinking of the risks and rewards of YaYa's offer. Sure, she was getting money, but nothing like the offer that YaYa had proposed. Working with Chase and Indie in the past looked like small time compared to this. She looked up at the apartment building that she lived in and looked around the dilapidated neighborhood that she called home. She didn't want her son growing up here. She didn't want her mother struggling to take care of them. To make a long story short, she just wanted more. She wanted more than fly clothes and spending money, more than money rolls. Miesha needed long paper, security, the type of cash that would relieve the burdens of her struggling mother. She needed what YaYa was offering her. She pulled out her cell phone and dialed YaYa's number.

"Hello," YaYa answered.

"I'll do it," Miesha agreed.

Click.

Miesha looked at the phone. "Hello? Hello?" she said. She was sure that YaYa had heard her. What she didn't know was that no more words needed to be spoken. Miesha was in, and that's all YaYa needed to hear.

***

YaYa looked out over the city and finished the bottle of wine as she sat with murderous thoughts running through her head. Leah's fate was one that she wanted to hand deliver, but she was too impatient to wait for the opportunity to arise. Leah was locked up, and there was no way to get to her personally, unless she went inside herself. YaYa couldn't do that, but Miesha could, and if she succeeded YaYa would forever be grateful to her.

She smiled, knowing that karma was a bitch. The day she read Leah's obituary would be the best day of her life.

"What are you doing out here?"

Indie's voice startled her, and she turned around to face him.

"Hey, babe," she said. "Come here."

She pulled at his arm until he was standing directly in front of her.

He picked up the bottle of wine. "You drank all this by yourself?" he asked.

"I did," she replied. Her eyes were low and heavy. The mixture of pills and alcohol had her on cloud nine. Indie had no idea how high she truly was, because he blamed her current state on the wine alone.

He picked her up and carried her back inside the penthouse. "Is everything okay, ma? I know you're nervous. Your first run is coming up, but everything will go smoothly. I've paid off some of the TSA workers here in Houston. Everything is good to go," he assured. Her head leaned lazily against his chest. "YaYa, are you sure you can handle this? It's not too late to back out."

"I'm fine," she said. "I don't want to think about any of that. Right now I just want to think about you and me. You inside me . . ."

Her words drifted off, and he knew that she was in no state to make love. "You're drunk, ma," he said with a slight chuckle. It reminded him of the very first time they had met. They had sat up all night talking and drinking together. It was back in those days when their lives were so uncomplicated and their attraction to one another was fresh, untainted by treachery.

"And?" she challenged.

"And I'll wait until you're in your right frame of mind," Indie said. He placed her on her feet and kissed her lips. He unbuttoned her blazer and slid it off of her shoulders, then grabbed the waist of her leggings and rolled them down. She stepped out of them one foot at a time. "I need you to sleep this off, a'ight? I need your head clear. You're a thinker, YaYa. You can't be the brains if your judgment is clouded," Indie said. He undid the clasps of her heels and took them off of her pretty feet. He kissed her ankles, causing YaYa to smile.

"You sure you don't want to take advantage of me?" she asked. "I give you full permission."

Her voice was low and sexy as Indie looked up at her. He pulled her panties to the side and licked her clit slowly. The drugs in her system had her entire body sensitive to the touch, and blood rushed to her love button, instantly making it throb with passion.

"Ooh, Indie. Yes, baby. Lick it," she whispered. Her head fell back as he pulled her flower between his lips and ran his tongue down her slit simultaneously. She creamed instantly as her legs shook. Indie pushed her down onto the bed and went to work, seducing her womanhood. He was reintroducing her to pleasure as he sucked and nibbled, tugged then pulled, on her most sensitive spot. YaYa's nipples hardened, puckering up so tightly that she rubbed them softly between her fingertips to relieve the aching feeling. Her back arched, and Indie wrapped one arm around her waist as he pulled her body into his mouth, applying more pressure.

She was speechless, breathless, and all she could do was gasp. No words were needed for the way that he was making her feel. Indie was an excellent lover. He always made sure that she was satisfied. He was unselfish. He was rugged, handling her with just enough masculinity to let her know he was in control, but still gentle and expressive so that she knew he loved her. Indie blew her mind the way he went from kissing her inner thighs to sucking the sweet nectar from her pussy.

As her legs began to tremble uncontrollably, he coached her to the finish line. "Cum for me, ma," he whispered, his breath hot, soothing as she moaned his name.

Her body went limp, and he stood to his feet while wiping his mouth with his hand. "Take a shower with me," he said.

"Hmm, I can't move," she groaned. She was stuck—partly from her high, partly from her orgasm. Either way it didn't matter. She couldn't move from that spot.

She turned over on her side, and Indie went to the bathroom to retrieve a warm towel. He opened her legs and gently wiped her clean, then tucked her into the bed before retreating to the shower.

He had no idea the types of demons she was battling. She hadn't come out of the fire unscathed. YaYa's revenge was pushing her toward an addictive personality. She couldn't let go of the idea of getting back at Leah. Her thoughts were constantly in a dark place, and the only way to counter the unhappiness was to take pills that made her happy, that made her feel good. They brought her bliss, but she had no idea of the price that she would eventually pay.

***

Trina didn't know how to feel about YaYa or her proposition. It seemed to her that YaYa's new team wasn't a team at all. It all seemed to be about her and no one else. Trina wondered if YaYa had even considered that she was putting Miesha's life at risk. She was glad that the proposition hadn't been for her, but she knew that one day YaYa would ask her to cross a similar line. The only question was if Trina would be able to be bought as easily as Miesha had.

She wasn't exactly sure what had happened to YaYa while she was away, but it had changed her. When they had first met, YaYa was sweet, considerate. She had become family. Now she was merely a shell of the person she used to be. Everything on the inside had changed. The power had changed her. She was selfish and cunning and ruthless. It was all about revenge to YaYa, and Trina no longer felt as if the loyalty was a two-way street. It wasn't a family, or at least it didn't feel like one to Trina. It felt like she was a pawn in a chess game. She didn't want to be sacrificed in YaYa's quest to get to Leah, but she knew that if she didn't get out, eventually she would be.

"Chase!" she shouted as she rushed into the apartment that she shared with her brother. "Chase!" She had to voice her concerns with him; had to tell him that she thought YaYa would lead them straight into the fire if they stuck around too long.

"Yo, Trina, what's up with all the yelling?" he asked as he came waltzing out of the kitchen.

"I just came back from a meeting with—"

She stopped speaking abruptly when Indie came walking out behind Chase.

"You had a meeting with who?" Indie asked.

"Um, nobody. Just a potential buyer out of Fort Worth," she lied quickly. She wanted to express her concern to Indie, but she didn't think it wise to speak ill about the woman he loved. If it got back to YaYa, then Trina would be labeled untrustworthy. So, instead of speaking up, Trina said nothing at all and said her good-byes as Indie made his exit.

Once he was gone and she was alone with Chase, she asked, "How much do you trust YaYa? How well do you know her?"

Chase's brow furrowed in concern. "What's wrong, Trina? Where did that come from?"

Trina shrugged. "I don't know. I just feel like we're all a means to an end for her. That any of us are disposable. It doesn't seem like YaYa cares about anything. Not the money, not us, just about getting to Leah," she said. "I just want to get enough money and get out fast. I just want you to know where I stand. My loyalty is to me first."

Chase didn't like what he was hearing. He had never known his sister to go against the grain. "As long as you keep it one hunnid and keep what you know to yourself, I don't see a problem with it. I'm in it until the death of me, though. You know how I move. Just remember I'm your brother. I wouldn't have brought you into the fold if I thought anyone would do you dirty."

"I just think that you're loyal to a fault. Just make sure the team is still a team and you're not just carrying out somebody else's agenda," Trina said. "I love Indie and YaYa, but I know this is only temporary for me. I'm getting to the money and getting out before she asks me to do something that I don't want to do."

Chapter 12

Miesha watched the speedometer go from sixty to seventy to eighty, and her heart beat rapidly as she checked her rearview. She glanced at the gun that sat on the floor of her passenger seat and then took a deep breath as she floored the gas even harder, pushing the car to ninety then one hundred. As she ripped through the city streets of the fifth ward, it didn't take long for a police officer to pull out and give chase. She didn't slow down when they turned on their lights and the siren rang out. She pushed the car to the max, figuring if she was going to do it, she may as well go all out.

She pulled out her cell phone and speed-dialed YaYa's number with one hand as she maneuvered the vehicle with the other.

"Are we on?" YaYa asked as soon as she answered.

"We're on. They're on my ass now. I'm pushing a hundred and five through the hood as we speak," Miesha answered. Her voice shook slightly and YaYa heard her fear.

"Don't be scared, Miesha. Trust me. I have the best lawyer in the South waiting to work everything out for you. Don't overdo it, though. A high-speed chase could turn bad quickly. I don't need you or anyone else getting hurt. Is the gun on you?" YaYa asked.

"Yeah, it's on the floor," Miesha answered as she checked her rearview. "They just added a second car. I have two of them on me now."

"Did you empty the clip like I told you to?" YaYa inquired. She knew that getting caught with a fully loaded clip would be much worse for Miesha.

"Yeah, yeah! I followed your instructions to a tee," Miesha yelled. "They're on me. I can't keep this up much longer." She hit a corner and her car tipped on two wheels as she never cut her speed.

"Okay, Miesha, slow it down and don't resist arrest," YaYa said. "When they take you in, your attorney will already be waiting for you. Don't worry. I've got you."

YaYa disconnected the call, and Miesha brought the car to a reasonable speed as she pulled over to the shoulder of the road.

The two country hick officers hopped out of the car with red faces that stared at her in anger as they trained their guns on her. "Put your hands on the steering wheel now!" one of the cops yelled aggressively.

Miesha knew to do as she was told. She was in fry-a-nigga Texas, and the police wouldn't hesitate to pop her if she gave them even the smallest reason to. She placed her hands on the steering wheel in clear view as they snatched open both of her doors. They pulled her out of the car as if little old Miesha was a threat. They dragged her across the gravel, making it hard for her to keep her footing.

"We've got a gun!" the second cop announced.

"You're going to jail. You have the right to remain silent . . ."

Miesha turned deaf as handcuffs were placed on her wrists. They pinched her so hard that she winced. "Ow!" she cried out as they bent her arm back as far as it would go then forced her toward the back of the squad car.

She hoped that she had made the right decision. YaYa had guaranteed her that she wouldn't do more than six months for a first-time offense of carrying a concealed weapon. It would be the longest she had ever been away from her mother and son, but when she emerged a new woman, a paid woman, it would be all worth it.

***

"Make me understand this, YaYa, 'cause right now it's not adding up," Indie said calmly as he leaned over the dining table in the penthouse suite as YaYa sat at the head of it, calmly eating her dinner.

"What is there to understand, Indie?" YaYa replied.

"Why would you send Miesha in? Of all people? She's eighteen!" Indie said through gritted teeth. YaYa had put a play down that had been stupid. "What makes you think she can even pull this off? Huh?"

"She's hungry," YaYa replied as she stopped cutting her chicken and looked up at Indie as she cocked her head to the side. "She has every reason in the world to pull this off. She's a mother," YaYa said, enunciating her words. "I made her a proposition that she couldn't refuse. She kills Leah, I'll personally see to it that her and her son want for nothing."

"You manipulated that girl, YaYa," Indie said. "You stay loyal to the team. You do right by your team, ma, because without them you're nothing. Without your soldiers you become touchable. You don't play off of their weaknesses in order to get what you want!"

"As long as Leah gets hers, that's all that matters," YaYa replied.

"You should have run it by me, YaYa. What if she murders Leah and gets caught? That's more than six months, ma. That's life. You have to think about the play from all angles. If this thing goes bad, Miesha won't ever get out. You will have taken someone else's mother away from them the same way Leah tried to take you away from Skylar."

"If that's the cost I have to pay to get at Leah, then so be it, and for the record, Indie, I don't have to run things by you," YaYa said snidely.

Indie looked at her in disbelief. He didn't even recognize the look in YaYa's eyes. This wasn't the fly girl that he had fallen in love with. YaYa was cold since the fire. She seemed preoccupied with her thoughts most of the time, and although she was there with him physically, she seemed so far away. She had always known how to play her position by his side, but things were different with her now . . . awkward. They weren't vibing to the same rhythm anymore. She was ruthless, more cunning and selfish than he ever remembered.

"Don't play that boss shit with me, ma. I know you. I know you better than you know yourself," he said as he leaned over her as she sat perfectly still. "Get your mind right, YaYa. It's too early in the game for you to be power drunk. I love you, ma," he said.

YaYa refused to look at him.

"What's over there? I'm right here. Look at me," he requested as he pulled her chin toward him. She resisted and snatched her chin away, but he gripped it with more authority. "This is me, YaYa. Look at me."

She did this time, but her bottom lip quivered in anger, in resentment, in sadness. YaYa hated Leah for what she had done to her. Through the cat and mouse games, YaYa had built up a wall of bitterness that was so hard for her to tear down. She was going through a thing that no one, not even Indie, seemed to understand. Not power, not money, not anything could cure her. The only remedy to her ailment was revenge.

"How could you not understand my need to get at her? She ruined me," YaYa said with tears in her eyes.

"She tried, ma . . . but you're here and free and breathing while she is rotting in a cell. The only person who can ruin you is yourself. Revenge is sweet, but it can make you rot, too. I just got you back, so tell me why it feels like I'm about to lose you again," he asked. "There is something in between us. What is it?"

"It's Leah," YaYa responded truthfully.

"Let it go, ma. Let all of it go," Indie said. The scent of her invaded his nostrils as he inhaled her Donna Karan fragrance while planting kisses on her neck. His lips left tingles behind as he blazed a trail from her ear to her collarbone to her chin, and finally their mouths met.

The electricity that flowed through her when Indie's strong hands caressed the back of her neck made her flower bloom. She was high out of this world on Vicodin, and it intensified every sensation. Pleasure was sinful as Indie rubbed her nipples through the thin fabric of her silk blouse, turning them into little torpedoes. Her legs instinctively spread as she re-familiarized herself with Indie's way of lovemaking.

He was an artist when it came to cunnilingus, and his tongue was like brush strokes as he painted a canvas on the way down. He went from her neck, ripped the buttons of her expensive shirt so that he could leave his mark on her breasts, then blazed a trail to her navel, before finally landing on her clitoris.

She inhaled as he exhaled hotly onto her love button, and her hips arched upward to meet his face as he ate away at her as if she were his favorite dessert.

"You've got a wall up, YaYa," Indie whispered as he was drowning in her wetness. "You've got to let me back in."

She moaned and her head fell back as he folded his lips over his teeth then closed them on her clit. YaYa almost lost her mind as he went from sucking to biting her flesh gently. It had been so long since they had indulged in one another. She had forgotten how skilled her lover was, and she was giving him total access to her body as she opened her legs wide and grabbed the back of his head.

"Agh, Indie, wait. I don't want to cum yet," she protested.

"Let it go, ma. I hit more than one homerun. I'm not a rookie," he said. His arrogance sent YaYa over the top, and her love melted against his warm tongue as her back arched and her mouth opened in ecstasy.

Indie stood and pulled her into the master bathroom. Their kisses were endless as he pulled his shirt over his head and then stepped out of his pants with ease. He reached for her clothing and felt her go stiff.

"My burns," she whispered. It was easy for her to fake confidence when her hands and arms were covered. The majority of the damage had been to places she could conceal, and she had become good at hiding her insecurities. Naked, she was vulnerable, she was ugly. Her arms and hands were exposed; the scars from skin grafts that had been taken from her back could be seen. Each time they made love, she cringed at the thought of Indie seeing her that way.

"I don't care about the burns, YaYa. I don't know how many times I have to tell you. I love every part of you. Once you realize that, you'll be okay," he said as he massaged the back of her neck while looking her intensely in the eyes.

YaYa lifted her arms and closed her eyes as tears streamed down her face. Indie slowly peeled the shirt off of her. He hurt just from seeing her so unsure of herself.

He positioned himself behind her and then walked her over to the full-length mirror. "Open your eyes, ma. Look at yourself," Indie said.

She was choked up and couldn't speak, but she opened her eyes. Her reflection was so flawed.

"What I see is perfection. Everything happens for a reason. I don't know why God chose you to bear these scars, but every single one makes you who you are, YaYa," Indie said. "I'm so attracted to you. You're the most beautiful girl in the world to me."

He was chipping away at the hard wall that she had built around her heart to protect herself. He loved her still, but could she love herself? YaYa didn't know, and the longer she looked at herself the more disgusted she became. Instead of being grateful that her face had been repairable, she was angry at the parts of her that were still marred.

Indie kissed the nape of her neck and wrapped his arms under her arms as he cupped her breasts. One hand stayed on her nipples, while the other slid down her flat stomach until he reached between her legs. He licked his fingers and then played with YaYa's pussy, rubbing in circles and applying pressure until she was soaking his hand.

"Make love to me, Indie," she said.

Acting in compliance, he bent her over the sink and entered her from behind. His thickness parted her southern lips, and her pussy immediately molded around him. She had always been the perfect fit. He gripped her hip with one hand, and pulled at her shoulder as he moved in and out of her to a slow, intense rhythm. His stroke was so official that it took her breath away. There was no theatrics, no name-calling, no faking, just straight lovemaking as his grunts and her moans filled the air.

The sound of skin slapping skin intensified her pleasure as she felt the pressure building between her legs. He had her bent over at the perfect angle, hitting her spot. Indie's dick was wide, strong, thick . . . it was everything, and YaYa hadn't realized how much she had missed his touch until now.

He was never too rough with her, but not overly soft either. He was in control, and he kept the pace while making her do no work. All she had to do was enjoy it. It wasn't long before she exploded. She squirted, and it wasn't long before he came too. He pulled out, and she turned to face him.

"I'm sorry," she said. "About Miesha."

"What's done is done," he said. "Let's just hope she pulls it off. It's time to head back to New York. That's home for you. Skylar is there. Ever since you came back you've been like a blank canvas, ma. Being around her, around family, will remind you of who you are and how much you mean to those around you. New York will put the color back into your life." He gave her shoulder a gentle squeeze, kissed the nape of her neck, and then grabbed a towel off the rack before stepping into the shower.

YaYa quietly opened the drawer and pulled out her pills. She popped three quickly and then watched her reflection sadly until the steam from Indie's hot shower no longer allowed her to see.

Chapter 13

Trina entered the crowded airport with Chase by her side. She was still a minor, seventeen, so she couldn't travel alone, and honestly, she didn't want to. Having Chase by her side made her less nervous. This wasn't fun and games anymore. She wasn't just hanging out on the block, getting money anymore. She was risking her life. YaYa was paying all of the girls $5,000 per trip, but Trina was getting fifteen racks just because she was a part of the team. With two trips per month, she knew that she would be getting money; she just had to get used to the flow of things and make sure that she could handle the pressure. She had a lot riding on this. Chase had all but given up on their drug-addicted mother, but Trina had hopes of making enough money to get her out of Houston and clean her up in a new environment.

"Relax, T. Don't let your thoughts psych you out," he said. "This is the easy part. We're not doing anything hot on the way there, so just chill out and enjoy the free trip to Italy. It's the trip back that is the challenge."

They checked in, and Trina looked around. She immediately noticed that YaYa had several other mules on her flight. She took a deep breath, closed her eyes, and said a quick prayer. She knew that she was asking God to ignore her sin and that it was pointless, but she did so anyway.

The uneventful trip to their destination was boring and long, but when they arrived in Italy it was show time. They made their way out of the airport and hailed the first cab they saw sitting curbside.

"You know you don't have to do this if you don't want to, Trina," Chase said. "You're my baby sister. You're going to eat regardless."

"And what about Mommy?" she asked. "Because it seems like you've washed your hands of her."

Chase opened the door for his sister and motioned for her to get inside. She did, and he walked around the back of the cab then entered from the other side. He was silent as he looked out of the window.

"Don't avoid the question, Chase. What about Mama?" Trina asked. "She's addicted to the shit that we're selling."

Chase shot Trina a sharp look and then nodded his head toward the driver. "Not the time or the place," he said.

"It's never the time or the place," Trina replied as she folded her arms in disappointment and looked out the window. "I miss her, Chase. I know she's fucked up and she's strung out and she's done some selfish shit. She's neglected us, beat us, and everything else under the sun, but she's our mother. She's the only one that we have, and she needs us."

"I've been there, Trina. I've tried to help Mama countless times and it's gotten me nowhere. Every time I would pull her off the block, she would just sneak right back. I was fighting niggas left and ride, creating enemies for myself just because niggas was serving her. And guess what she would do? She'd be right back on the corners begging niggas to suck they dick for rocks. So I stopped fighting over her. I gave up. Mama gon' do what she want to do, and right now she want to get high."

Trina had tears in her eyes hearing her brother's words. She knew that they were true so she didn't dispute them, but inside she hoped for change, prayed for God to heal her mother and release her from the demon of addiction.

"We can help her. How do you know that things haven't changed? When's the last time you tried? She's not a young girl out here no more. The street life has to get old one day and when it does, when she's ready, I'm going to have my money right so that I can help her," Trina said.

Chase shook his head. "Yeah, good luck with that. Messing around with Mama you're bound to wind up with your feelings hurt. My only responsibility is you and making sure you're straight out here. Everybody else . . . fuck 'em. So I'm going to ask you again. Are you sure you want to do this?"

Trina nodded. "Yeah, I'm sure."

Trina and Chase were dropped off at their five-star hotel. Chase checked in while Trina waited outside. They didn't want to draw any attention to themselves. Two young black people in such an expensive hotel was sure to make people wonder. He retrieved the keys to the room and then headed up before calling Trina and telling her the room number as well.

She discreetly headed toward the elevators and found their room, where Chase waited, holding the door open for her as she made her way inside.

"Did they ask you any questions?" she asked.

"Nah, we're good. They don't give a fuck as long as the room is taken care of. I just want to make sure we are dotting our i's and crossing our t's. I would rather be safe than sorry. The moment we get too relaxed or used to the routine is the moment we get caught up," he said.

She nodded.

"Now get some rest. It was a long trip. We can't go through customs tomorrow. That'll throw red flags. So we'll pick up the package tomorrow and catch a train to Florence, then fly out from there the day after . . . maybe even two days from now to be safe," Chase said.

"That wasn't in YaYa's plans," Trina said.

"Maybe it should be. I'm teaching you to think for yourself. You're the one taking the risk, so you have to make sure you're moving smart. Flying in and out of the same airport within days of each other is stupid. Most travelers coming to Europe for vacation stay at least a week. You're a tourist not a drug smuggler, so your schedule has to match. Every detail counts. And next time no five-star hotels. Security and scrutiny in here is top notch. Student hostels will work better, especially for you because no one will question your age. You'll look like just another American kid backpacking through Europe."

Trina was soaking up her brother's knowledge like a sponge, and she nodded her head as she listened.

"As long as the product gets back and it gets back on time, that's what counts. If you have to make a few adjustments to the plan, then that's your call. Always remember that it's your life that's at stake," Chase said.

***

There was no need to set up a fake shoot with Trina. She was the only girl that actually knew what she was carrying, so she wasted no time. She got right to the money. She was given an address to a small shoe shop, and as she dressed, her hands shook. Chase noticed immediately. He knew his sister, and her normal chatty persona was now stoic and quiet.

"I'm going with you," he said.

"Chase, no . . . you don't have—"

"I'm not asking," Chase said sternly.

Trina didn't argue because inside she was grateful for his presence. She had the most pressure riding on her shoulders. *All of them other bitches have no idea. I know it all, so I feel it all, too,* she thought as her heart beat rapidly. Adrenaline made it feel as though she had thoroughbred horses racing inside of her chest.

The shoemaker's shop was outside of the city, nestled in the folds of Italy's mountainous countryside. YaYa had arranged for a driver to take them to their destination and as they rode, silence in the interior of the car was deafening. The car stopped at a small storefront in the middle of nowhere. There was nothing but miles of nature around. Trina and Chase stepped out of the car. Trina was so nervous that she held her breath.

"Breathe, T. This is your show; I'm just a costar," Chase said. He placed his hand on her back. If he hadn't been pushing her forward slightly, she probably would have never moved her feet.

She entered the shop as Chase played the back and stood near the door. He wasn't strapped, and without the pistol sitting on his hip, he may as well have had no clothes on. He felt naked, vulnerable, like any nigga lurking could see all his weak spots.

An elderly man stood behind the counter, reading a newspaper. He never even looked up when he heard the little bell above the door announce their presence.

Trina cleared her throat to get his attention, but still she was ignored. "I'm here for Bruno," she said.

The old man lifted his eyes and glanced back and forth from Trina to Chase then back down to his paper.

"Nobody here by that name," he huffed as he began to cough in his hand. He picked up the half-burnt cigar in the ashtray that sat on the countertop beside him and took a long drag of the cheap tobacco.

"I'm here to see Bruno about a package," she said again.

"You hard of hearing a' something? Eh? I said you got the wrong place," the man replied.

Chase came up off the wall. "Ayo, homie, why don't you go to the back and make a call. Verify that we are who we say we are. Do whatever you need to do. We're in the right spot and we're not leaving until we see Bruno," Chase said as he stepped up. He was halted by the revolver that the old man pulled from behind the counter. He pointed it at Chase as he leaned forward slightly.

Chase's hands went up in defense.

"I was expecting a girl and she was supposed to come alone. She's the only one with a pass. Who the fuck are you? You don't call any shots here," the old man said harshly with a heavy Italian accent. "You come here uninvited you might not get to leave."

Chase didn't fear death; he half expected it in the business he was in. It came with the territory, and as he stared down the barrel of the gun, he made atonement in his head as his life flashed before his eyes.

***

"I'm not crazy," Leah said as she sat in front of her lawyer. Her hands were handcuffed in front of her as she slouched in the metal chair.

"You told me to get you off. This is the only way I see to do it," her attorney replied. "After what you did to that little girl, a jury is going to convict you without thinking twice."

"I didn't harm Skylar!" Leah protested. "I took her from her whore of a mother because she didn't deserve her. That stupid bitch had everything; she has always had everything and everyone to love her. So I took what she loved most."

Her lawyer looked at Leah, perplexed. "You're sick, Leah. You need help, not to be locked up in a prison for the rest of your life. I've looked at your record. The things that you've done, mentally stable people do not do. You killed your mother, you put staples in your teacher's coffee, when you were placed in foster care you put the family dog in the clothes dryer. You're accused of murdering a man in New York, and that's not even mentioning the unhealthy obsession you have with Disaya Morgan," he stated.

Leah sat, growing angry as she listened to him lay out all of her dirty deeds.

"You think you know me?" she asked him. "You don't know the half. That's not all I've done, but you only see my actions. You reading about it in a fucking folder doesn't tell you why I did that shit. Everything I did was a repercussion to something that someone did to me. So fuck you. I'm not crazy."

"You're mentally unstable, and it is my opinion that you are unfit to stand trial. That's the defense that we're going with or you will have to hire other representation," he said.

"I didn't hire you," she remarked. "You were assigned to my case, and since you think I'm so crazy, I would think twice before you pissed me off."

Leah's eyes were so dark and cold that her attorney was sure that she meant the threat. He stood to his feet, grabbing his briefcase as he hastily shuffled his paperwork together.

"An insanity plea will get you off," he said. As he exited the room, a cold chill ran down his spine. He had never worked with anyone as evil as Leah. She truly had no remorse for her actions. It was unfortunate, because his personal opinion conflicted with his job. He thought that she deserved to rot underneath the jail, but it was his responsibility to play the cards he was dealt and get her treated in a mental facility rather than sentenced to spend hard time in a federal prison. He opened his cell and phoned the district attorney.

"I don't think my client is fit to stand trial. I need to order a psychological evaluation for her before we proceed," he said as soon as the D.A. answered the phone.

"You're telling me Ms. Richards is crazy?" the D.A. answered skeptically.

"Leah Richards is a sociopath, but I don't think it is entirely her fault. She's dangerous to herself and to others. There isn't a sane thought running through her mind, and if that's the case, you can't convict her."

***

"Wait, wait!" Trina said in alarm as she held her hands up in Chase's defense.

"Be quiet, Trina," Chase said, not wanting his sister to face a similar fate. "It's his move. Let him pop off. There are repercussions to those actions though. All it takes is one bullet to start a war. You sure you want to do that? I'm no threat. I came here to do business. You might want to ask who I am before you pull that trigger. I'm good. I'm just here for her protection," Chase said calmly.

The old man yelled to the back in Italian and another man emerged. This one was younger, early forties, and stood in a sweaty white wife beater and brown trousers that were held up by suspenders. The little bit of hair he was holding onto on the sides of his head had started to gray, and his large belly hung over his pants.

"Papa, I see we have a problem?" he said.

"We've got an extra guest," the old man spat.

"Well, let's see who he is," the younger man said.

He picked up the old rotary phone that was attached to the wall and made a call directly to YaYa. He would get to the bottom of this, and if he didn't get an answer, he would shoot first and ask questions later.

"Bruno, to what do I owe this unexpected phone call?" YaYa asked as soon as she answered the phone. She knew the restricted call was only coming from one place. She also knew that Trina was making her first run, so she hoped that there were no hiccups in the first pickup.

"There's an extra person here with your girl. A guy. Says he's—"

"Her brother," YaYa said, finishing Bruno's sentence. "He's good. I need them both returned to me safely. I vouch for them both."

Bruno hung up the phone abruptly and turned toward the old man. "He's good," Bruno said. He then turned toward Chase. "Today's your lucky day. Next time let somebody know you're coming."

Trina sighed in relief as she looked back at Chase. His facial expression hadn't changed. In his eyes she saw no fear.

"Can we get down to business now?" Chase asked snidely as his jaw tensed in anger.

Bruno nodded reluctantly and pointed to the doorway that led to the rear of the store. The old man still followed them. "This way. The product is back here."

Trina and Chase followed him to a small workshop in the back where hundreds of pairs of shoes were lined up on shelves. He grabbed a pair and pulled the platform out of the bottom to show the cocaine package that was stuffed inside.

"Practically undetectable," Bruno said. "The new technology in the airports won't pick it up. Body scanners, X-rays, it can get through all of that. Now, if you ever see dogs, you get out of there. The dogs pick up the scent of the cocaine. They don't have to see it to know it's there."

Trina nodded. "I can take back more than two," Trina said. "One on my feet and one in my luggage."

Bruno shook his head. "No, that wasn't what I was told to do, sweetheart."

Chase agreed. He leaned in to whisper in Trina's ear. "This is just the first run. Don't get cocky. We don't know shit about customs or the airports here. Just take one."

Trina conceded and the shoes were handed over in a box and a shopping bag as if she had just purchased them.

"None of the other girls will come directly to you. You'll send the shoes to the photography studios. That will be prearranged," Chase said.

Bruno nodded and Chase gave him a long stare then said, "Next time you pull a gun on me, you better make sure you pull the trigger."

Bruno scoffed and the men had a battle of egos as neither of them refused to back down or break the intense stare. Trina knew that this could easily go left, so she pulled Chase's hand and forced him to follow her out of the shoemaker's shop.

***

It took two days for Miesha to be let loose into general population. Waiting to be arraigned was torturous. In a city as crowded as Houston, she was lost in the sauce of an overpopulated jail. She had been housed in a bullpen with petty drug dealers, prostitutes, traffic offenders, drug addicts, and anyone else who had happened to commit a crime on the same day as she did. All types of characters surrounded her, and the moment they closed the gates around her, she began to fear incarceration. The thought of being locked up was much different than the reality of it, and she had to admit that she was terrified.

What the fuck was I thinking? she thought. She regretted her decision almost immediately. Instead of chasing fast money, she should have been starting a new life. She was a young adult and had the world at her feet just waiting for her to conquer it, but growing up in the slums of Houston she had developed a different dream. She craved the fast life, the street life. It was what she had chosen, and there was no turning back now. She had already landed herself behind bars. If she didn't finish the job, she would be foolish. She would have a record and come out and be broke. Miesha had already ruined her life; she may as well get paid for it.

YaYa had remained true to her word and had hired the best attorney in the city. Miesha had agreed to a plea deal and was expected to get six months from a judge whose pockets YaYa had greased. That was a light sentence compared to her charge. When she got out there would be no parole, just community service, and she would have a misdemeanor on her record instead of a felony. Her lawyer had worked miracles considering the hand that she could have been dealt.

It seemed like Miesha was the youngest girl in the system. Every other woman around her seemed hardened, as if they had been in and out of the brick and steel for their entire lives. She was sent inside to attack, but instead Miesha felt like a sheep as she walked past the cells of the other inmates. She didn't look left or right, only straight ahead, following the line of new inmates as they were assigned to their blocks. Her stomach turned from intimidation, but she kept her face in control. She didn't wear her heart on her sleeve because she knew the first time she showed fear that she would become a target. Fear was like one drop of blood in the water; it attracted the sharks. So Miesha played hardball. If somebody did test her, they would

be in the fight of their lives, because Miesha wasn't letting anyone chump her.

It had been prearranged that Miesha would share
a cell with Leah, so that she would have direct access
to her at all times. All she had to do was wait for the
right opportunity to present itself, and when it did, she
would snuff her lights out. But when the CO escorted
her past Leah's cell, Miesha became alarmed. She
looked inside and saw Leah crumpled up in a tight ball
on her bunk.

"Miesha Patrick, you're in here," the male CO barked
sternly as he hit his billy club against the metal bars of
her new home.

Miesha looked back at Leah's cell. "You skipped a
cell," she said casually.

"Don't worry about it. You don't want to be in there
with that loony bin anyway. She's on suicide watch.
No bunkmates for her. She will be shipping out of here
soon. Sending her to the nuthouse once she gets evalu-
ated by a shrink."

Miesha didn't respond, but instead took her state-
issued belongings and entered her cell.

Fuck, she thought. YaYa had laid everything out
from A to Z, but now things were all twisted up. Miesha
would have to plot out her own way to touch Leah, and
she didn't have much time to do it. If Leah got sent out
before Miesha could put her play down, then things
would be all bad. Time was of the essence, and Miesha
had to act quickly if she wanted to earn her keep.

Chapter 14

Bark! Bark! Bark! Bark!

Trina's eyes bulged when she stepped off of the plane and saw the extra security that had been added to the Houston Hobby airport. They had just stepped off of an international flight from Italy. Things had gone smoothly, and she thought that she was home free until she saw that the passengers were being lined up and searched. Trina could hear the drug dogs coming, and she looked back at Chase in alarm. Her worst fears were coming true, and when she saw the uncertainty in her brother's stare, she could see her freedom slipping away.

"Why the fuck are they searching us? They don't do that when you get off the plane. What's going on?" she asked in alarm.

Chase quickly replied, "I don't know. Just stay cool."

This is my first run. This can't be happening! she thought as her breathing became labored. She was so close to freedom. All she had to do was make it out of the airport and she could hightail it out of there, but as she stood impatiently, shifting from foot to foot, she heard the dogs getting closer. The commotion could be heard all the way down the concourse.

God, please, God, please, God, please, she thought. She wanted to take off the loaded high heels right there on the spot, but she was stuck. She had two kilos on her. That was life. Her life hadn't even truly begun yet and she was already facing the end. Three men in jackets came with two trained canines, and when Chase saw Agent Norris's face, he knew that something wasn't right.

"He's FBI, not DEA. Fuck is he doing here?" Chase whispered to Trina.

"I don't want to go to jail, Chase," she whispered fearfully as tears filled her eyes.

"You won't," he promised. "Take the shoes off and put them in a bin on the conveyor belt. Hurry up!" Trina's hand fumbled as she unclasped the shoes. She practically threw them into the bin. She quickly removed her flip-flops from her carry-on bag and slipped them on her feet. Just as she stood up the feds made their move.

"Ladies and gentlemen, drop everything in your hands and line up against this wall. FBI. We have reason to believe that illegal drugs are being brought in on this plane!" Norris yelled.

Trina's hands shook so badly that she had to clasp them together to avoid looking hot.

"Play it cool, T. Play it cool," Chase said. She couldn't take her eyes off of the conveyor belt.

Agent Norris ice-grilled Chase as he walked up and down the long line of travelers, allowing the dogs to sniff freely. When they got to Trina, the dogs went wild as they picked up the scent that was lingering around her.

"Take her," Norris said. He nodded to Chase. "Him too." The dogs went haywire on ten more passengers, and they all were thrown into separate rooms to be searched more extensively. "Grab their belongings."

Trina was panicking inside as Norris cornered her inside of a private room. There was a female agent present as well, and the woman began to search Trina from head to toe, placing her hands in Trina's most private of places. She then emptied the contents of Trina's backpack, turning up nothing. Trina glanced at the shoes that still sat inside the bin. The female inspector bypassed them, not even thinking to check them.

"She's clean," the woman announced.

"Clear the room," Norris told his colleague. The woman reluctantly removed her rubber gloves from her hands and left Norris alone with Trina. It wasn't protocol, but Norris outranked her, so she followed instructions.

When Norris was alone with Trina, he locked the door and turned toward her.

"Take off your clothes," Norris said, determined. He knew that Chase and Trina were directly affiliated with Indie. There was no way they were traveling abroad for pleasure. He wasn't buying it. So as they came back into the US, he was waiting for them. Whatever they had going on, he was either going to bust it up or become a part of it. The choice was Indie's.

"What?" Trina asked.

"You heard me," Norris said. "You can either take off your clothes or I'll take you in."

Trina bit her cheek to stop her lip from getting flip. She wanted to tell him to kiss her ass, but she was in a delicate position. If he caught her up, she had more to lose than just her pride. She sighed and began to peel out of her clothes. Her young body was flawless, and Norris enjoyed the show as she removed everything but her panties and bra.

"You like what you see?" she snapped with an attitude as she crossed her arms across her chest and turned her head toward the wall. Norris stepped toward her and unclasped her bra, freeing her perky C-cup breasts. Her nipples hardened as soon as the cold air hit them, and Norris licked his lips out of pure instinct.

"I'm going to search you," he said, his voice full of lust.

"Don't act like this is legal," she whispered harshly. She closed her eyes as his hands cupped her breasts and circled them in his hands. She cringed as he moved closer to her, pressing his hard-on into her. Tears came to her, and she let them slide down her face, feeling completely violated, but she knew that she couldn't stop him. She would rather take some unwanted dick than unwanted time, so she remained quiet. He slid her panties to the side and quickly unbuckled his belt. The scent of him disgusted her. Just as he positioned himself to enter her, the handle of the door turned.

Knock! Knock!

"Norris, how's it going?"

Trina heard the voice of the female agent, and she was so grateful for the interruption that she burst out crying.

Norris's hands stopped abruptly and he quickly adjusted his clothes. "Get dressed," he whispered harshly.

Trina snatched away from him and hurriedly put on her clothes. She just wanted to get out of there as quickly as possible. She slipped back into her flip-flops and darted for the door.

She spilled out as the female agent spilled in.

"Is everything okay?" she asked once she noticed Trina's teary face.

"She's clean," Norris stated. "Let her go!"

Trina was halfway out the door when the female agent stopped her. "Hey, don't forget your shoes."

Trina turned around and grabbed the high heels then rushed out, where Chase was waiting for her at the terminal.

"What's wrong? What happened, Trina?" Chase said when he saw her.

She shook her head, humiliated. She didn't want to tell anyone, not even her brother, what had almost happened. "Nothing. I was just terrified. Let's get out of here."

They turned to leave, but before they could step one foot outside of the airport, Norris shouted after them. "Hey!" He jogged until he caught up with them. He grabbed Chase's arm roughly. "I don't care what you say. I know you weren't going to Italy for fun. This is business for you. You tell Indie he either cuts me in or I'm going to search the incoming foreign flights so much that he won't be able to get an ounce into this country, let alone a brick." Norris poked Chase's chest hard as he practically spat the words in his face. "You fucking tell Indie to call me. Sooner rather than later."

***

Kitchen detail. That was the way that Miesha planned to get to Leah. It wasn't hard to get assigned to it. Nobody wanted it, and as Miesha fought off the cockroaches and mice, she understood why.

Leah was in general population, but it was as if she had completely checked out of reality. She spoke to no one, she walked with her head down, and she barely interacted with the COs. The few times that Miesha had seen her she cringed. Leah was hard to stare at for too long. She was healing, but prison was not the best place for medical care. Her scars were hideous, and what once had been a beautiful girl was now an ugly sight. Miesha almost felt sorry for her. It seemed as though killing Leah was actually doing her a favor. Living life with a face as hideous as Leah's was punishment enough, but it wasn't her call to make.

Miesha had thought of every possible way to murk Leah. She didn't have the stomach to do anything that required close contact. She wasn't a killer. She never proclaimed to be gangster. She needed to play her hand close to her chest and move in silence. If she hurt Leah physically, then there was a chance that she would be caught. So the simplest way to get the job done was to get to her food.

Thanks to the pest problem the prison had, she was able to get her hands on rat poison quite easily. While cleaning the kitchen at night, she smuggled it out of the storage closet.

Now all I have to do is get it into her food, Miesha thought.

She stood behind the serving line watching Leah as she entered the cafeteria. Miesha took one of the bowls of chili and looked over her shoulder before putting in the powdered rat poison. She mixed it quickly, hoping that she hadn't put too much in. If Leah didn't eat it, she would be back at square one. When Leah came through the line, Miesha handed her the tray.

She didn't say anything as Leah walked away with the poisoned food in her hand. Her life was on an official countdown. As Miesha dusted off her hands she smiled. It was the easiest money she had ever made.

Chapter 15

Leah shot up out of the bed in excruciating pain as she clenched her stomach. "Aghh!" she groaned as she doubled over while crying out. Her mouth was as dry as the Sahara and she was soaked in a cold sweat, causing the prison clothes to cling to her. A small fire seemed to be ablaze in her stomach, and she tried to stand, only to be knocked back to her bunk by sharp pains. It felt as though she were being stabbed by a thousand tiny needles. Her throat was so dry that she couldn't scream for help. She fell to the floor, using her shaky limbs to drag herself across the floor and to the toilet. She sat down to relieve herself, thinking it had to be something she ate. Her stomach exploded, but when she stood up, she saw blood dripping down her legs. Her stomach lining was being eaten away by the toxic rat poison.

It took everything in her to speak as she mustered up her strength. "CO!" she screamed from her gut. The pain became unbearable, and her vision was suddenly blurry. A splitting headache threatened to cripple her as her knees gave out. She hit the concrete floor hard. The last thing she saw was the blurry sight of the officers rushing into her cell before she passed out.

***

"It's done," Miesha said.

YaYa gripped the phone tightly in her hand and her breath stopped when she heard the words. She wanted to say thank you, but she didn't. She didn't even want her voice on the recorded line of the prison's systems. So instead of showing Miesha her appreciation, she gave her the dial tone.

"She did it," YaYa whispered in disbelief. Miesha had just moved up the ranks in YaYa's organization. She would forever be loyal to her, and as long as YaYa was in a position of power, Miesha would always be taken care of. She was a woman of her word. An account had already been set up for Miesha in the Cayman Islands. The bricks were coming in effortlessly, and as soon as she moved them she would make Miesha's first deposit, which would be more than she could ever spend.

***

"I'm telling you, fam, we barely made it through the airport. The pig mu'fucka Norris was on us. He didn't find the work, but what if he had? Me and my sis would be sitting in a concrete cell right now," Chase stated as he sat in Indie's passenger seat as they sat hidden from view inside the closed garage doors of the car wash.

"How the fuck did he even know we were putting that play down?" Indie asked. "He's been watching me. He has eyes on us. I'ma have to cut him in. If everybody eats, then nobody is complaining. I cut him in, record the conversation, and then the ball will be in my court. I'll have something over his head," Indie stated.

"Question is, can you trust him?" Chase asked.

"No. That's why we'll have him on tape. That's my insurance. The only thing worse to the feds than a drug dealer is a drug dealer with a badge," Indie stated.

Indie wasn't stupid. He knew that getting in bed with the feds was risky, but at this point it was necessary. Norris had connections within the bureau, and he also had the power to bring YaYa back to life officially if the time ever came for her identity to reemerge. Norris could prove valuable as long as he knew his position on the team.

***

The sound of Norris's hard-bottomed dress shoes echoed against the floor as he entered the empty warehouse where Indie wanted to meet. He kept his hand on his holster as he looked around. He half expected to be shot when he walked through the door, but instead he saw that Indie had come alone. He stood waiting for him in the center of the empty space.

"I have to admit," Norris started as he stood in front of Indie, keeping a comfortable distance between them for good measure, "I was surprised to hear from you. I thought maybe you wouldn't take me seriously."

"I take all threats extremely seriously, and I don't appreciate them either," Indie replied.

"Well, you forced my hand. I tried to get on your team the nice way. You turned me down," Norris stated.

"Agent Norris, why would a man in your position want to step on the wrong side of the law? I thought you were supposed to arrest the bad guys," Indie asked. He knew that it was all being caught on the tape he had in his pocket. He wanted to make sure that he had enough on Norris to keep him on a tight leash.

"Turns out the good guys make shitty pay," Norris replied.

"I'll put you on payroll. Ten thousand dollars per month," Indie stated.

Norris's eyes lit up like a Christmas tree. He had come ready to negotiate, ready to barter with Indie, but there was no need to.

"In return I want to know everything you know about any cases relevant to me or any of my people," Indie stated. "I'm talking investigations, raids, open files . . .

If my name or any of my team's names are a whisper on the crusty donut breath of one of you pig mu'fuckas, I want to know about it. You got me?"

Norris nodded his head. "Yeah, yeah, I got you," he agreed.

"There's one more person that you need to meet," Indie said.

"Who's that? I thought you were running the show," Norris said. "I don't want too many people knowing about my involvement with you. I just want to fly under the radar. Nobody else needs to know I'm on your side."

"I need to know," YaYa said as she walked up behind Norris.

Norris's face turned pale white as his eyes widened in shock. "I thought you were—"

"Things aren't always what they seem," YaYa said. "To the rest of the world I am dead. I trust that you can keep this under wraps. If you keep my secret, I'll keep yours," she said. "Wouldn't want anyone at the FBI to know that you're dirty, right?"

Norris nodded and swallowed the lump that had formed in his throat. "Yeah, yeah, we're good," he assured her.

YaYa smirked and joined Indie by his side as they prepared to make their exit.

Indie looked at Norris in pure disgust. He wasn't naïve. He knew that he was on the other side of the law and that it was the job of the police to keep things in their proper order, but men like Norris made him sick. He wasn't in it to clean up the streets; he was in it for greed. He was loyal to the dollar, not the job, so whoever had the most to pay him was the one who had his allegiance.

Indie began to walk away, but stopped and snapped his fingers as if a light bulb had just gone off in his head.

"Oh yeah, one more thing," Indie said. He turned to look at Norris. "I heard you had a run-in with one of my lil' mamas at the airport.

Norris's face turned beet red and he laughed uncomfortably. "No, I . . ." He cleared his throat. "I don't know what you mean."

Light came spilling into the darkened warehouse as Trina came walking into one of the rear doors. Her high heels clicked as she made her entrance.

"Maybe she'll refresh your memory?" Indie responded.

"Take off your clothes," she said.

Norris scoffed as that same nervous laugh escaped him. "You can't be serious. Indie, come on, I thought we just made nice."

"We did," he said. "But you two haven't. Now, if you want it, you take off your fucking clothes."

Rage flashed in Norris's eyes, but he was too thirsty for dough to say no. He snatched his jacket off and tossed it to the ground angrily. "This is bullshit, Perkins!" he barked, calling Indie by his last name.

"How do you think I felt when you tried to fuck me?" Trina said harshly. "Now shut the fuck up and run them clothes, you perverted, little-dick mu'fucka."

Agent Norris removed his clothing down to his tight white drawers, and Trina walked up to him. She spit directly in his face then brought her knee up hard into his groin. He doubled over instantly.

"Asshole," she barked before walking away. Indie followed behind her and gave Norris a pat on the back as he left.

"You disrespect her again and I'll cut off your dick and make you swallow it," he said calmly. He pulled out $10,000 and tossed it on the ground near Norris's feet. "That's a bonus. Welcome to the team."

Norris waited until he heard the clang of the doors signal that they had exited before he wailed in pain, "Son of a bitch!"

Chapter 16

YaYa took to the drug game like a fish to water. She was too good at it, actually. She had chicks that were so loyal to her that even if she hadn't lied to them about what they were doing, they still would have done anything she asked. YaYa was moving weight without ever ruffling one feather. She didn't need the streets; the streets needed her because she supplied every major hustler in Houston. She started out slow and tried to only deal in territories that she was familiar with. Texas was eating her product up, so she saw no need to expand, but when Indie approached her about upping the ante, she knew it was time for her organization to grow.

"We need to move bricks into Georgia, Florida. We're missing a lot of money by just sticking to one place. You've got a goldmine, ma. Let's tap into it," Indie said as he lay between her legs and she rubbed her hands gently over the top of his head.

"I don't know," she said. "Are you sure we can handle that? I mean, it's just Chase and Trina. The other chicks aren't involved like that. We've got a good thing going. It just seems like if we expand too fast we'll crash and burn."

YaYa was timid in the way that she moved to avoid conflict. She would rather play it safe than to move sloppy and be sorry, but she also trusted Indie. She was bringing bricks into the country faster than she could get rid of them. The Texas buyers she had on deck couldn't keep up.

"So you cut some of the chicks in. Build the team," he said. "It's also time to let Chase do what he does best. We're missing money by not breaking the product down. Put him on the streets. Have half of the chicks running weight up and down the highways, and have the other half whipping up the product in the factory."

"I'll call a meeting," YaYa said.

***

YaYa popped three pills to calm her nerves as she prepared to approach the roomful of women. YaYa had been watching all of her mules closely since the very first run and had weeded through the pack, separating the weak from the strong. It was time to cut off those who could be potential liabilities and then elevate her game to the next level.

She remembered her elite days when she had been lured into a money scheme. She had done the dirty work, while niggas on top had gotten most of her pay. She wouldn't do that to these girls. The ones who joined her circle would be well taken care of. She would be loyal to them so that they would feel the same loyalty to her. It was a two-way street and she understood that.

She stepped out and noticed Chase, Indie, and Trina standing in the rear of the room. Marco and a few of his Italian goons were also present. Courtesy of Zya, Marco had been sent to aid YaYa in whatever she needed done. If YaYa was going to expand, then Zya would see to it that her investment was protected. Marco would be at YaYa's disposal. It never hurt to have soldiers on deck. In the game she was playing, she never knew when she would need to be ready to war.

"I've called you all here to thank you for the work that you've put in with my company, but I feel like it's time to present a new opportunity to you and to be honest about the real reason that you are here," she stated. YaYa grabbed one of the platform high-heel shoes that sat on a table beside her. "You've been going overseas doing business, and each time you came back with a package for me. This is what you've been bringing back." YaYa popped the bottom out of the shoe and pulled out a tightly wrapped package of cocaine. Chatter erupted in the crowd as the girls gossiped among each other, some intrigued, some in shock, some slightly afraid because of the risks that they had unknowingly taken.

"At first you didn't know what you were doing; now I need you to know because I have a proposition for all of you. It's time that our business grew, and it's time to fill new positions. For those of you who are still willing to make the trips overseas, you will be paid triple. Fifteen thousand dollars for every successful trip. You have to know that this is your risk to take. If you are caught, you won't speak to anybody about me or this organization. It will be your burden to carry. I will take care of your legal expenses, and your family will receive assistance for their inconvenience. If you speak one word about me or my business, then it would put everyone you love in danger," YaYa said seriously. The crowd grew silent.

"I'm telling you both the good and the bad so that you can make an informed decision. I'll also place some of you in the factories. Some of you will hit the roads running the product to different cities and states. I've already said too much, so before I continue, I need to know who is in and who is out," YaYa said.

YaYa had only chosen twenty-five girls to come to the meeting, and out of the ones chosen, three stood up to make their exit. YaYa nodded at Marco, and he and his goons quickly gathered the women and escorted them out, undoubtedly escorting them to their deaths. YaYa hated this part of the game, but it was necessary and she understood that. One loose set of lips could sink their money ship, and YaYa couldn't have that. Anyone who posed a threat to her budding empire would be handled accordingly. She couldn't afford to have liabilities. The new throne that she sat on suited her well.

"For those of you who are still sitting here, let's get money. We move smart, we move silently." She looked around the room at the women who had committed to stay. She had been them once upon a time—hungry, ambitious, but also lost. She had been down to make a dollar any way that she could, until she met Indie and he revealed her own worth. Now she was the boss, and as she remembered how it felt to be at the bottom, she promised to take care of these girls. She would help them clean up their money and take away some of their risk of being caught. It was the least that she could do.

She introduced them to Chase, who would take a third of the girls and use them in the cook-up factory. Trina took a third of them, and together they would continue to cop overseas. Indie would handle the remaining women by putting them on the road to make connections to other hustlers in other states, expanding their buyers.

Indie watched YaYa command the room, and an odd feeling swept over him. He was proud to hold her down and proud of the hustler's spirit that she had, but he also worried about her wellbeing. She hadn't chosen the game; the game had chosen her. Indie wasn't sure that she knew exactly what she was getting herself into, and he would protect her as much as possible to make sure that she remained untouchable. To everyone around her she seemed as if she had everything together, but he knew her well, and could see the internal struggle that she was going through. He knew that there were weaknesses that she was trying to hide. He didn't know if was from her new reign of power or if she was simply having trouble adjusting to life after the fire. She wouldn't open up to him; no matter how much he tried to reassure her that everything was okay, she was like a locked box and Indie didn't have the key.

He didn't expect her to be a machine. She went from being victim to Leah's tyranny to fighting for her life after the fire to queen pin almost overnight. Her world had to be spinning. He just wanted his old thing back, the woman that he had fallen in love with. She just wasn't the same, as if the doctors hadn't put her back together quite right.

It wasn't the life that he would have chosen for his lady, and it certainly wasn't something that he wanted for the long term. Part of the reason that he had pushed YaYa to expand was so that they could make the money and make their exit sooner rather than later. Indie had plans to take them legit that would keep them rich for generations.

Indie knew how addictive getting money could be. He only hoped that when it was time for YaYa to give it all up, she understood the bigger picture and let it go without a fight.

***

"Leah Richards was placed in protective custody after an attempt on her life was made at Harris County Jail. Allegedly, rat pesticide was put into her food. Doctors say she would have died if one of the guards hadn't found her and rushed her to the infirmary. Richards is on trial for the kidnapping of Skylar Perkins and has a pending murder charge waiting in the state of New

York. She is no longer among general population at Harris County, but has been transferred to a local mental institution, where she is being held until her trial begins. There is a good chance that Leah Richards's counsel will change their plea to not guilty by reason of insanity or mental defect, as it has been determined that she qualifies for this disability. . . ."

YaYa couldn't believe what she was hearing as she watched the news story play out before her very eyes. How Leah had survived she didn't know, but the way the news spun the story made Leah seem more like a victim than an actual criminal.

"Aghh!" YaYa screamed as she knocked the television off of the TV stand, causing it to shatter on the floor. "This bitch has nine lives!"

She was like a tornado as she picked up everything in sight, tossing it in frustration around the room. Leah had survived. Leah always survived, and her existence was taking a toll on YaYa. How long could they play this cat and mouse game? The back and forth was more torture than if she had just given up herself.

She grabbed a bottle of vodka from the mini bar and retrieved her bottle of pills. She popped three as if they were candy then washed them down with the liquor. She took a deep breath and shook her head as she waited for her mind to go to a happy place.

She didn't even know how she had gotten to this point. This certainly wasn't supposed to be her life. She had an obsession for payback. She was addicted to Leah in the same way that Leah was addicted to her, and she couldn't let it go. The world was too small for them to coexist.

She heard Indie open the door, and she turned to him with a tearstained face.

"What's wrong?" he asked as he rushed to her. She broke down in his arms.

"She lived! The bitch is alive!" YaYa informed. "They saved her and now she's in some fucking mental hospital. The bitch is going to get off. I know it. She's going to play crazy and get away with everything she's done. She lived." YaYa said the last two words in disgust as she put her hands over her face in distress.

They spoke about Leah so frequently that he didn't even have to ask who or what YaYa was talking about. He gripped her face gently. "So let her live, ma. Fuck her. She is not a part of our lives anymore. Do you really think she will ever be happy after what she's done? Her face is like a Halloween mask now. She will get hers. Life has a way of making sure that things even out. You're trying to force it, ma. You're trying to make something happen that isn't in the universe. Let this shit go. It's consuming you. You're obsessed, YaYa. You think about Leah so much that you hardly have room to think about Sky. You haven't even asked to see her. Do you know that? All of this is about our daughter, but you haven't seen her. Haven't asked how she's doing. Focus, YaYa!"

"I know . . . I know," she cried. "I just want revenge for my baby. For me. For—"

"Ma, I need you to promise me that you'll let this go. Just let go. It's changing you, YaYa. I want my old thing back. You can't even go through a day without the negativity bringing you down. You're drinking, taking more pills than I think you should. I haven't said anything because I don't want to believe that what I'm seeing is true, but I need you to get a grip on shit, ma. Come back to me. We have everything at the tip of our fingers. How you gon' lead a pack of bitches when you letting one make you weak? Huh? That makes no

sense. You're stronger than this. We're building an empire together and you want to risk it all . . . let it all slip
away trying to live in the past. Walk forward with me,
YaYa. Trust me," Indie said. He was practically plead-
ing with her to move into the future, and as she stared
into his eyes, she saw that she was causing him pain.

"Okay," she whispered. "I'll let it go . . . I trust you."

Indie pulled her into him and held onto her as she
cried on his shoulder. "Let it out. Get it all out of your
system and that way we won't have to revisit it again.
Let the pain go," he whispered in her ear.

He held her in his arms until she cried herself to
sleep, and then he made the decision in his head that
they were leaving Houston. Indie was taking YaYa
home to their daughter where she could have balance
restored to her life.

***

Miesha sat with tears in her eyes as she watched her
mother and son enter the visiting room. She wanted to
hug them, to run to them, but she couldn't even touch
them, so she sat still and waited as they made their way
to her.

"Mi-Mi!" her son yelled. She wished that she could
hear him say the word "Mama," but that was a special title that he reserved for her own mother, his true
grandmother.

"Hey, big man! How you been?" she asked.

"Good! When are you coming home?" he asked.

"Soon," she promised. She hadn't heard from anyone
on the outside. She had tried to reach YaYa but could
never get through. News had spread through the prison
like wildfire that Leah was still alive, and Miesha knew
that she had failed to deliver. She had risked it all and
come up short, so she was sure that YaYa had cut her
off as a result of her fuck up.

As she sat in front of her mother, she couldn't read her expression. Marilyn Patrick had always overextended herself for her daughter, had tried to provide the best under the most dismal of circumstances. Miesha knew that she had disappointed her greatly. Instead of relieving the pressure from her shoulders, she had added more.

"Mommy, I'm so sorry, I thought I had a plan. I thought that I would come out of here and be able to take care of the two of you, but I messed up. I was wrong," she stated.

"No, baby, I understand. I understand everything. I got a visit from your friend YaYa," she whispered as she looked around and lowered her voice. "She delivered a package. She said that you earned it."

Miesha looked up in surprise.

"It was half a million dollars, Mi-Mi," her mother revealed. "She told me to tell you that when you get out, there is more where that came from and that she appreciates you for trying. She's moving us to New York, baby. Says there is a little house waiting for us in Brooklyn . . . safe neighborhoods, nice schools. I tried to thank her, but she told me to thank you instead."

Miesha was floored at the loyalty that YaYa had displayed. She was generous and compassionate. Miesha was more than grateful and couldn't stop the tears from slipping down her cheeks. There weren't many people like YaYa in the world. Most would have forgotten about Miesha and written her off, but YaYa embraced her. Miesha was a part of the team, and for that she was taken care of.

"Now, I don't know what you had to do to get that money, Miesha, but know that Mommy loves you and I thank you, my daughter," her mother said.

"You're welcome, Mama," she replied. Sacrificing the next few months of her life was worth the relief and thankfulness she saw in her mother. It was as if a huge burden had been lifted from her shoulders, and it was in that moment that all regret left from Miesha's body. She would do what she had to in order to make sure that those she loved were taken care of, and now that list included YaYa. Leah had hurt her, so she deserved whatever she got. Miesha only wished that Leah had not been spared by the guards. Maybe next time she wouldn't be as lucky.

Chapter 17

YaYa didn't know how much she missed New York until she smelled the stench of the city as she exited the airport. The cold winter wind bit at her jacket as she held her head low to avoid the winter hawk. Everything came alive inside of her as the blares of the car horns rang in her ears. It was like her senses were awakened from a long slumber as she was led from the lobby of LaGuardia into the private car that was waiting for her curbside.

Trina and Chase followed behind her and entered the car with her, while Miesha's mother and son trailed in a car behind them. Indie had business to attend to and would join them later. Everything had already been arranged for YaYa's return. Indie wanted to make the transition as seamless as possible for her. Her business in Houston was put on hold, leaving the streets dry as she relocated to New York. She had no idea that Indie was shutting her down for good. She assumed that she would pick up where she had left off, but Indie had other plans.

She picked up her cell and dialed his number. Even if he didn't answer, she just wanted to hear his voice. YaYa felt as if she was disappointing Indie. She knew that as much as they had endured, she should be stronger by now. She was in too big of a position to be so weak, and even though the outside world couldn't see her falling apart, she was, and Indie knew her too well to hide it from him. As she suspected, he didn't answer, and a hollow pit filled her stomach.

I'm going to lose that man if I don't get my shit together, she thought.

They drove to the prestigious St. Regis hotel, where they planned to stay temporarily until Indie joined them at the end of the week.

***

The flight to Italy was long, but Indie emerged refreshed as soon as the Tuscan sun warmed his skin. His driver wasn't a minute late, and he entered the black Maybach that Zya had sent for him. He rode in deep contemplation, his head spinning as he planned YaYa's exit from the game. He had come to the conclusion that she couldn't handle it. She was genius when it came to mapping out the game plan. She was surprisingly and disturbingly phenomenal at the hustle, but the pressure that it put on her shoulders made her fold. She was on edge, snappy, and extremely paranoid.

YaYa had been through too much in such a short period of time. He wanted her to have the luxury to just chill. His lady deserved to sit back and enjoy life without worry, financial or otherwise. Her circumstances were always so traumatic, and although she seemed to be resilient because she always just picked up the pieces and kept it moving, YaYa's demons were ganging up on her.

Sometimes he couldn't even imagine the horrible memories that played inside of her head. She needed a break, and it was his job as her man to give her one. He had every intention of making her his wife, but he wanted a woman who was able to be just that—his woman, nothing more, nothing less.

Most men would be intimidated by a woman like YaYa. The fact that his connect had chosen to replace him with his woman would have sent most men into a bout of insecurity, but Indie felt nothing of the sort. He was proud of her. At times he felt the pedestal he placed her on was unfair because he saw so much perfection in her that her imperfections caused him disappointment at times. She was exquisite in every aspect, and her wit kept him on his toes, but the light inside of YaYa was fading. He rarely saw her smile. Indie couldn't even remember what the melody of her laugh sounded like. He would do all that he could to spark the flame of life inside of her again.

The car pulled up to Zya's villa and Indie exited. He was greeted by the butler before he even had a chance to ring the doorbell.

"Ms. Miller is expecting you, Mr. Perkins. This way," the man said.

Indie followed him through the opulent estate and out to the back, where Zya indulged in the cool waters of her Olympic-sized pool. Indie walked along the edge as he watched her move gracefully through the water. She was like a fish as her brown skin glistened and her arms and legs worked powerfully. Zya came up at the end of her lap and wiped her wet hair off of her face, sweeping it to the back as she came up for air, gulping it in.

"You're good in the water," Indie said as he bent down and extended his hand.

She looked up at him and smiled, then took his hand. He used his strength to pull her out of the water.

"Yeah, well, I'm used to being wet," she replied with a smirk. Indie blushed slightly at Zya's flirtation, then pinched the bridge of his nose. He reached past her and bent down to pick up the towel that sat on the chair. He held it open for her.

"You're a true gentleman, Indie. YaYa's a lucky girl," she said as she stepped into the towel and took it from his hands as she secured it underneath her armpits.

"No, I think I'm the lucky one, but so is Snow," Indie said, referring to Zya's husband.

"Indeed he is," she replied.

"So why are you here? Something wrong with my coke?" Zya asked. "The first pickup went smoothly. I wasn't expecting to hear from you or YaYa until she moved the work. I know it's not gone already. She's good, but she's not that good."

"No, everything is good on our end. Product isn't gone, but it's moving. We'll have that off in no time. A few weeks at most. I'm here about something else, but before I speak on it, I need your discretion," Indie said.

"You've always had that. What's on your mind?" Zya asked as she led him to the patio table. She motioned for him to have a seat.

"I want YaYa out of the game. She's not built for it," Indie said. "I need you to stop doing business with her."

"Why would I do that?" Zya asked seriously. "She's the sharpest person I've ever come across in this business. YaYa can move a hundred kilos through international airports without blinking. Do you know the potential she has? What her hustle is worth?"

"It's not worth her life," Indie replied sincerely, causing Zya to look up at him in concern. "She can't handle it. She's good at it, but it's changing her. She's been through too much to take on something like this. All it takes is one little fuck up, one little slip for everything to go bad. She's snappy lately, distant. It's like she withdraws inside of herself. Sometimes the look in her eyes makes me fear her thoughts. It's like she's obsessed with something so sinful that she can't share it with anybody," Indie said.

"Wow," Zya said sincerely. She was impressed with the way that Indie was so in tune with his lady. She could tell that he loved her dearly and missed the innocent chick she used to be before Leah tore her down and Zya bossed her back up. "You know your woman well."

"I know her well enough to be able to see that if she stays in this game too long she'll get lost in it. After what she's been through she needs to heal, and I'm not talking about the burns. She's emotionally vacant, damaged. The only thing she speaks about with passion in her voice is killing the bitch Leah. That's the only thing she's living for, ma. Revenge. Our daughter isn't even her focus anymore. She moves weight effortlessly, but it's time consuming, it's dangerous, and I don't want that on her shoulders . . . the pressure."

"Makes diamonds," Zya said.

"Or bursts pipes," Indie countered.

"I am sympathetic for you, Indie. I really am. I admire you as a man and I respect you as a friend, but during the time that YaYa was here in Italy, I also developed a friendship and respect for her. Even if you take the friendship part out of it, how could I possibly cut her out, Indie? The revenue that I stand to make with her is irreplaceable. It doesn't make good business sense for me to cut ties with her. Even you can't bring me as much money as she will. You're good at what you do, Indie, but YaYa is a different breed. She's me all over again," Zya said with a chuckle.

"You see where I am. Living here in complete luxury. The life that I've built for myself, for my family, is so grand, Indie. We vacation on yachts in the south of France, we eat from the spoons of the finest chefs, we want for absolutely nothing. My kids and their kids will want for nothing. She can make it this far if you don't get in her way. Face it, Indie. She's a queen pin in the making."

"I don't want this for her," Indie said. "You're beautiful, Zya. You're rich, you're powerful. You've got it all. You live in the hills of the most beautiful country in the world, but to me this isn't an option for you. It's the only option. It's a prison. This is nothing but a rich man's prison. You're wanted back home. You can't walk down the streets of Harlem no more, ma. You can't visit family, friends . . . to them you're just a memory. You can't feel the love of your legend because you're too far away from it. Niggas in Harlem talk about you in rap songs, Zya. Everybody remember how you was selling ounces out of that Italian joint, whipping all the foreign shit through the hood. They worship you in New York, ma, but you can't feel it. You're disconnected from it because you can't ever step foot back in the streets of New York. Feds want you too bad, and even if you do sneak in and out, you can't ever stay. You can have all the power in the world, but you can't tell me you're not lonely . . . that you and Snow don't miss home."

Zya's eyes turned sad, and her silence was admission enough that he was right. She shifted uncomfortably in her chair. "What do you want from me, Indie? This seems like it's a conversation that you should be having with YaYa. I'm her partner. I do good business with her. You know how the game goes. Once you're in, you're in. We're just as addicted to the flip as the addicts are to the product."

"I've got something big working, something legitimate. Something that makes the drug game look like it is for little niggas. I'm trying to step into the pharmaceutical business," Indie said.

"You're talking pills?" Zya asked curiously as she sat up in her chair, intrigued.

"I'm talking stocks and bonds, ownership of the drug companies," Indie said.

Zya raised an eyebrow as she intertwined her fingers and placed her chin on top of them. Now Indie was speaking her language. She had tried to tap into the corporate drug market numerous times before, but she always hit a glass ceiling. If Indie had a way in, she was definitely taking it.

"They won't let you in. That's a white man's game," Zya said.

"I know someone. A friend of mine just happens to be a minority share owner in Vartex," he said.

"That's one of the biggest drug companies in the world," Zya replied in disbelief. "I've been reading up on the new drug that they have. The one that they claim can reverse Alzheimer's if taken in its early stages. They stand to make billions." Zya's mind was turning, and she had money schemes on the brain. "If you can get me at least ten percent of the share, I'll cut YaYa loose. You will have my word that I won't do business with her," Zya assured. "If you can get us through the door, I can get us leverage. Their FDA approval will depend on them letting you buy in. You're not the only one with valuable friends. I have a friend at the FDA that can pull the plug on Vartex's entire little project if they refuse you," Zya said.

Zya couldn't legally hold stock because she couldn't take the risk of tipping her hand to the DEA. If her name came up as a shareholder in Vartex, it would give the feds clues in finding her whereabouts. Indie however hadn't been convicted of anything. Although the feds wanted him badly, they hadn't been able to make anything stick, so there was less risk for him. As long as he stayed true to his agreement with Zya and kept his word, they could split the profits.

"I'll make the call immediately," she said.

"And I have your word that you'll cut YaYa off?" Indie asked.

"As soon as the deal is done, I will discontinue all business with her. I'll only deal through you," Zya said as she stood to her feet. "But let me ask you something, Indie. Are you sure you want to do this behind her back? You're cutting her off. You're taking her power away. That girl Leah from the fire made YaYa feel helpless, defenseless, like she was backed into a corner. Are you sure you want to do the same thing? She's a big girl. You should give her a choice instead of making it for her. You're trying to save her, but after this you just might push her away."

Chapter 18

Sleepless nights turned into restless days as YaYa waited impatiently for Indie to arrive in New York. She hadn't heard from him. It had been four days and she was beginning to fear the worst. She stayed high off pills just to distract herself from his absence, but lately she had to take more and more of them just to get a decent high. Her system was getting used to the drugs, and instead of making her float, they only irritated her because she couldn't reach the level of unawareness that she sought. YaYa was running through prescriptions so frequently that she had to switch pharmacies often just to avoid arousing suspicion. Zya's doctors were being paid too well to concern themselves with her growing addiction, so they just kept writing more prescriptions for her.

Her red eyes were puffy from crying, and despite the fact that she had every reason to celebrate, she felt numb. She wanted to see Skylar, to go and get her daughter from Indie's parents, but she couldn't pull herself together long enough to even pretend that she was okay. She couldn't stop taking the pills until Indie was back by her side, and she knew that Elaine would be able to tell that something was awry.

YaYa looked like shit. She was tired, her body begging for a break as heavy bags decorated her eyes. She was restless because she wasn't sure if Indie would ever return.

I need you. Where are you? YaYa thought.

A knock at the door caused her to jump out of bed.

"Who is it?" she asked.

"It's me, YaYa. It's Indie. Open up."

His voice calmed her soul, and she quickly opened the door. Her disheveled appearance alarmed him.

"Where were you? I called you a thousand times," she whispered.

Indie held her, concerned. He had never known YaYa to be so clingy. Her sloppy clothes, messy hair, and bloodshot eyes caused him to frown. It was uncharacteristic of her to be anything but flawless, so seeing her in such a state of disarray immediately let him know that something was wrong. He knew her too well not to see that she was unraveling more and more, day by day.

At first he had felt guilty about going to Zya behind YaYa's back. He didn't want her to think that he was jealous of her come-up or that he wanted sole control over their budding empire. Indie was all man. He wasn't threatened by YaYa's new status in the game. He hoped that she could see that it had nothing to do with that. Despite the purest of intentions, his conscience had eaten at him during his travels, but as he stared into her eyes, he realized that he had made the right decision. He had her best interests at heart.

"I'm right here. I had to handle something very important, but I'm here now," he said while gripping her shoulders and staring her in the eyes curiously. His gut told him that YaYa was high, but he didn't want to admit it. He attributed her strange behavior and sullen mood to stress, giving her the benefit of the doubt.

"Everything is okay, ma. I'ma always take care of you," he said. He kissed her forehead and nodded toward the bathroom. "Now, go get gorgeous. I've got a surprise for you."

YaYa smiled, and Indie watched her disappear from sight. As soon as he heard the water begin to run, he went across the room and opened her handbag. He pulled the prescription bottle out and noticed that it was almost empty.

YaYa's not a pill head. I know her. She's just going through a hard time, he thought, obviously in denial. Everything in him wanted to confiscate the rest of the medicine, but he wasn't ready for the argument that would surely come with it. To accuse her of something that heavy would cause her to feel resentment toward him if he was wrong. It appeared as though her physical ailments had healed, but he didn't walk in her shoes. He had no idea how it felt to be disintegrated in a fire and then put back together again. Who was he to measure her pain?

***

"Where are we going? I thought you said we were going to get Sky," YaYa said as she noticed that Indie was driving in the wrong direction. She was so anxious to see her daughter that it felt like a wall of tension had built up inside of her chest. It had been way too long, and she couldn't wait to set her sights on her beautiful child.

"Just ride and relax," he said as he reached over and gave her hand a reassuring squeeze.

As they exited the chaos of the city, the highway gave way to suburban living and entered the affluent neighborhood of New Rochelle. Posh and well established, the homes were built with old money. It was the neighborhood of families who had been rich for generations. Indie pulled into the driveway of a two-story 6,000-square foot home and YaYa frowned.

"What are we doing here?" she questioned as she lowered her neck to peer out of the front window at the beautiful Victorian home. "My mother used to drive me through this neighborhood all the time and admire this exact same house," she said, unable to take her eyes off of the exquisite piece of architecture.

"I know," he replied.

YaYa frowned. "What do you mean you know? How could you possibly? Who lives here?"

"You do," he answered. "We do."

She glanced at him in shock. "What?"

"This is our new home, YaYa. Welcome home, baby girl," he said.

She laughed in disbelief. Indie hadn't just purchased any old house. He could have built her a mansion anywhere or bought her the entire top floor of a Manhattan sky rise, but instead he touched the core of her, purchasing a modest yet expensive piece of property that meant more to her than he could ever understand. This was the home that she and her mother had fantasized about living in when she was just a little girl. She had dreamed of her mother baking cakes while wearing flower aprons in the kitchen. In her mind she had planted a garden in the backyard. This home had been what she thought of on nights when she had lived through unspeakable pains. Through rape, through abandonment, through loneliness . . . YaYa had let her mind wander back to this very brick structure. Her imagination had kept her sane, and now Indie was presenting it to her as a gift. The emotional value that this house held for her was priceless. It was more than enough to buy her love forever.

Her mouth fell open, but no words came out as her eyes flooded. She was speechless. She could not even attempt to put her emotions into words. There wasn't a phrase created yet to show how appreciative she was. So instead she reached over and kissed his lips. She

kissed him fully, intensely, submitting herself to him
as he stroked her wet cheek with his thumb. He was
such a beautiful man, inside and out. YaYa felt so lucky
to have him in her life, when she herself was so flawed.
His selfless love for her was so great that it filled her
heart with joy.

At times she felt guilty because she knew that she
was too selfish to ever love him so purely. If she loved
with the same devotion that he did, she would never
have allowed herself to succumb to the temptation of
drugs. She would have stayed too high off of Indie to
ever chase the sweet satisfaction of the sinful bliss.

She looked at the house, enthralled by her new
home. As a kid it had seemed like a castle. She had
never imagined that she could one day own it. To a little ghetto girl in the hood, a house in New Rochelle was
everything. YaYa had truly found her Prince Charming
when she met Indie; he had made her every dream
come true.

"How did you know about this?" she asked, dumb-
founded. It was as if Indie lived in her thoughts and
knew her deepest secrets without her ever having to
tell him.

"A friend of mine helped me pick it out," he replied
vaguely. He nodded toward the house. "Go ahead and
check it out, ma," he said softly as he removed the key
from his ring and handed it to her.

She snatched it up giddily and hopped out of the
car as she bounced happily to the front door. She admired the yard that was blanketed in snow. She could
see her children growing up there, building snowmen
in the winter and running through sprinklers in the
summer. This home was so sentimentally valuable
for her that she felt overwhelmed by it. It meant security, it symbolized love . . . it was the perfect gift.
There wasn't anything greater that she could have

been given because Indie had done his research. It was heartfelt, and the intention of the gift outweighed everything else.

She placed the key inside the lock and leaned her shoulder against the door as she turned the knob. Inside stood a giant Christmas tree. It was so huge that the star almost touched the ceiling as it illuminated the foyer. The smell of pine needles filled her nose as she turned to Indie and smiled. "Thank you," she said.

"You're welcome," he replied. "I love you, Disaya. I want to love you forever, ma. I know things haven't always been simple between us, but when you're in my life I feel complete." Indie reached into his inside jacket pocket and pulled out a black ring box. He got down on one knee and grabbed her hands into his.

She gasped, then laughed, then gasped again. "Boy!" she screamed in delight. YaYa could not fathom what was happening. This scene, this proposal was something that other girls got to experience, not her. This was too grand; Indie was too good for her.

Indie chuckled slightly and flashed a charming grin. It was the same crooked smile that had hooked her from day one.

"Ain't you forgetting something, young'un?"

The deep baritone voice echoed through the home, and Indie gave YaYa a wink before she turned toward the voice. Before her stood Buchanan Slim, the only father she had ever known.

"Daddy?" she whispered. She looked back at Indie then to Slim. Her hand covered her mouth in utter disbelief.

"This is the friend I was telling you about, the one who helped me choose this house," Indie said.

She remembered the day she had lost him. YaYa had never expected to see him again, never expected to face him. She had grown so much resentment toward him in the years that he had been absent from her life, but none of it seemed to matter now that he was standing in front of her.

She ran to her father and hugged his neck tightly. Losing him had caused her so much confusion. The day that he was taken from her life she became another lost little girl with no direction. Without a mother or a father to guide her, she wandered through life, figuring everything out by trial and error. She hadn't realized how much she missed him until this very moment.

He wrapped his arms around YaYa, embracing her in a large hug as she bawled into his shoulder.

"I love you, YaYa. I know we have a lot to talk about, and we will get our chance, but I think right now Indie has something he wants to finish," Slim said. She sniffed and nodded her head as she stood between the only two men in her life that she had ever loved.

"With your blessing, Slim, I would like to ask your daughter to marry me," Indie said.

"I couldn't have chosen a better man if I handpicked you myself, young'un. My blessing is easy. I just wish I hadn't been trapped in the system, so I could give my daughter to you the right way and pay for your wedding," Slim said.

"Your blessing is more than enough," Indie said. He turned to YaYa, focusing all of his attention on her. "How about it, ma? You want to kick it until forever with me?" he asked.

YaYa nodded and couldn't stop the laughter from escaping her. Only Indie would put it so eloquently. It wasn't cookie-cutter, it wasn't the corny, begging, Keith Sweat proposal. It was done in true gangster form, and in YaYa's eyes it was absolutely perfect.

"Yes," she replied.

He stood to his feet and scooped her up in his arms as he shouted, "That's a yes, people!"

Suddenly applause erupted in the house and Chase, Trina, and Miesha's family came entering the room, all elated. YaYa looked around and then asked, "Where's Skylar? Where are your parents? Why aren't they here?"

Her voice was so eager it was as if she were feenin' for her daughter's presence. It had been too long since the last time she had seen Skylar's precious face.

"They're running a little late. They got caught in traffic, but they will be here," Slim spoke up.

Disappointment filled YaYa's expression, but Indie gave her hand a gentle, reassuring squeeze. "Why don't we get dinner started," he suggested. YaYa pulled away from him and pointed toward the stairs.

"Is the bathroom this way?" she asked.

He nodded his head and said, "Take your time, baby girl. Get acquainted with your new house. We won't get started without you."

"You better not," she replied with a smile as she ascended the stairs. She couldn't help but admire what Indie had done with the place. It was fully furnished with the finest pieces that money could buy. He had taken care of every detail, down to the white Audi A8 that he had waiting for her in the three-car garage. All it needed was her touch to make things complete.

She peeped into every room until she located the master bedroom. She flopped down on the plush king-sized bed and pulled the pill bottle out of her Birkin. Her smile disappeared as she looked at the orange bottle. Indie had just proposed to her. He had just professed his undying love. Why wasn't that enough to erase all of her pain away? She knew that Indie made her happy, but lately she was so up and down that she was tired of the roller coaster ride. She wanted to feel nothing but bliss. This was a day that she would remember forever, and she didn't want any negative thoughts to creep into her mind and spoil her mood, so she opened the bottle and swallowed three pills without water.

YaYa could feel herself slipping further and further into the comforting arms of addiction. She had underestimated the drug's ability to hook her. For some reason, in her head prescription pills were the lesser of two evils. It was okay because a doctor had given them to her, but her misuse of the drug had created a vice. She had developed a nasty habit, but it was one that felt too good to let go of.

What Indie doesn't know won't hurt him, she thought. *I've got everything under control. It's not like I can't stop.*

***

By the time she made it back to the dining table she was on cloud nine. YaYa sat at the head of the table on a mental and physical high as she felt the effects of the pills coursing through her body. At this point YaYa was mixing Oxy with Vicodin, which was a deadly combination, but she didn't care. YaYa no longer took the pills for pain; she took them for pleasure. They gave her a calm that she had never experienced before, a certain orgasmic experience that made her entire body pulse with pleasure. It provided her with a confidence that no one could break. She had gone from taking one whenever her pain was at its peak to taking three to four at a time every few hours. The feeling was euphoric, almost orgasmic. It was like breathing in warm air after being locked out in the freezing cold. Like having her skin massaged by the warm currents of the Caribbean waters. It gave her balance, made her hectic life easier to manage and her past easier to forget.

This dinner was for celebratory purposes. They were toasting it up to the good life, but also commemorating the hard times of the past and putting them to bed. YaYa had made her first million almost effortlessly, and it was finally time for her to be reunited with her daughter. She would have been full of nervous energy if it had not been for her magical little pill that helped her maintain her cool.

She wasn't sure how Skylar would react to her. It had been too long since she had last bonded with her baby girl.

Will she remember me? YaYa thought. The devil had been busy at work, separating her from her child, but God's mercy had brought them back together. YaYa vowed to never allow anyone else to keep them apart. Now she was powerful enough to have her enemies touched before they got an opportunity to touch her. Get or get got: That was her new motto, and anyone who posed a threat to her family would be made an example of.

Indie sat across from her at the other end of the king's table, while the others sat around them. A celebration was in store. Their first flip had been flawless. Not one of YaYa's mules had been caught, and now they were sitting on a stash of cocaine that was worth millions. The streets were ready for the taking, but first they were going to feast like royalty as they lived it up for the night, celebrating YaYa and Indie's engagement.

"How is Miesha holding up on the inside?" YaYa asked.

"She's good. She's just biding her time until she is released. Six months is nothing. She's staying strong," Trina said.

YaYa nodded. "Good. Make sure she has everything she needs in there. Keep her books on full. When she gets out, we'll move her here to New York."

"Thank you," Miesha's mother said.

"You're welcome, Marilyn," YaYa said as she reached over and squeezed the woman's hand.

The doorbell rang and Indie arose, knowing that it was his parents. YaYa stood eagerly.

Indie rounded the table and grabbed her hand. "You ready?"

YaYa nodded as she flashed the brightest smile that had ever decorated her face. He escorted her to the front door and opened it.

"Oh, YaYa," Elaine exclaimed as she hugged her tightly. "You don't know how good it is to see you standing here in front of me."

YaYa hugged her tightly. The two women had formed a bond of love and respect. It warmed her to see Elaine again.

"My baby," she whispered as she set her sights on Skylar, who lay asleep in Indie's father's arms.

"Good to see you, YaYa," Bill greeted.

There was always some tension whenever the two interacted, although they both had made an unspoken pact to never admit why. She gave him a nod and opened her arms to receive her flesh and blood.

Holding Skylar in her arms again warmed her to the core, and YaYa couldn't help but cry. Her makeup ran down her face as streams of emotions fell down her cheeks.

"I love you, Skylar. Mommy loves you so much," she whispered, rousing the toddler from her sleep. "Oh my God, she's gotten so big," she noticed aloud as she held her closely to her chest. She could feel the beat of her tiny heart, and it warmed her soul. "It feels like

I've missed so much." YaYa took in all of her daughter. She inhaled her scent, caressed the natural curls of her delicate hair, and kissed the top of her head as she cradled her back and forth in her arms. She savored this moment, wishing that she could make it last forever. In that exact moment of time, nothing could have been more perfect. With all of her loved ones around her, YaYa felt complete for the first time since her mother had died, and she was overcome with emotions as she reveled in her own joy.

The sight pulled at Indie's heart strings, and as he looked around the room, everyone had tears in their eyes as they witnessed a mother's true love. All of YaYa's emotions were enhanced by the drugs that coursed through her system, but she didn't mind. She enjoyed the overwhelming love that flowed from her to her daughter, and she cried freely. It didn't matter who was looking. She let the crystal clear tears flow down her face.

Skylar rubbed her doe-shaped eyes as she awakened slowly.

"Hi, Mommy's Girl. Hi, baby," YaYa whispered.

As if no time had passed at all, recognition lit up Skylar's face and she called out, "Mama."

It was the first time YaYa had heard that word. It was the sweetest melody she had ever heard.

"That's right, Sky. I'm Mama. I missed you so much," she whispered. Now that they had been reunited, she would never let her daughter go. The fact that Leah had even been able to get to Skylar meant that YaYa was slipping. It would never happen again. She was more determined than ever before to make sure that Leah no longer posed a threat to her family. Being locked up wasn't enough; being burnt up wasn't enough. Leah deserved to take a dirt nap, and YaYa was just the person to put her to sleep.

One glance was all it took to reestablish the connection between mother and child. Despite Leah's efforts to break their bond, Skylar remembered YaYa. She knew whom she belonged to. No matter how much time had passed or the amount of distance that had come between them, she could never forget the woman who had birthed her. Their bond was unbreakable.

Indie came up behind them and kissed the top of YaYa's head. Slim walked up behind the couple and interrupted. "Do you mind if I have a moment with YaYa?" he asked.

"Not at all," Indie said. He shook Slim's hand then led everyone else into the dining room.

This father and daughter moment was long overdue, and as Slim admired his lovely YaYa, he regretted all of the time that he had missed in her life. He didn't know what had led her to this point. He had no idea how she had become the woman she was today, and it pained him.

"You look good, baby girl," Slim said. "It's so good to lay eyes on you."

"You too," she replied. Her voice trembled because she knew how much she used to love him, knew the admiration that she had held for him in her heart.

"You can be upset with me, YaYa. You deserve to be upset with me," he admitted. "I was a selfish young man. My ways hurt a lot of people, including your mother, including you. I promise you that I will make this up to you. I will try to right my wrongs," he said.

She admired Slim. His promises still meant everything to her, despite the ones that he had broken in the past. She had tried to convince herself over the years that she hated him, that he had never truly loved her, but she knew that it was false. He wasn't even her paternal father, but he had loved her from day one. As she witnessed tears accumulating in his eyes, she saw nothing but genuine emotion.

"Are you Leah's father?" she asked.

"Everyone else who asked me that, I've told them no. I just got back into your life, YaYa, so I don't want to start out lying to you. Honestly, I don't know. I could be. I always thought I was sterile. Doctors told me that a long time ago. But who really knows? I used her mother, had unprotected sex with her mother. I very well could be, but I'm not certain," he answered.

"So you shunned your possible daughter and doted all over me? Why? I'm not even your blood," she asked.

"But you're the blood of the woman I loved. I have only truly loved one woman, and that was your mother. The moment that she had you, I thought you were more precious than gold. Seeing her carry you in her belly, aw, man, what a sight," Slim said, staring off in space briefly as he drifted back down memory lane. "She was the prettiest when she was pregnant. It suited her. I used to place my hand on her belly and tap a little rhythm as I sang to you. It always seemed like you danced to my tune, because I would feel you moving around in there. You see, baby girl, I was there with you from conception. I rubbed your mama's feet, made late-night runs when she had cravings for peanut butter and bananas," he said, causing YaYa to smile.

"Witnessing your birth, waking up for late-night feedings with you, I was there for all of that. You and your mother had locks on my heart that no other girl or woman could remove. I didn't have any room for Leah in my heart because I only had eyes for the two of you."

"So you weren't grooming me? You wouldn't have put me to work the moment my ass started to sprout or the curves of my body came in? I wasn't just an investment?" she asked.

Slim placed a hand over his heart as if her words had wounded him, and he shook his head. "Oh no, baby girl. You were the only evidence of purity I ever saw. I would never ruin that. Ever. I know that I did some bad things in the past and I wasn't there for you as a child, and if you don't want me here, I understand."

"I want you here," she replied quickly. "I would like to get to know you if that's okay."

She hugged Slim, and he grabbed both shoulders and said, "I will try to make this right. I'll do everything in my power to heal the wounds that I left open all that time ago."

They walked hand in hand into the dining room and joined in on the feast.

***

All of the pieces of the puzzle seemed to come together. Indie sat back and watched as YaYa transformed before his eyes. Where there had been sadness, he now saw extreme happiness. She was drunk on love, and as their eyes met from across the room, he gave her a wink. It was satisfying seeing his incredible woman thrive again. She had been down for so long that she deserved this come-up.

They feasted over a five-course meal as they popped bottles, living it up among themselves. They were all that they had. The people sitting around the table were family and had proved their loyalty to the team. Her heart felt full, overflowing with an emotion that was so overwhelming that she had to let some of it out. She wiped her eyes as tears involuntarily fell. Things felt normal for the first time in her life. She was surrounded by people who loved her, and her family was intact. Life couldn't be better, but if things were as great as they seemed, why did she still have the overwhelming urge to pop pills? She was becoming frustrated with the short-time highs. She needed something stronger.

YaYa handed her daughter off to Elaine and she snuck away from the crowd to gather herself. *I just need to take the edge off,* she thought as she rushed over to her leather Birkin and spilled the contents out onto the bed. Every pair of eyes in the house were on her. So many people had so many expectations of YaYa. It was as if at any moment they thought she would crack and nobody wanted to miss it.

She located the pill bottle and unscrewed the top. The more often she took them, the shorter her high lasted. It was as if she could never get the same high that she had gotten the very first time she had taken them. She needed something stronger, something that lasted longer, so that she didn't have to take them so frequently. She popped two into her mouth and swallowed them dry, forcing them down her own throat.

"I didn't know you were still taking those."

Indie's stern voice startled her and she jumped, causing the bottle to spill out over the floor. She turned to him and immediately got defensive.

"I didn't think you had to know," she snapped back, with a little more bite to her words than she intended. She bent down and began to pick up the pills. Her mood had changed just that quickly. She was coming down from a high ride, and her irritation caused her to mistake his concern for contempt. She was on the defense because she knew that she was wrong.

Indie was hit with her sarcastic comment as if it were a slap in the face. He peered at her in concern.

"Yo, hey, ma, come here," he said as he went to her side and knelt to help pick her up off the floor.

She exhaled and came to her knees and rested in the space between his legs as he sat on the bed in front of her. Her head hung low.

"Are you okay?" he asked simply.

"I'm fine," she replied. She wanted desperately to tell him that she felt empty inside . . . that despite all of the positivity around her, she couldn't stop thinking of Leah. It was as though the tables had turned. At first it was Leah's obsession that kept them linked, and now it was YaYa who couldn't let go. She couldn't release the hatred that dwelled inside of her, and it was slowly beginning to rot. The power. The hustle. The money. The love. It was all just a distraction from the vendetta she harbored against Leah. She knew that she would have to let it go in order to move on with her life, but it was so much easier said than done.

"Should I be concerned about this?" Indie asked as he pointed at the mess she had made.

She shook her head. "No. I just have pain some days. It's not as bad as it used to be, but sometimes I do need to take something for it. That's all. I promise," she lied.

Indie pulled her close and held her tightly, hugging her as if he were afraid to lose her once again. "You will tell me if you're in over your head, right? You can talk to me about anything. You do know that, right?" he asked.

She nodded. "I know." She said it, but she didn't really believe it. How could she tell him that she thought about killing Leah every second of every day? What words could she use to make him see that as long as Leah breathed, she would never be able to truly live without fear? And even if she could tell him those things, she would never have the courage to tell him that she really felt no physical pain. She had healed from the fire. It was the emotional pain that she was trying to numb by taking the pills.

"I want you to do me a favor and stop taking these," Indie said. "If you're in pain, we'll find a doctor here in

New York. This is Oxy, ma. That shit is just as bad as
taking heroin. The dosage is too high for you now. You
shouldn't be on the same dosage as you were right after
the fire. I've seen pill heads, YaYa, and I know the damage that these can do to you, ma. Stop taking them, and
I'm not asking. I would never tell you anything wrong."
His words were stern, chastising, but also caring.

She wanted to open her mouth and have the truth
spill out of it, but she wasn't ready to stop. So instead
she told a lie. "I will, Indie," she said. She touched his
face lovingly. "I'm so lucky to have you."

YaYa had been through so much in such a short period of time, and Indie could see it taking its toll on her.
Life had beaten her up, and a lot of times the recovery
was harder than the actual circumstance. "Nah, you got
it wrong, ma. I'm the lucky one." He stood to his feet.
"You stay up here. I'm going to go clear everyone out.
Then it's me, you, and Sky, a'ight? Our family is back
together again, and nothing or nobody—not Leah, not
the game—will ever tear this apart."

She nodded, and he planted a soft kiss on her forehead, causing her eyes to close in appreciation.

She watched him leave the room then looked at the
pills on the floor. She bent down and picked them
up. *Get yourself together,* she thought. *He loves you.
Sky is healthy. They are all you need to take the pain
away. Get rid of the pills,* she thought, silently scolding
herself for being so weak.

YaYa had never cracked so badly under pressure.
She had raised herself since childhood, and her path
had always been hard. Allowing herself to break now
made no sense. She walked into the bathroom and
emptied the bottle of pills into the toilet, flushing them
and her fears away.

Chapter 19

Leah had been unresponsive since she was transferred to the mental hospital. If she hadn't been crazy before, the padded room that they kept her in would have surely driven her insane. She had seen countless therapists, had been doped up on antidepressants, and still she hadn't spoken to anyone. She was far from stupid; Leah knew what game she was playing. It was called survival of the fittest. If she showed that she had the smallest ounce of good sense, then they would put her on trial for her life. They couldn't prosecute the mentally ill, so Leah kept up the charade day and night. What she didn't realize was that it wasn't so farfetched.

She lay on the white bed with her eyes locked on the wall in front of her. Since the fire, she had been experiencing a confusing mixture of emotions. Resentment had built up inside of her, and she secretly wished that she had died in the blaze. Her entire existence would never be the same now. Leah knew that it was vain, but she would rather be beautiful and dead then ugly and breathing.

A nurse came into the room and said, "Leah, you have your very first visitor."

Leah didn't respond. She didn't even sit up because there was no way that anyone was coming to see her. There wasn't a soul on earth that cared enough to visit her.

"Get up. Maybe this visit will snap you out of your funk. It's your father, and he came here all the way from New York," the nurse said.

"My father?" she whispered. Her raspy voice could barely be heard, and the nurse looked at her in surprise.

"So she does speak?" she asked. "The doctors will be so glad to hear about your progress."

Leah stood to her feet and walked out of the room. Her lace-less shoes slipped off her feet with every step she took. She didn't know who was playing such a cruel joke on her, but curiosity drew her toward the visiting room all the same. She stepped into the crowded space and immediately felt insecure as all eyes fell upon her. Insecure in her own skin, Leah felt cornered. Her eyes cut through the crowd with precision, and when they fell upon Buchanan Slim, the man whose love she had always yearned for, her heart began to spasm as she fidgeted.

"He only likes the pretty girls."

The words that her mother had spoken to her as a child echoed in her head and she knew that if that was the case, then there was no way that he could possibly love her in her current state. Leah took a deep breath and approached Slim's table. He didn't flinch when he saw her. He had gotten used to her burns when she was trying to pass for YaYa. It wasn't Leah's physical health that disturbed him; it was her mental health that was hideous.

"Now that you know who I really am, what are you doing here?" she asked defensively.

"I'm here to make amends, to make things right. The things that you've done are ugly. I can't imagine what you must have seen or lived through to make you hate another human being so much. I know that you feel jealous of YaYa because of the relationship that I had with her. I was young and I was irresponsible. I don't know if you are my daughter, but I don't know that you're not either. This fight over me, this war you've waged on YaYa over me . . . it makes me believe you when you claim to be my daughter. I've denied you for a long time, and because of that you lashed out at YaYa. Your hatred for her landed you both in a bad place. You're locked up here, while YaYa lives in fear," Slim said sincerely.

Leah looked up but hid her shock. *YaYa is alive,* she thought in disbelief. *I thought she died in the fire. I'm locked up here and she's out there living free.*

"I know that what I did was wrong," she lied. "I just wished that I could have you in my life the way that she did. She wasn't even your real daughter, and I felt cheated . . . robbed. But I took things too far. I hurt a lot of people. I'd give anything to be able to make things right."

"You need to let the past go. I'm willing to do my part and get to know you, but your vendetta against YaYa has to end. It's a dangerous and unhealthy fixation. If you looked through YaYa's eyes, you might real-ize that you didn't miss out on much. I was a ruthless man. I was a pimp who disrespected and manipulated women, including your mother, including her mother. I wasn't the best father. In fact, I was the worst kind of father," Slim admitted.

Leah felt the tears accumulate as she thought of how rejected she felt as a child. So many bad things had happened to her because she felt that she had no father to protect her. She had been raped, neglected, beaten, when all she had ever wanted was her daddy's acceptance and love. Now he was sitting in front of her, within arm's reach, telling her that he accepted respon-sibility for her pain.

"The things that you are blaming YaYa for is really my fault. I ask you not to hurt her anymore. Don't hurt yourself anymore," Slim said.

Leah's expression changed when the conversation went from "I'm sorry" to defending YaYa. *He's not here for me. He's here for her. He doesn't want me to hurt her. It's always about YaYa.*

Leah wanted to let her rage show, but she stayed reserved and turned on her sympathy. Before Slim's visit, she hadn't even known that YaYa was still alive. She had figured her for dead. Now she was going to play a role to find out where to find her.

"Hopefully one day I can look YaYa in her eyes and," *slit her throat,* she thought bitterly, but aloud she said, "say I'm sorry."

"You just focus on getting better and maybe one day you will get that chance," Slim said. He knew that it would never happen. YaYa would never forgive Leah for the things that she had done, but he didn't want to make his visit a negative one.

"Can I write to you? I don't know how long I'll be in here. They act like they never want to let me out, but it would be nice to send you a letter every once in a while," Leah said.

"Sure. I don't see why not," he said.

Leah slid him a piece of paper and Slim wrote down his address. Leah knew that she would never lift a pen to a piece of paper to start one letter. She had nothing left to say. Now that she knew where Slim lived, it wouldn't be hard to find YaYa. They were all in New York together, and the first opportunity she got, that's where she would be as well. Leah's hatred for YaYa was just as deep as YaYa's hatred for her, and both of them were too obsessed with each other to let go.

***

YaYa awoke to the soft kisses of her daughter, and she smiled as she noticed that Indie was still asleep. It should have been the perfect awakening, but the pounding headache that she had distracted her from the bliss. This was the scene that she had pictured in her head for so long—comfort, security, and happiness with the two people that she loved most in the world. But now that she had it, she couldn't appreciate it. YaYa hated to be out of control, but she had to admit to herself that she had an issue with prescription pills. She had become dependent on them for emotional stability. Her happiness had been superficial, and now she was so far in that she was craving something stronger.

She was grateful that Indie had left to handle business. He had been up in her shit ever since he asked her not to take the pills anymore. He thought that he was discreet, but she saw him checking her purse when he thought she wasn't looking, to see if she had refilled her prescription. The first few hours had been easy. She hadn't even noticed a difference, but by day two YaYa's body rebelled. The bouts of diarrhea were enough to send her running right back to the pharmacy, not to mention the intense stomach pains, cold sweats, and irritability.

She grabbed Skylar and quickly threw on their clothes. She grabbed the keys to her brand new car and rushed out of the house.

Her eyes were barely on the road as she dialed the number to her doctor while she drove. To her dismay, the number had been disconnected. What she didn't know was that he had been commissioned by Zya to render his services for her treatment. When the job was done, he had severed all ties. Unless she picked up the phone and called Zya herself, then her prescription had just been canceled.

"It's so damned hot in here," she yelled as she blew out a breath of air and rolled down the window. "Damn it!" She had tried her best to keep it together, tried to walk a straight line, but not only did she need the medication to keep her out of the threshold of depression, she now needed them physically.

She took a deep breath and calmed her racing heart. She really didn't want her thoughts to drift in the direction they were going, but she couldn't help it. If she couldn't get what she wanted, then she would get what she needed. She turned the car around and headed toward the city. YaYa was about to pay an unexpected visit to Chase.

***

When Chase opened the door to the trap house and saw YaYa standing on the doorstep, he was thrown off guard.

"You looking for Indie?" he asked, puzzled.

"No, umm, I'm looking for you," she said. "Can I come in?"

He held open the door for her and moved aside as she and Skylar entered. He felt awkward being alone with YaYa, and he had no clue why she was there. He folded his arms across his chest as he observed her. She seemed nervous as she stood bouncing Skylar on her hip and patting her back. "I need to speak with you about something, but first I need to make sure you know who you work for," she finally said.

Chase and YaYa had never spoken more than pleasantries to one another. He had nothing but love and respect for her off of the strength of Indie. "I don't know what you mean," he replied.

YaYa sighed and looked over her shoulder. "I mean you work for me, Chase. The cocaine that you move comes from me. So what I'm about to ask you cannot leave this room. I need you to keep it between us. Not even Indie can know," she whispered. It wasn't until she said those words that she knew how awful she truly was. She was about to make Indie's most loyal confidant become disloyal just to get high. She was caught in a web of lies and didn't know how to break free.

"Whatever it is, I'm sure you don't got to hide it from Indie," Chase said. He was completely uncomfortable with the position that she was putting him in. It was true that YaYa was the boss, but it was Indie who had saved him from a life of poverty. It was Indie who had put him on and showed him the rules to the game. It was Indie who he owed his life to, not YaYa. Telling her no was like a catch-22, so instead he said nothing.

"Indie can't know," she barked. "I'm still in a lot of pain from the fire." There it was . . . the excuse that she used to justify it. She knew that she was wrong, but it didn't stop her from continuing. "The doctors won't refill my prescription. I need something."

"Maybe you should talk to your doctor, ma," he said. He frowned.

I know she's not coming here to cop. She know what I deal in: cocaine and heroin. She can't be asking me for that, Chase thought.

"I'm asking you because I respect you, Chase. Do you know anybody who sells pills or anything similar to it? I just need it this one time," she said. She tried her best to sound normal, but she was giving off all the signs. Chase's mother was addicted to drugs, so he knew what to look for. YaYa was jonesing, and it may not have been for crack, but a jones was a jones.

"Nah, I don't know nobody like that," he replied. "Let's just call Indie together. If you need help, he can—"

"Forget it," she said. "Let me just use your bathroom. Hold Sky." She handed Chase her daughter and then went to the back of the house.

Chase couldn't believe what was happening. The pit in the bottom of his stomach made him feel like he would throw up. "Damn," he muttered. If he told Indie about this, YaYa would undoubtedly cut him off, but some things were deeper than money. This is when loyalty came into play. If YaYa had been a busto or one of Indie's little side chicks, Chase wouldn't have given two fucks, but she wasn't. YaYa was Indie's rib, his everything, his future wife, and this was a problem.

He picked up his phone and shot a text to Indie.

> Big homie I need you to swing by here like right now. It's 911. I've got to talk to you about something.
> –C

He didn't know how YaYa had gone from boss chick to this, but he suspected that the prescriptions she had been taking were the spark that started the fire.

That's why I don't fuck with it. A drug is a drug. All of that shit will fuck up your life. Don't matter if it comes from the dope man or the doctor, he thought.

YaYa emerged from the back of the house and grabbed Skylar from Chase's arms. He wanted to let her leave, but he couldn't.

"YaYa, why don't you let me drive you home," he suggested.

"Mind your business," she said, looking him dead in the eyes. "And keep your mouth shut."

She stormed out quickly. Chase didn't have to help her. She had gotten what she had come for. She couldn't find any pills in the house, but she had grabbed a sand-wich bag full of cocaine off of the kitchen counter. She was so desperate that she didn't even care that she was graduating to illegal drugs. She just needed to shake the kinks off. She would think about the consequences later.

Chapter 20

There was nothing like New York City, and being back home lit a fire in Indie. He had come up on these streets, hustled its blocks, chased its bold women. Indie was East Coast through and through. From hopping the gates in the subway to shooting cee-lo in pissy halls in the ghetto, Indie was bred in the greatest city in the world. Clad in Versace slacks and matching vest, he fit in nicely as he walked into the Empire State Building where Frank Needleman's office was located. The finest CPA in the city, he kept the books for every major businessman in Manhattan.

Indie clasped a brown leather Louis Vuitton briefcase in his hand as he made his way to the thirty-fourth floor. The average hustler would have been intimidated by the fancy degrees that hung on the walls, but Indie wasn't fazed by corporate America. He had seen more money than most of these nine-to-fivers would ever make during their careers. They had yet to live the type of lifestyle that he had experienced. While they worked eighty-hour weeks, slaving behind desks to maintain their plush lifestyle, Indie enjoyed life. He worked smart, not hard.

He was greeted by a young blond woman who sat behind a neat desk. Her hair was swept up in a tight bun, and her plainly manicured fingers tapped the keys on her computer efficiently. She looked up at him. "You must be Mr. Needleman's eleven o'clock?" she asked. "He's expecting you. Right this way."

Harry Needleman was the top-rated investment banker in the entire city, and if anyone could help Indie go legit, Needleman could. His client list was so prestigious that Indie was lucky to even get a meeting with the man. Their paths had crossed by chance years before, and Indie still remembered it like it was yesterday. He had saved Needleman from a robbery in Harlem years ago, and ever since the two had shown a mutual respect for one another. Indie had never called upon his old associate for any favors, but today it was time for Needleman to show good faith and return the favor.

Indie followed the receptionist down the long corridor that led to Needleman's office. She entered first, announcing his arrival, and then he was ushered inside.

"Mr. Perkins," Needleman said. "It's good to finally have the opportunity to do business with you."

"Likewise," Indie replied. He took a seat and placed the briefcase on Needleman's desk. He popped it open, spinning it toward the white man so that he could see the treasures that were hidden inside.

Needleman's eyes widened in surprise—a good surprise, but still an unexpected shock nonetheless.

"You told me you were down to your last two hundred thousand dollars," Needleman said. He glanced at the money, and his experience allowed him to immediately estimate the amount of money in the case. "There is at least three million sitting here. My fee goes up."

Indie smirked. He had already known that Needleman would double, perhaps even triple, his going rate. It was one thing to balance the books for a legit company, but to cook up false documents and cleanse street money was an entirely different ballgame.

"I'll be bringing you that amount weekly, maybe biweekly, so set your price accordingly. Whatever amount we agree to today will not increase," Indie said sternly.

Needleman stood and closed his office door, not wanting anyone to overhear the illegal conversation that they were about to have.

"I thought this would be a one-time thing. Covering up this much drug money is not easy," Needleman said, prepping Indie for the large number he was about to deliver.

"How much?" Indie asked.

"Fifty grand for every transaction," Needleman said.

Indie sat back in his chair and crossed his legs as he pondered the numbers. "I tell you what. I'll give you the fifty thousand, but I need this done right. I have a lot at stake here. I can't have anyone asking where this money is really coming from. I want it to be so clean that we have tax returns, employees on record, whatever it takes to make this thing legit."

"That won't be a problem. We can incorporate you. Filter the funds you make as profit from your company. The DEA isn't whom you should fear. The IRS is much worse. They're the real threat. But as long as they're getting their piece of the pie quarterly, and you maintain a level of discretion on your end regarding the questionable practices in which you make your money, then you should fly under the radar," Needleman schooled.

"And this will work? I can't beat another federal case. I barely walked away from the first one unscathed," Indie admitted.

"This has been the practice of many men in your *line of work*," Needleman revealed. "The biggest gangsters in the world are the ones dressed in suit and ties. They are the ones you never hear about because they pay guys like me to make sure they are never caught. It is all about making the right investments, Mr. Perkins. You grease the right palms and make the right connections, you'll never have to worry about your freedom ever again."

Needleman peered curiously at Indie. "You could have gotten incorporated at any half-ass accounting firm though. Come on, Indie. Shoot straight with me. Out of all of the time I've known you, you have never come to me about anything. Why is it that you're really here? Because it for damn sure isn't just to S-corp a phony company for you. You gave me the fifty K without even blinking, no negotiation or nothing, and you're a stickler for the hard bargain. You're the best negotiator I know. I can tell by the look in your eyes that you've got something on your mind. This little side deal was just the Vaseline. Go ahead, bend me over, because I feel like I'm about to be fucked," Needleman said jokingly.

Indie chuckled because Needleman knew him too well. The S-corp was important to cover their dope tracks, but that was only the tip of the iceberg for the reason why he had visited. Indie reached into his inner jacket pocket and removed a folded up page of the *New York Times*. He placed it on top of Needleman's desk and pointed to the headline.

It read:

VARTEX PHARMACEUTICAL COMPANY WAITING ON PENDING FDA APPROVAL FOR THEIR NEW WONDER DRUG, DIPROXIL.

"You're on the board," Indie stated.

"I am," Needleman said.

"I want on the board. I want ten percent of the stock," he said, finally revealing the real reason why he was there.

"You can't afford ten percent of the stock," Needleman said.

"Try me," Indie said. Between the money they were making from their new setup and his new deal with Zya pending, he was more than confident that he could come up with the buy in.

"One hundred fifty million," Needleman said cockily. "Ten percent is a bit ambitious. The company is made up of thousands of stock holders. Even I only own two percent. You would be one of the major share holders. Not the largest, but certainly not the least. You would have a say in what goes in. If you're just looking for a sound investment, you can go lower."

"I want ten percent," Indie said. He stood to his feet. "You'll have your money by the end of the month."

"It's not that simple. The majority share holders will want to meet with you," Needleman warned.

"Then set up the meeting for the end of the month. I read the article. As long as the FDA is delaying approval of this drug, the company is losing money. Vartex is in a delicate state right now. They can't turn down my money right now if they wanted to," Indie said.

Needleman loosened his tie and leaned back in his seat. "No offense, Indie, but they might not want you in their arena. You're from the streets. What do you know about business?" Needleman asked.

"I know enough to cover my bases. The sudden delay in FDA approval wasn't a coincidence. They turn me down, I make one call and the FDA denies Vartex. Don't underestimate my reach. I always have insurance," Indie said with a smirk.

"I'll be damned," Needleman said with a chuckle. "I'll set up the meeting."

Chapter 21

When Indie exited the meeting and went to his car, he had three missed calls from Chase and an urgent text. He frowned, knowing that Chase wasn't big on phone conversations. Plus, he knew the rules. Anything said over the phone was dangerous. Indie knew plenty of good men who had gotten locked up by talking too much through a filter. Anything Indie said would be said in person.

He dialed YaYa's number to let her know that he wouldn't be home directly as expected.

"Hello?" she answered.

"Hey, beautiful," he greeted.

"Hey, yourself," she replied. "Where are you?"

"I just finished handling some business. I know things have been rough on you. I'm going to make everything better though, ma. I've got a plan for us," Indie said hopefully. He was so optimistic about the future. He had no idea that the moves YaYa was making had the potential to destroy everything he was trying to build.

"I love you," she said. "And if I ever do anything to disappoint you, please know that I don't mean it."

"You never will, so don't worry about it, baby girl," he replied. "I'll be home soon. I've got to swing by and see Chase."

"Chase?" YaYa blurted out more urgently than she meant to.

"Yeah, Chase. What's wrong with that?" he questioned.

YaYa knew that if Indie met with Chase, then he would spill the beans about her. She couldn't let that happen. She closed her eyes and lowered her head in shame. What she was about to do was grimy, but she had warned Chase. She had told him to mind his business. Now she had to protect herself by telling lies to cloud the truth that Chase was trying to reveal.

"I didn't want to tell you this, but I think Chase is out for self. I got a phone call from Bruno when Trina made her first run. He said Chase tried to cut a side deal. He wanted to take more coke on consignment. He was trying to cut us out and get straight to the connect himself," YaYa lied. The words tasted bitter on her tongue, but doubt in Chase's character had to be established. When it came down to it, all Chase had against her were empty accusations. He had no proof. It would be her word against his, and it would all boil down to who Indie trusted most. She loved Indie and hated to manipulate him the way that she was, but what was the alternative? To come clean? She already had too many flaws. She wasn't about to give him one more reason to leave her.

"Why didn't you tell me?" he asked. "I gave li'l homie a way to eat when he was starving and getting bullied on the block."

"I didn't want to hear the hurt in your voice that I hear now," YaYa said. She was laying it on thick, using his love for her to cloud his judgment against someone who was like a brother to him. YaYa was reverting to her old ways. She thought she had outgrown her treacherous ways, that Indie's love had healed her, but she was still the same ol' girl from the hood. *Maybe I am my mother's child,* she thought.

"I thought you should know. Just be careful with him. Everybody ain't as loyal as they seem," she said.

Yeah, bitch, because you're a snake, she thought, knowing that she was the lowest of the low right now.

"I'll be home soon. Let me pull up on him," Indie replied. "Just when you think you can trust the people around you, they show you that you can't." He sighed and finished, "As long as I got you and Sky, that's all I need."

He hung up, and YaYa tossed the phone across the room in frustration. She didn't know what was wrong with her. She was spiraling down and down and down. She wanted someone to blame, so she blamed it on Leah, but now she was beginning to think that she was just a bad seed. Her thoughts haunted her as she realized she was ruining lives the same way that Leah ruined hers.

Maybe I'm just like Leah. I'm no better than her. I'm willing to hurt innocent people just to get my way too.

***

Disappointment filled Indie as he pulled in front of Chase's home. It took him fifteen minutes just to get out of the car, because he didn't quite know how to approach Chase about the subject. Chase was like a brother to Indie, and he didn't want to believe that he had been disloyal. Indie was cutthroat, many would even call him heartless, but when he embraced someone as family, it was hard to bring them harm. His loyalty was sometimes a fault, because he seldom got the same in return.

He checked his anger, making sure that he wasn't irrational before he went inside. He wanted to be clearheaded. He would give Chase a chance to share his side of the story, but if he lied, even once, then Indie would cut him off.

He knocked on the door and greeted Chase with a stiff handshake when he opened up.

Indie looked around Chase's plush brownstone and couldn't understand why Chase would go behind his back. Indie was fair and loyal. He made sure that his team was comfortable and well fed.

Every nigga want to be the chief. Nobody wants to put in they time as an Indian, Indie thought. He was feeling a type of way about the information YaYa had told him. He was almost sick to his stomach, because Chase had become dear to his heart. Chase had shown so much good faith. He had remained loyal to Indie when others like Khi-P had jumped ship. Just as Indie was planning to take them all legit and establish them as business minds, Chase had shown his hand. Or so he thought. He trusted YaYa too much to ever question her or figure out her agenda. If she said it, it was law, so he had already marked Chase as guilty. The fact that Chase couldn't look Indie in the eyes only added confirmation to YaYa's claims.

Chase's heart was heavy. He could barely stand to look at Indie as he tried to think of a gentle way to deliver the news that YaYa was stumbling down a slippery slope of addiction. He wanted to come right out with it and give it to him square, but he knew what it was like to have someone poisoned by drugs. He knew the hurt that Indie was about to feel. His own mother had put the burden on his heart.

He took a deep breath and began. "You know I've got nothing but love and respect for you, but I've got something to tell you."

Indie's jaw tensed.

"I already know what you're about to say, Chase. I want to know to why. After everything that I've placed in your lap, you betray me? That's how it's laying between brothers now?"

Confusion crossed Chase's face. The conversation had gone bad before it even begin. "What? What are you talking about?"

"You saying you didn't try to back-door me when you snuck off to Italy with Trina? You didn't try to take more bricks than you were supposed to? Huh? You wasn't trying to steal the connect for yourself?" Indie asked.

Chase chuckled in disbelief before anger sparked ablaze in his chest. "That's bullshit and you know it," Chase spat.

"Fuck you was doing in Italy in the first place? Your position is here. You move the work through the streets. How come no one knew about this mysterious trip?" Indie grilled.

Chase could see Indie growing cold. Just the look in his eyes warned Chase to tread lightly on the subject. "Look, fam, you got the shit all wrong. I went there because Trina was going. That's my sister. I'm not gon' send her into the fire solo on her first run."

"Yeah, that ain't what I heard. I heard something different," Indie stated.

"Yeah, from who?" Chase asked defensively. "From YaYa?" Chase smirked as he put two and two together. YaYa was trying to burn him so that he couldn't rat her out.

"Might want to check with your source, bro. She got an agenda like a mu'fucka," Chase said.

"You lie to my face after everything I've done for you?" Indie barked. His bark was low, but it still hurt all the same.

"Only person who's lying to you is your bitch," Chase responded.

"Watch your mouth, li'l nigga. Don't make me body you in this bitch," Indie spat. "Only reason you're not floating in the East River is because I had love for you, but from this point on you're done. You're cut off. I've never kept anybody in the shadows. If you wanted to shine, all you had to do was say so."

Chase was floored that YaYa had poisoned Indie against him. He never pegged her to be that type. She was tearing down a friendship and a prosperous business relationship just to keep her dirty secret.

"Yeah, a'ight, Indie. You let YaYa plant that seed all you want to, but don't assassinate my character, homie. Don't speak ill on me. I've earned every stripe on my vest. You need to go home and ask wifey why the fuck she bring that ass to the trap today trying to cop! Ask her that! A young nigga put in work for you, and when it's time for you to judge me, you go in without proof? YaYa behavior been shady ever since she came back from the dead. You just blinded, bro. The love got you feeling instead of thinking."

Indie had no more words for Chase. "You're lucky that you were loyal to me for as long as you were," Indie said in a low tone. The implied threat that lay beneath the surface of his words was like a punch to the gut. Never in a million years did Chase think he would see the day when his mentor would become his adversary.

"I guess there's nothing left to say then, homie," Chase stated. "When you find out the truth, though, you can keep the apology. I don't want it. Loyalty goes both ways."

Indie turned solemnly and walked ou the door. He didn't even have the itch to murder Chase. It felt as if he were walking out of a funeral. He had just lost a brother.

***

YaYa heard the snow crunch as Indie pulled into their driveway. She looked at the bag of cocaine in her hand. She hadn't touched it. Not yet. After lying on Chase, she knew that she had taken things too far. She fought the urge and told herself that she could create her own solace, without any help from a narcotic.

I threw shade on a real nigga today, she thought sadly. *All because of this.*

She placed the bag of cocaine in her panty drawer, telling herself that she would do better, but if she really wanted to walk a straight line, she would have flushed it. Her downfall was inevitable, because she was her own worst enemy.

She met Indie at the door and saw the inner turmoil that he was going through. As soon as he greeted her, he stared deeply into her eyes. She knew what he was looking for—clues, any indication that she was high—but she wasn't stupid. She knew the accusations that Chase would defend himself with, and that was the real reason why she hadn't put the cocaine to use.

Indie gripped her face tightly and stared deeply into her eyes. His force was rough, almost as if he wanted to snap her neck for throwing shit in the game. "You better not ever lie to me, YaYa. I will go against a thousand armies for you. All you got to do is say the word, but I don't want to have to second guess anything that you say to me. All I've ever asked is that you keep it real with me. Never lie to me," he said through clenched teeth.

He hated that he loved her so much in that moment. He missed the old days when he had no vices. YaYa was his weakness. She could lead him in whatever direction she wanted to because of his affection for her. He was vulnerable with her and only her. He only prayed that she didn't prey upon him.

YaYa reached for his coat and took it from his shoulders, tossing it to the side. Then she went for his tie, then his shirt, then his wife beater as she kissed him without reservation. The sweet taste of her tongue invaded his mouth as they ravaged one another.

"Where's Skylar?" he growled.

"She's asleep," YaYa answered in between breaths as she frantically reached for his hardness and stroked it, rubbing his balls and pulling the shaft, causing him to groan. He turned her around. His frustration and anger was evident in the way that he handled her. He bent her over the Italian sofa and entered her. She was dripping wet. Hot and tight. She needed the dick. If she couldn't have her first drug of choice, she would surely take this. His strong ass muscles worked as he moved in and out of her, hitting the back of that pussy like an all-star hitter.

"Agh," she cried out in pure ecstasy. "Get it out, baby. Get it all out," she whispered. She knew that she needed punishing. Her bad-girl deeds deserved the bruising that he was putting on her sex.

Indie grabbed her shoulder for leverage and gave her all of him, putting all of his length inside of her then taking it out to the tip, only to go back in again and again. YaYa's ass rippled as she took the dick. There was no running from it tonight. She owed him this debt. After what she had caused Indie to lose, she knew that she had to take it. It was a plus for her, because he was working her body over so good. This wasn't love-making; it was fucking at its finest. This was an animalistic man-to-woman interaction.

YaYa came all over him, causing her juices to coat him and sending him over the edge. She felt the warmness spill into her as she caught his orgasm. Spent, she didn't move as he pulled out. She turned to look at him, but the hurt she saw in his face broke her heart.

She didn't speak, and neither did he as he gathered his clothes and ascended the steps, leaving her alone and clueless as to what he was thinking.

Chapter 22

With Chase no longer in the fold of things, Indie knew that it was only a matter of time before his old protégé became his new competition. Indie was easing out of the street aspect of the game anyway, so he wouldn't rival with Chase over street blocks and cocaine wholesales. He would simply graduate to the next level and move on to greater things. If Chase had been anyone else, he would have starved him out just because of the principle of things, but because of their past, Indie would allow him to eat. He would even move over to allow him room to grow.

Truth was, the streets were for the young hustlers. Chase was in his prime, whereas Indie had matured. He had a child and a woman to think about, which forced his aspirations to change. He no longer wanted to be the dope man; he would settle for businessman instead. But before he made the transition, he had to ensure that he had the buy-in for Vartex. He had to become a shareholder in the company to secure his financial stability. He would do what he did best to make the dough, but he vowed that this was his last run. He couldn't force YaYa out of the game if he was still trying to play it himself.

They had barely spoken since she had given him the bad news about Chase, and the tension between them was growing by the day. YaYa seemed on edge, and Indie was too preoccupied to figure out why. Keeping up with her changing moods was almost impossible, so instead he gave her space, because in all honesty he needed it as well. He just didn't know how to tell her.

YaYa entered his office and stood near the doorway. She didn't speak, partly because she didn't know what to say. She was ashamed of her actions, but couldn't admit that to Indie because she was still living a lie.

Indie looked up at her, knowing that they couldn't avoid each other forever.

She's not the one who crossed you. She's just the messenger, he thought, knowing that he was taking out his loss of a friendship on her.

"Sit down, YaYa. I want to talk to you," he started.

She slowly walked over to the chair in front of his desk and took a seat.

"I spoke with Zya and I asked her to stop doing business with you," he said honestly.

YaYa didn't respond immediately. A part of her felt betrayed, but the part of her that had betrayed him couldn't protest. She had wanted to be like Zya, to command an army of goons like Zya, to get money like Zya for one reason and one reason alone: to get to Leah. But here she was, a few flips later, and she was still no closer to Leah than she had been when she was living regular. Her net worth had increased, but her self-worth had diminished, and she was still just as weak as before. Leah was in a place where security was too tight for anyone to infiltrate. She couldn't be touched as long as she was within the walls of a mental hospital. YaYa had no wins. It was like she was stuck, glued to the hurt of her past because she couldn't forgive the people who had wronged her.

"Honestly, Indie, I don't even care anymore," she said. She stood and began to walk out of the room.

"Disaya," he called.

Her breath caught in her throat because she knew that he was serious when he used her full name. She turned to him feeling defeated. Defeated by Leah, by life, by Indie, by Zya, even her own mother. She blamed everyone for everything bad that had ever happened to her, but she refused to see the parts that she had played in her own demise. Her story hadn't even ended yet, but she was slowly giving up.

"I love you," he said.

She paused, and the doubt that he saw in her eyes stabbed him in the heart.

How can he love me? I don't even love me. I don't deserve to be loved by a man like him, she thought.

The sound of the doorbell saved her from having to share her concerns. Indie checked the monitors and saw that Agent Norris stood at his doorstep.

He stood and walked past YaYa, stopping momentarily in front of her. He grabbed her chin gently. "I do love you, ma."

"I know you do," she replied softly. He walked past her and went to answer the door.

"Norris. What are you doing here?" he asked sternly as soon as he opened the door.

Agent Norris stood shivering and blowing hot air into his hands as the bitter wind blew fiercely around him.

"Can I come in?" Norris asked.

"No need for that," Indie replied. "This will be short and sweet. The ten thousand I pay you doesn't require us to be friendly. Why are you on my doorstep?"

"Always busting my balls," Norris mumbled as his face began to turn red from the cold. "I just thought you might want to know that the Richards girl? She escaped. Crazy bitch drugged a psychiatrist with the same medication they were supposed to be giving her then snuck out. The cops have been on her, the bureau . . . hell, everybody wants a piece of this girl, but we have no leads. I think she's going to come for your girl. We found a New York address among her things, so we know she's headed this way," Norris admitted.

"Then let her come," YaYa said.

Indie turned around, realizing that she had heard the entire thing.

"YaYa . . ." he said.

"No, I'm fine. If she wants to come at my head, let her. This is what I've been waiting for. I couldn't get to her when I wanted to, so I'm going to let her get at me. This time I'll see her coming, though." YaYa turned around ascended the steps with tears in her eyes.

This was the same bitch that had made her weak and destroyed her life. YaYa didn't know it before, but she had let Leah instill fear within her. Times were over for that, however. She was tired of the same bum bitch winning. YaYa had asked for this moment for too long not to come out on top in the end. She welcomed the showdown and mentally prepared herself for it, because she knew that one of them wouldn't walk out alive. When it was all said and done, one of them had to die.

Chapter 23

YaYa felt as if she were having a panic attack as her chest tightened to the point where it hindered her breath. She clasped her chest as she rushed through the house and staggered to her bedroom.

How could they let her escape? How did she just slip through the cracks? She ruined my fucking life! she thought as she rushed to her nightstand. She pulled the drawer all the way out and emptied it onto the floor. The dark orange bottle spilled out among the contents, but when she picked it up and heard the rattle of one small pill inside, she tossed it across the room in frustration. YaYa was feeling too much at once. Leah's face, the sly grin that always wore on her face, her evil eyes, it all plagued YaYa's mind. She was losing it.

She choked on her own emotion as she stood to her feet and went to her dresser drawer. She pulled out the bag of cocaine that she had stolen from Chase. She had promised herself that she wouldn't touch it, and for a while she had done good. She had focused on her family, on her upcoming nuptials and on being a better woman, a stronger woman for Indie, but in the end she always felt weak. She was a victim. The roles had been established when Leah first targeted her. YaYa was a victim of life, of Leah, and of herself.

Her hands trembled as she looked at it. YaYa was no longer in denial. She knew that she had a problem. She had tried to mask her turmoil and hide her weakness

from everyone around her, but as she sat on her bedroom floor contemplating the unthinkable, she realized
that she needed help. Ever since Leah had crossed the
line and kidnapped her child, YaYa hadn't been the
same. Something inside of her had shattered. Prescription drugs were like the ice on her emotional bruise,
only it didn't work anymore. It wasn't strong enough
and YaYa found herself chasing a stronger high.

She set up three large lines, using a card from her
wallet to evenly distribute the white powder. She lowered her head over the lines with a rolled-up hundred
dollar bill pinched between her fingers.

You don't have to do this, she thought. *Just tell Indie
you're hurting.*

Leah's face flashed before her mind, and it was all the
push she needed to lower her head and inhale the powder up her nose. The powder hit her like a Mack truck,
and her mouth fell open as her nipples hardened and
her entire body tingled. Euphoria flooded her senses as
YaYa slumped to the floor. This was unlike any feeling
that any pill had ever given her. She sat there as all of
the world's ills escaped her mind and she was suddenly
wrapped in a comforting cocoon. Nothing in her world
mattered at the moment—not Leah, not her failures
as a mother, not the pressures of being a hustler. It all
seemed to fade to the background.

"Mama."

Skylar's tiny voice caused her to look up. "Oh my
God, what am I doing?" she asked herself. Suddenly
she felt ashamed. Despite the fact that her adrenaline
was on ten, she couldn't enjoy the high. YaYa was becoming a liability to herself and the ones she loved.
Using drugs in Skylar's presence confirmed what she
already knew: she had lost herself in the fire. Her physical appearance had been repaired, but on the inside
she was still a mess.

"Come here, Sky. come to Mommy, baby girl," she whispered as she came to all fours and reached out to her daughter.

Skylar walked clumsily to her mother, and YaYa pulled the little girl into her arms. "I love you, Skylar Perkins. I'm so sorry, baby girl. I let her hurt you. I'm so sorry. I won't ever do this again. I promise," she whispered.

***

Indie entered the boardroom with a cool confidence as the subtle scent of his Armani cologne announced his presence. The board of corporate figures around him watched him sternly, sizing him up as he took a seat at one of the leather executive chairs that surrounded the rectangular table. Everyone else around the table possessed a degree in business, finance, marketing, or had some other formal skill set that they had acquired from a fancy university. Indie's only experience was the school of hard knocks. He had learned the art of negotiation on the street corners of New York City. He had taken Ls that would make the average Wall Street broker put the barrel of a gun in his mouth and pull the trigger, yet Indie had bounced back.

His intellect always allowed him to stay on top and ahead of the game, but the risks he took were astronomical. He could see the game swallowing YaYa whole. They were international. If one minor thing went wrong, the empire that they were building would crumble. Indie couldn't allow that to happen. The money that they were making was too good to be long term. It was only natural for every good thing to come to an end, but Indie would much rather walk away from the game than to let it lead to his demise.

He unbuttoned his suit jacket to make himself more comfortable as he took his seat.

They had accumulated the buy-in with ease. With the money their team was getting, it was easy to come up with his half. Zya was already papered up, so once he came to the table with his portion, they were good to go. Zya was cut from the same cloth as Indie, and she realized a good opportunity when she saw one. A percentage at a pharmaceutical company had the potential to make them much more money than the streets could ever offer up.

The others seated at the table threw him subtle glances. They were curious about his identity and skeptical of his involvement in their business. Upon FDA approval, they knew that they would have a goldmine on their hands, and nobody wanted to bring one more person into the fold. Needleman was the bridge between Indie and the other partners at the company.

They could give him all the dirty looks they wanted, but they weren't going to stop him from staking claim. They needed him. The truth of the matter was that the delay of FDA approval of their newest drug was draining their pockets. The prices of their stocks had fallen, and they were losing money by the day. Indie had money, a lot of it, and he would use it as his buy-in. There would be no way that they could deny him after they found out his worth.

"This is Indie Perkins," Needleman said. "He is a long-time client of mine and a business owner in the community. He is interested in buying shares of the company."

"It's a pleasure to have you here, Mr. Perkins. I'm Ian Douglas, CFO of Vartex. What percentage are you interested in buying?" the CFO asked as he sat at the head of the corporate table.

"Ten percent," Indie said, speaking up for himself as he crossed his hands on top of the table.

"No offense, Mr. Perkins, but ten percent is quite expensive. That would make you a majority shareholder. This company is made up of thousands of smaller shareholders. There are only a few of us sitting at this table that have majority vote," the CFO said.

"I'm not here to ask permission to buy into Vartex, Mr. Douglas. It's a public stock, so as long as I have the hundred fifty million, that shouldn't be a problem. I do know that office politics of an organization can keep me out of the loop on a lot of things. I'm here to make sure that I don't run into that problem. Truth is this company needs me more than I need it," Indie stated calmly, as he commanded the suit-and-tie bandits with authority and confidence.

"Is that so? Please continue, Mr. Perkins. I think we are all interested to hear more."

Indie cut to the chase. "I have influence at the Federal Drug Administration. Once I become a shareholder, your new Alzheimer's drug will be approved," Indie stated.

Ian Douglas looked around the table at the rest of the board. He was a young, ambitious white boy who happened to be the son of the CEO. He was the youngest on the board and wasn't too fond of the idea of letting Indie eat off of his plate. He smelled a drug dealer from a mile away and knew that Indie was bringing dirt to the dinner table. But at such a critical time, he knew that Indie's connections could solidify them. He would welcome Indie with open arms until they received their FDA patent.

"I guess the only thing left to say is welcome to Vartex," Ian said.

***

Indie kept his cool until he entered the Maybach that was waiting for him curbside. As soon as he was behind the black tint, he loosened his tie and exhaled in relief as the driver rolled away. "Yes, yes," he whispered as he pumped his fist in triumph. He picked up his cell phone and sent a text to Zya.

Welcome to the country club.

***

YaYa sat at the dining room table nervously as Skylar played at her feet and they both waited for Indie to come home. YaYa felt like a little girl waiting for her father to come and chastise her. She had finally realized that she was out of control, and as soon as Indie walked through the door, she was going to confess everything. Her lies were beginning to change who she was, and guilt plagued her. YaYa had done the unthinkable by using drugs in front of her daughter, and she needed Indie to help her get her life together. She couldn't continue to pretend that everything was okay, and Indie was the only person who could save her from herself.

She feared what his reaction would be. *What if he looks at me differently?* she thought. She didn't want the context of their relationship to change, but it had to, because she had changed. Every single dramatic event that had occurred over the course of her life had changed her, so she couldn't expect their relationship to remain the same. Everything had to evolve; she only hoped that with evolution came growth. She wanted to grow with her mate, not apart from him.

YaYa had taken Indie through much worse. In the past she had contributed to the death of his own brother under Leah's manipulation, she had made her body available to the highest bidder when working as an escort for Elite. Her closet was full of skeletons that he had forgiven. If he could get over all of these things, then surely he would be willing to deal with her current dilemma.

Or it could be the straw that breaks the camel's back, she thought.

She battled with the idea of coming clean, of admitting her sins. Once she said them aloud, Indie would take control and any further drug use would be impossible. His eyes would be on her at all times. YaYa had to be ready to let the drugs go for good because once Indie found out about them, it would be a wrap. She no longer felt that she could handle things on her own. She didn't even recognize herself. She loved her daughter dearly, but her selfish ways had caused her to cross the line.

When she heard his keys in the door, she stood nervously.

As soon as he set his sights on her, he kissed her lips. "We on, ma. You're looking at a majority shareholder in Vartex Enterprises," he said. "We ain't got to do this no more. No risks, no trips overseas, no bricks, Pyrex jars and baking soda," Indie said. "We're all the way legit, YaYa. Nobody can take that away. I don't have to worry about one of us standing before a judge and jury ever again. You can just sit back and be my lady . . . my wife. You ready for that?" he asked.

He was so happy that YaYa couldn't bring herself to tell him. It wasn't the time. It didn't feel right and she felt that if she opened her mouth to admit that she had just used drugs hours ago, he would leave her. YaYa needed Indie the way that she needed air, and although she knew that he loved her, everyone had limits. Her drug use just may be the one thing that Indie would not accept. Indie would never look at her the same if he knew exactly how pitiful she had become.

I don't have to tell him. What he doesn't know won't hurt him, she thought. *I'll never touch another drug again.*

"Of course I'm ready," she said in a low tone. Shame plagued her. How could she even think about sabotaging such a marvelous man? Her drug use would be his downfall, especially now that she was beginning to have interest in the drug that their entire empire was built upon. Indie was only as strong as the woman that stood behind him, and if she showed her weakness, she felt like she would become his liability. He required a bad bitch on his arm, not some strung out girl from the hood that was a borderline pill head. He could only prosper if she kept things intact at home. Behind every great man there was an even greater woman, but at the moment YaYa was anything but. She was living a lie, but it was then that she decided to be his strength instead.

This will be the last lie I ever tell him, she thought sincerely.

"Start planning that wedding, ma. The world is ours, and I want you at my side as my wife and nothing else," he said. "That's all I want you to concern yourself with: making a home for our family. I want to fill this house with babies, ma. Little girls that look like you and little boys that I teach to how to be men. I want Sunday dinners, happy holidays, all that, ma. I just want you. You're my foundation. I want to build a future with you, and I don't want to wait."

His words were bringing her to tears, and she closed her eyes in guilt. *You don't deserve him,* she told herself, but now that she had him it was her responsibility to give him all of the things he desired. His requests were pure, simple, and good. All he wanted was a life with her, and YaYa vowed that she would give him that.

"Let's get married, ma. I don't care where or how. I just want to do it soon. Like tomorrow. Let's hop a flight, go to Vegas."

Indie was so in the moment that she had to laugh. "Vegas! I plan to get married one time, and it will not be in some cheesy chapel in Vegas!" she said jokingly.

"Well, whatever you can plan in a week is what we'll do. I don't want to spend too many nights sleeping next to Disaya Morgan. I'm ready to meet Disaya Perkins," he said. "You've got a week. Money can make anything happen. Just tell me when and where to show up," he said with a wink as he walked away.

YaYa shook her head. The ups and downs of her life kept her on an emotional roller coaster. There was no middle ground with YaYa. It was almost as if she were connected to two different people: one pulled her toward bliss, while the other tried to tear everything apart. Leah and Indie, that's who she was torn between, but today she was determined not to let Leah ruin this moment.

YaYa pushed all negative thoughts out of her mind. It was true that Leah was out and that she went unpunished for the things that she had done, but YaYa knew that it was only a matter of time before Leah showed her cards, and when she did, this time YaYa would be ready. Until then YaYa would focus on her family and focus on strengthening her mental. If she was stable, then Leah or anyone else would never be able to get inside of her head and throw her life off balance. When the time came to face her, YaYa would make sure she was ready, but she wasn't going to continue to live her life in chaos, consumed by the tragedies that had occurred yesterday.

I've got to stop letting that bitch break me, she thought. YaYa picked up her daughter with renewed faith. She didn't have to tell Indie about the cocaine. She could handle it herself. YaYa was no longer going to be a burden on his shoulders or proclaim to be a victim any longer. She had come too far to let everything fall apart now. She would be exactly who he needed her to be and become the woman that she always knew she could be. The only way for her to do that was to bury the past and forget about all of the people who had done her wrong, including Leah. She was looking forward to tomorrow, forward to her upcoming nuptials. She would plan an intimate ceremony that she would never forget; one that would be the beginning of her new life.

Chapter 24

YaYa had no idea when Leah would come back into her life, but she was definitely coming, and YaYa was only biding her time before she faced off with the bitch that had ruined her life. The planning of her wedding served as a good distraction, but she would never truly let her guard down. Although she no longer feared Leah, she also would never underestimate her. The last time she had done that, her daughter had ended up missing. YaYa wouldn't make the same mistake twice. She was always acutely aware of Leah's impending return. It was as if she could sense her, and she seemed dangerously close.

She was exhausted from the constant state of paranoia that she lived in. YaYa had been prey and Leah her predator. She almost welcomed the day that Leah would make her move, because at least then her enemy would be in her sights and not stalking her in the shadows. YaYa hated that every significant moment in her life was overshadowed by such intense negativity because Leah was always in her thoughts. Even today, on the eve of her wedding, her mind was consumed by Leah. Knowing that she was free and roaming somewhere in the world caused extreme paranoia in YaYa.

She stared out of the window at the snow that fell from the sky. She could barely see to the end of her driveway. It was like a white blanket covered the earth. Nothing moved and everything was calm, except for her racing heart. Her breath froze on the windowpane as she admired the winter wonderland that was her front yard.

"Are you ready for tomorrow, Mrs. Perkins?" Indie said as he came up behind her and wrapped his arms around her slim waist.

She smiled and leaned her head back against his chest. "That sounds so weird to me. Mrs. Perkins," she said aloud. "I can't believe we're actually doing this . . . that you actually want me for the rest of your life."

"There's no doubt in my mind," he assured. "Are you sure you don't want me here with you tonight? I can tell you have some things on your mind. I don't want you here alone if you can't handle it."

"She's just out there. Watching me. I know she is," YaYa said.

"I can put goons around the house. No one will get in or out unless you want them to," he said.

"No, that's not necessary. I don't want my house to start to feel like a prison. If she finds me, then it'll be judgment day for one of us," YaYa replied.

"Don't talk like that. I won't let her or anyone else hurt you. You shouldn't be thinking about the negative right now. All I want you focused on is looking beautiful for me tomorrow," he said. He kissed the top of her head and she turned to face him.

"I can do that," she promised. "Now, get out of here. I don't want you to lay eyes on me again until I'm walking toward you to say 'I do.'"

She was putting on a good front, but truth was she was terrified—not of the commitment of marriage, but of the possibility that Leah just may show up and ruin it all.

"You call me if you need anything. Sky is with my parents. They'll bring her to the ceremony tomorrow. All you have to do is relax," he said.

She nodded and watched as he pulled out a long silver jewelry box.

"I know you're supposed to have something new, something old, something black and blue, or however the saying goes . . ."

She chuckled as she corrected him. "Something borrowed, something blue."

He smiled and opened the box, revealing a white gold diamond bracelet. "This can be your something old. It was my grandmother's. She wore it on the day she married my grandfather. She gave it to me when I was a kid. Told me to make sure I gave it to someone who deserved it. You deserve it, ma. It's not as flashy as some of your other pieces. It's only one karat of diamonds and some of them are cloudy, but my grandfather saved up for months just to get it for her. She treasured it."

"And so will I," YaYa said with a smile as she held out her wrist and watched him clasp it on. She knew how much his grandmother meant to him and was honored to accept the gift.

"I just have to pack a bag and then I'm out of here," he said, bidding her adieu as he left the room.

Indie wouldn't let YaYa know, but he would put one of his goons around the house just to make sure that she was safe. She thought that she could handle herself, but Indie knew that YaYa wasn't as strong as she would like the world to believe.

He went into their bedroom and pulled out his Gucci duffel bag. His custom suit was waiting for him at his hotel room, so he only packed the essentials. When he was all set, he looked over his shoulders before pulling out another jewelry box containing a pair of beautiful diamond earrings, another wedding present for YaYa. She wouldn't find them until she dressed in the morning. It was her something new.

He opened the top drawer to her bureau and froze when he saw what lay inside. His heart dropped because he immediately knew what the bag of white powder was. Cocaine.

He wanted to ask her what she was doing with it, but he already knew. *Chase was telling the truth,* he thought. He grabbed the bag out of the drawer and tossed the earrings on the bed.

Tears stung Indie's eyes as he remembered Chase's warning. He knew that the accusations had been true, but because he didn't want to taint the perfect image that he had painted of YaYa in his head, he had lived in denial. YaYa was hooked on prescription pills, and as he gripped the bag of cocaine in his hand, he realized the problem had escalated. The pills were nothing but a gateway drug that had led her to something much darker. Whatever demons she was fighting, she was losing the battle, and Indie's heart broke into irreparable pieces as he realized how far his queen had fallen. She was too tormented to tell him the truth. There was nothing lower in his book than a liar.

I asked her if anything was wrong. I asked her repeatedly, he thought in disappointment. The fact that she hadn't come to him broke him in half. He thought that they had come so far together, accomplished too much to ever harbor secrets that could destroy them. If they didn't have trust they didn't have anything, and it was clear that he couldn't trust YaYa. He wasn't even sure if he recognized her at this point. He had extended his offer to help her should she need him, but she always turned him down . . . she always reassured him that she was okay, that she had everything in control. What hurt the most was that she had lied to him.

How can I trust her? he asked himself. The night before their wedding day he had found out her biggest flaw: she was an unremorseful liar.

He found her still staring out of the same window, lost in thought, but instead of feeling the intense love that he had just moments before, he felt disgust.

"Chase never tried to cut in on the connect, did he?" Indie asked.

YaYa turned to him in shock and said, "What? Yes, I told you—"

"You told me what, ma? Huh? Tell me again," Indie grilled in a low, no-nonsense tone. "Tell another lie. A new lie to cover the old lie. You seem to be good at it, so tell me another one."

YaYa folded her arms across her chest and shuffled from foot to foot nervously. "I didn't . . . I . . ." She didn't know what to say.

"What, you don't want to talk about that?" he asked condescendingly. "Then let's talk about this." He pulled the bag of cocaine from behind his back and tossed it to her. YaYa let it fall to her feet as her eyes widened in panic.

No, no, no! Why didn't I just flush it? she thought.

"It's not what you think," she said.

"Really? So you didn't lie on Chase? You didn't try to cop from him? You wasn't getting high?" he asked.

"Indie, please!" she begged. "Just let me explain."

Indie shook his head as he stared at her. Her tears did nothing to move him. He had seen them before, heard the excuses from her before, forgiven her before, and his kindness always proved to be his weakness. YaYa always wounded his heart every time he took her back. Animosity built around his heart like a fortress and allowed no room for sympathy to cloud his judgment.

"You let me cut him off. You let me accuse him of going against the family when it was you all along who had been disloyal," Indie said. He shook his head in disbelief.

"I had to. I was in over my head, Indie. Please just hear me out. I was hurting. I was depressed. I was angry that Leah was still alive. So I continued to take the pills even after the physical pain went away. They made me feel better. They made it easier to cope with everything that I was feeling. I ran out, and by then I was too far gone to stop, so I asked Chase to give me something."

"Chase served you? He gave you drugs?" Indie shouted.

"No, baby, no. Please just listen," she cried as she reached for Indie.

He removed her hands from his body. YaYa could practically see the end of their relationship, and as she fixed her mouth to tell a lie, she stopped herself. It was time for the lying game to end. She had too much love and respect for this man to continue to litter their union with the pollution of dishonesty. If she placed any further blame on Chase, Indie would kill him. She could see it in his eyes. They were ablaze with hatred, the same way that they had been when he had beaten her while she was pregnant with Sky. In that moment, she feared him. She remembered just how ruthless Indie could be. Somewhere along the way she had lost respect for him, enough to think that she could get over on him . . . that she could lie to him without consequence. She had taken him for granted, but now as he stood before her with such rage in his heart, she remembered exactly who he was. Indie was a boss, and no matter how well connected she became, her new status didn't trump the work that he had put in or the amount of respect that he deserved. She had been given her place in the streets, whereas Indie had earned his. As much as he had done for her, she owed him the truth. YaYa's lips quivered as she began to speak.

"Chase didn't serve me. He refused to. He threatened to tell you, so I stole it from him. But I didn't touch the stuff. I swear to God, Indie, I never used it. I felt too bad. I just kept it because . . . I . . . I don't know why. But I wasn't going to use it," she said. "You have to believe me!"

He scoffed sarcastically. "You're still lying, YaYa. Is that what you've turned into? A liar, ma? You can stand here in my face and it just comes out effortlessly. You fidget when you lie. You twiddle your fingers and your eyes lower, almost like you're ashamed of yourself. I saw it the night I asked you about Chase, but I forced myself to put it in the back of my mind, to believe you in spite of what I already knew. Not this time, ma. I want to hear the real. Now, tell me the truth," he said.

"I just wanted to feel better. I came back from the dead, but I didn't feel alive. I felt lost, afraid, scared, angry. I just needed something to help me cope," she admitted.

YaYa looked so fraudulent to him.

"Please. Leah ruined my life. I just wanted to escape reality," she said as she grabbed his arm desperately.

He shrugged her off of him and stormed out of the room, headed for the front door. YaYa chased after him.

"Indie, don't do this! What about tomorrow?" she shouted at his back.

He stopped and turned toward her. YaYa was a mess as snot and tears mixed on her face. He was the love of her life, and she had fucked it all up.

Indie's heart bled out for the woman that he loved. She had her hooks in him. Indie was stuck on her like fish to bait, and it always hurt when he tried to pull away.

"You're a piece of work, ma. That Leah shit is getting old. She didn't ruin your life; you did by living in the past and letting old ghosts haunt you. I told you to let that shit go," he said.

"I couldn't! I can't! Not until she's dead and gone. Don't you get that? Every breath that she takes sucks the life out of me!" YaYa screamed.

"Yeah, well, I can't live like this. I'm not going to sit around and wait for you to self-destruct," he answered. "The wedding is off."

YaYa fell to her knees as she watched Indie walk out the front door, assuming that he was walking out of her life as well. She curled up in a ball on the floor and wept because after the fight that they had just had, currents of grief swept through her body and she was racked with sobs. She had lost Indie many times before, but this time felt different. This time YaYa wasn't sure if he would ever come back.

***

YaYa peeled herself off of the floor an hour later. Her eyes were so swollen that she could barely see through them as she stood to her feet. She felt weak as she thought of the mess that she had made of her life. Leah hadn't caused her to lose Indie; she had done that all on her own. She had made herself out to be a liar. Instead of going to him in her time of need and asking him to help her crawl out of the emotional hole she was stuck in, she had lied—lied about her misuse of prescription pills, lied about Chase's loyalty. YaYa had been stupid. Selfish. It took him walking out the door for her to see the error of her ways.

"What did I do?" she said. She yearned to feel numb at the moment. It would be so simple to hit one line and have all of her troubles melt away, but it would only solve her problems temporarily. It would only give her false happiness, when all YaYa truly wanted was the real thing. She grabbed the bag of cocaine and momentarily contemplated the sweet relief that it could give her. YaYa opened the bag and watched the pure white cocaine sparkle.

How could I have been so weak? Why would I jeopardize my family, my daughter? she thought. She went into the guest bathroom and opened the lid of the toilet, then finally did what she should have done a long time ago. She flushed the cocaine down the toilet. Yes, she was hurting, and yes, the past terrorized her, the unknown future intimidated her, but as she watched the powder flush away, she realized that the pain was an indication that she was still alive. She lived and breathed. YaYa was still standing after everything that she had been through, and in order to heal, she had to hurt. It was necessary to go through all of the emotions. The drugs had only picked at the scab and stopped her from moving on with her life.

She went up to her room and pulled her beautiful wedding gown out of the closet. She held it up to her body. YaYa didn't know if she would ever get a chance to wear it. Her happily ever after may never happen, and she had no one to blame but herself. She had to laugh aloud because she had no more tears to cry.

She went to the kitchen and grabbed the bottle of Dom that she had intended to share with Indie on their wedding night. She popped it open and white foam splashed from the top, only she had no reason to celebrate. She was in mourning, and at that moment she wished that Leah had killed her. She welcomed death because life without Indie was not worth living. She had tried it once before, and it was too hard.

YaYa poured herself a flute of champagne and sat at the head of her dining room table as she drowned her sorrows.

***

Indie flew down the highway into the city, navigating through the icy streets as he put as much distance between himself and YaYa as he could. He was so sick over what he had discovered that he wished he had never even unveiled the truth. The lies hurt much less.

He picked up the phone and called the only woman he could go to for advice. His mother would never lead him astray. He felt lost, so he went to her because her love was like a compass. She always helped him find his way. He needed the burden lifted from his shoulders, and when he couldn't reach her, he decided to pay Elaine an unexpected visit.

He didn't want to leave YaYa or give up on the love of his life, but he couldn't take any more. Her life was like a never-ending soap opera. The ups never lasted long enough, and the downs were too low. It seemed they were destined to be torn apart, and there was nothing that he could do to stop it. Indie knew that if he walked away, he would never love another woman with such intensity, but it was a risk he was willing to take. If he didn't love as hard, he wouldn't hurt as much. It was an even trade-off in his book.

It took him two hours to arrive at his parents' home as he fought the elements of the snowy winter night. He was supposed to be preparing for his wedding, but instead he was contemplating a forever good-bye. Indie got out of the car and rang the bell. The porch light came on and he heard the locks click on the door.

"Indie?" Elaine greeted. "What are you doing here?" All it took was one look for her to know that something heavy was on his mind.

"She's doing drugs, Ma, and she's been lying to me the entire time," he revealed. She could hear his devastation, and she stepped back to allow him into her home.

"Your father and Sky are upstairs asleep. I'll put on some coffee so we can have a nice, long talk," she said. Indie made himself comfortable on the couch and waited until his mother returned with two mugs. He accepted one gratefully.

"What kind of drugs is she using?" Elaine asked sadly.

"Pain pills. . . . She was prescribed some medication after the fire. She's been taking them ever since. I guess she ran out, and cocaine was her next drug of choice. She stole it from Chase and then turned me against him because he had her figured out," Indie explained. "How did I miss all the signs?"

"You might not like what I'm about to tell you, Indie, but it is my job as your mother to be straight up with you. Your expectations of YaYa are too high, son. No woman could live up to what you want her to be. That girl has been a victim her entire life. She's been to hell. Literally has been kissed by the fires of hell, Indie, and she was saved. I don't know how she survived a fire so bad, but she did . . . but she's not superhuman, son. Healing from that, from her daughter being kidnapped, from the ghosts of her childhood . . . that has to be hard. She turned to drugs because she couldn't turn to you, Indie."

"She could come to me, ma," Indie protested. "I asked her countless times if she was okay."

"If you asked, that means you were concerned. You weren't completely blind to the fact that something wasn't right. You knew all along that YaYa was struggling, but you sat by and let her handle things herself . . . her way. . . . Her way of dealing was drugs. But you can't be mad when you didn't offer an alternative. Tomorrow you were to be her husband. That means you are responsible for the livelihood, the protection, the stability of that woman, Indie. If she stumbled along the way it is because you didn't guard her steps or clear her path. You young people take this marriage thing as a joke. With that ring comes responsibility," Elaine said.

Indie honestly didn't know if he could handle the responsibility of being YaYa's husband, or better yet, if he wanted to. Loving her was like torturing himself because she could never fly straight for too long. YaYa always faltered, always crossed him, and each time he opened himself up to her she let him down. "Is she the right woman for me?" Indie asked. After all that they had been through, he was beginning to have doubts.

"Only you can answer that question, Indie," Elaine responded. "But I can tell you that a blind man can see that she adores you. You're ten feet tall in her eyes," Elaine spoke honestly. "It sounds to me like YaYa needs you now more than ever." She could see the mental battle he was having, and she took the coffee mug from his strong hands.

"Go home to her. If you truly wanted to let go, the decision wouldn't be this hard."

***

YaYa exited her home. She couldn't just let Indie go.

I know he went to talk to Elaine, she thought as she rushed to her car and got inside. The soft snow covered her windshield, and she turned on her wipers to clear her view as she backed out into the street.

I can't let him leave me. I love him too much. YaYa knew that she had done so many things to sabotage their relationship, but she couldn't let him slip through her fingers. He was the greatest man she had ever known, and she refused to give him up easily.

She pulled away from her home and picked up her phone to call him. The cold kiss of a gun touched the back of her neck and YaYa froze in fear.

"Put the phone down."

She pressed Indie's name and then clicked off the light on her screen all in one movement before tossing the phone in her passenger seat. She hoped and prayed that he answered. She needed him to come to her rescue, but after the blowout that they had just had, she knew that it was a long shot that he would even answer the call.

Leah's voice was one that she would never forget, and as she lifted her eyes, she saw pure horror in her rearview mirror. It was the first time that she had laid eyes on Leah since the infamous fire. She hadn't been so lucky to have her looks restored, and her gruesome appearance shocked YaYa.

"You bitch. We get burnt by the same fucking fire and you come out just fine, while I'm left looking like this," Leah spat venomously as she kept the gun trained at the back of YaYa's head.

"You ruined my life," YaYa whispered as she felt an involuntary tear fall. Her heart pumped furiously as her eyes met Leah's in the mirror. "If I die tonight, you're dying with me," she said. Her foot grew heavy on the accelerator, and the car lunged forward. "You pull that trigger, and I lose control of the car. You came here to kill me, but are you ready to die?" YaYa asked. Her voice was so steady that it alarmed Leah.

"Slow down the car!" Leah yelled.

"Drop your gun!" YaYa shouted back. YaYa's voice was firm, and Leah saw no fear in her eyes. "All this time I gave you so much more credit than you deserve.

I gave you power over me," YaYa spoke as she drove faster and faster. "When really you're just a bum-ass bitch who stalks my life because you don't have one of your own. Nobody loves you, Leah. Even if you kill me I'll get more love than you ever will."

Her words stung Leah, hitting home as she reflected on her life. "Shut the fuck up!"

"You took my life from me, stole my daughter from her bed while she slept. You should have stayed away from me and left well enough alone, but you couldn't help yourself. As long as we occupy the same planet, you will always come for me. I used to fear that, but you can't scare a woman who isn't afraid to die. Now that you're here, you're not walking away breathing. I'll die with you before I let you walk away."

"Slow the fuck down!" Leah screamed as she noticed that YaYa was about to fly across a bridge at high speed. The ice that had frozen on the roads plus the speed at which she was driving were a dangerous combination. Leah desperately wanted to pull the trigger, but if she did, then the car would spin out of control.

YaYa had pure hatred in her eyes as she thought of what she had to do. Leah had done too much harm, caused too much damage in her life, and YaYa didn't have a forgiving soul. It would end here and now, even if YaYa had to meet her end as well. Her vengeful heart held murderous intent.

The engine growled as her speedometer went from eighty miles per hour . . . to ninety . . . to one hundred. . . . She held the steering wheel so tightly that her fingers turned red.

"Stop the car!" Leah demanded. Her hard demeanor cracked as her voice gave away her fear. YaYa was in control, and anything Leah did to stop her would jeopardize her life. All she could do was hold on for the death ride that YaYa was taking her on.

As soon as YaYa got to the bridge, she rolled down her window, causing freezing air to smack Leah in the face.

"What are you doing? What are you . . ." Leah's words gave way to her screams as YaYa jerked the wheel hard to the right. She lowered her head and braced herself as the car went flying, crashing through the guardrail and into the river below.

YaYa's seat belt stopped her from hitting the windshield, but Leah went flying from the back seat to the front. She hit her head hard, knocking away her good sense as she closed her eyes from the pain of the blow. Blood trickled from her forehead as she reached up and touched her wound.

The car began to sink immediately, and the shock from the water temperature caused YaYa to gasp in horror as she went for the open window. The water that was pouring inside of the car made it hard for her to get out, and just as she found her footing, she felt Leah's hands pulling at her waist.

"Aghh!" she screamed as she tried to break free, but the water was now waist deep, and moving against the resistance of the current proved difficult.

"Why don't you just die already, you bitch!" YaYa screamed as she turned around, knowing that she would have to fight if she wanted to make it out of the car alive. She lifted her frozen hands and hit Leah with a haymaker that caused her head to snap back violently.

Leah's eyes widened in pain as she lunged for YaYa. They both knew that the stakes were high. Only one of them could leave the car breathing.

They wrestled each other as they both went for the window. YaYa grabbed Leah by the hair and pulled with all of her might, which only infuriated Leah more.

"You . . . fucking . . . crazy . . . bitch," YaYa shouted as she banged it out with Leah, crashing Leah's head into the steering wheel with all of her might. "This is for my daughter!" she shouted as she saw blood begin to mix with the river water. She pulled Leah's head back one more time. "And this is for me!" She slammed it against the wheel once more, using all of her strength.

Leah slipped under the water, dazed, as she tried to gather her bearings. She turned around, and insanity flashed in her eyes.

The car shifted, causing YaYa to slip under the water. Her hands reached out as her feet went up, but there was nothing for her grab on to. She gulped in a breath of air, but her body protested when she inhaled water instead. She was completely underwater as she struggled to come back up.

Leah's hands wrapped around her neck, and she pressed down with all of her might, making sure YaYa stayed under. She struggled, her body racked with spasms as it begged for her to inhale. She couldn't fight the urge to just breathe, but all she sucked in was water, flooding her lungs. Her insides felt as if they would burst as she dug her nails into Leah's hands. She was desperate for oxygen, but Leah's grip was so tight and YaYa was becoming faint.

The struggle was gruesome as Leah adamantly yelled, "Die already! Just fucking die!" She didn't care that the car would be completely underwater within seconds. She wasn't letting go until YaYa was dead.

YaYa's hands searched the passenger seat. She couldn't see, but she could feel and she frantically patted around. Desperate. Terrified. YaYa felt her life slipping away.

She's going to kill me. I'm dying. The realization hit YaYa like a ton of bricks as she felt the darkness closing in on her. *God, please take care of my daughter,* she silently prayed. Her life flashed in front of her eyes, and she closed them to enjoy the memories. Her hand searched the floor, but her persistence died down as she began to give up.

Her fingertips grazed something hard, something solid, and a tiny ember of hope came alive in her heart. She wrapped her fingers around the handle of the gun. She was so weak that she could barely grip it.

Pull the trigger, just pull the . . .

Water spilled into the car. It was chest high, and they were almost completely submerged, but Leah still wouldn't let go. She could feel the fight leaving YaYa as she drowned her.

Finally YaYa's fingers found their place on the trigger, and using all of her might, YaYa brought the gun up out of the water and fired. It was nothing but the grace of God that the water didn't cause the gun to jam.

Bang!

She didn't even have the strength to aim, but it didn't stop her from hitting her target. Leah's grip loosened instantly as she grabbed her chest, and YaYa popped out of the water.

"Huuuuu!" YaYa gulped in the air as she coughed and choked while water spewed from her mouth and nose uncontrollably. She waded through the neck-high water until she was face to face with Leah. Leah gasped as her own blood reddened the water around her and she went under. Moments later, she popped back up, struggling to keep her head above water as blood leaked from her mouth as she reached out her hand to YaYa.

"Help . . . me," Leah whispered as her eyes pleaded with YaYa.

As the water took over the car, YaYa had to make a split decision—to save Leah or to leave Leah to die. She didn't have time for hesitation; whatever she was going to do, she had to do it now.

Everything in her wanted to leave Leah there to suffer. This was the moment that she had obsessed over. It was what Leah deserved. So why was it so hard for YaYa to walk away? Revenge was bittersweet as YaYa's mind flashed back to the near-death experience she'd had after the fire, to the conversation with her mother where she had been labeled the devil's child. If she left Leah there, then she knew it would be true. Only someone destined for hell could leave Leah to die such an excruciating death.

YaYa hated herself at that moment for wanting her soul to be saved. It would do her great pleasure to leave Leah there, to punish her for all of the ways that Leah had ruined her life. To leave her would be poetic justice, but it would also be the devil's doing. She didn't want to be a puppet on the devil's strings. Her conscience was telling her that she couldn't do it. As much as she wanted to, she couldn't just leave. YaYa realized that it wasn't her place to play judge, jury, and executioner. She had spent far too much time trying to deliver her own version of justice, and by doing so she was writing her own future. She was ruining her own life in the process.

In a split second she thought, *Only God has the power to judge her. It isn't up to me.* YaYa moved forward to grab Leah.

"Damn it!" she screamed as she moved through the water until she was near Leah's side.

Leah gripped YaYa's hand and pulled YaYa into her with surprising strength. The sinister look in her eyes showed her true intentions. YaYa felt the hard steel of the gun press into her stomach as a twisted smile spread across Leah's bloody lips. Sadness filled YaYa's eyes as she realized the mistake she had made. People like Leah didn't deserve forgiveness.

Leah lifted the gun out of the water and pressed it point-blank range against YaYa's forehead.

"Burn in hell," Leah said as she stared YaYa in the eyes.

"I'll see you there," YaYa replied.

Leah pulled the trigger.

<u>Epilogue</u>

It had been a long night of indecision, but as Indie pulled up in front of the church, a calm came over his heart. He knew that he was making the right choice. YaYa was flawed, but his heart wouldn't listen to his head. He couldn't walk away from her. His grandmother had once told him to be the change he wanted to see in the world. It was a saying that he hadn't fully grasped until now.

If he wanted YaYa to be strong, then he had to be strong. He wanted her loyalty, so he had to be loyal. He wanted her unconditional love, so he had to give her his first. He had stayed up all night praying for an answer, but he realized that he didn't need guidance. He already knew what he wanted to do. His heart and mind were in conflict, but emotion overweighed logic whenever it came to YaYa.

He had wanted to call the entire thing off, but he loved her too much to leave her. Marriage was about more than the ups. It had its share of downs as well, and Indie wanted to withstand the trials and tribulations. Everyone in life was going to disappoint him; they just had to be worth it, and YaYa definitely was.

He hadn't spoken to her since he had stormed out, and they had a lot of things to iron out, but today wasn't the day for that. He would address the negativity later. On this day he was just anxious to see his bride.

He waited for the driver to open his door, and then he stepped out of the car. He headed toward the front door, but stopped as he saw Chase sitting on the front stoop.

"You're late to your own wedding," Chase stated.

"It's good to see you, fam," Indie said. "Can't say that I expected you to be here. How did you know?"

"Your mother gave me a call. Couldn't be a wedding without a best man," he said. Chase was so loyal that he had swallowed his pride to let bygones be bygones.

Indie embraced Chase. "I owe you an apology." He was man enough to own up to his mistakes.

"Remember I told you to keep that," Chase said. "It don't need to be said. I didn't want to be right about that one, fam. As long as YaYa gets the help that she needs, everything's love."

"Where's Trina?" Indie asked.

"She went to Houston to get our mama. She's determined to get her clean," Chase replied. "She says she's sorry she couldn't be here."

Indie clasped Chase's shoulder and they walked inside. His mother and father waited with Skylar. Buchanan Slim sat in one of the church's pews.

Indie wasn't a nervous man, but butterflies fluttered in his stomach. This was the biggest leap of faith that a man could make, and he had to admit that he was shook.

Elaine handed Skylar off to her husband Bill and walked over to her son. "YaYa isn't here yet," she said softly.

"I'm forty-five minutes late. What do you mean she isn't here?" he asked with concern.

"She isn't here and we can't reach her," Elaine said. "Did you tell her that you were still coming in? I know after last night—"

"Yeah, of course I did," he said. "I sent her a text. Told her I . . ."

Indie went inside his pocket to retrieve his phone, but realized that he had left it at his mother's home. He checked the Presidential on his wrist.

"She's not that late. We'll just wait. She's coming. She will be here," he said calmly.

Indie took a seat at the front of the church, and as the minutes ticked by, an elephant entered the room. His heart grew so heavy that it weighed down his chest as he realized that there wouldn't be a wedding on that day. If it were up to him, he would have waited all day just to avoid facing the reality of the situation, but when the pastor grew impatient, Indie knew that it was time to go.

He stood to his feet and tried his best not to wear his heart on his sleeve. Loving YaYa had been one of the greatest joys he had ever experienced, but now as he stood without a bride at the altar, he would have preferred to never have encountered love at all.

"I want to thank you all for coming, but there won't be a wedding here today. It's over," Indie said. He placed one hand over his chest and the other in his pocket as he walked out of the church, heart broken by YaYa's absence and defeated in spirit, gripping YaYa's wedding band in his hand.

The End . . . for now.

The Prada Plan 4 Coming January, 2014

ORDER FORM
URBAN BOOKS, LLC
78 E. Industry Ct
Deer Park, NY 11729

Name: (please print):_____

Address: _____

City/State: _____

Zip: _____

QTY	TITLES	PRICE
	16 On The Block	$14.95
	A Girl From Flint	$14.95
	A Pimp's Life	$14.95
	Baltimore Chronicles	$14.95
	Baltimore Chronicles 2	$14.95
	Betrayal	$14.95
	Black Diamond	$14.95
	Black Diamond 2	$14.95
	Black Friday	$14.95
	Both Sides Of The Fence	$14.95
	Both Sides Of The Fence 2	$14.95
	California Connection	$14.95

Shipping and handling-add $3.50 for 1st book, then $1.75 for each additional book.

Please send a check payable to:

Urban Books, LLC

Please allow 4-6 weeks for delivery

ORDER FORM
URBAN BOOKS, LLC
78 E. Industry Ct
Deer Park, NY 11729

Name:(please print):_____

Address: _____

City/State: _____

Zip: _____

QTY	TITLES	PRICE
	California Connection 2	$14.95
	Cheesecake And Teardrops	$14.95
	Congratulations	$14.95
	Crazy In Love	$14.95
	Cyber Case	$14.95
	Denim Diaries	$14.95
	Diary Of A Mad First Lady	$14.95
	Diary Of A Stalker	$14.95
	Diary Of A Street Diva	$14.95
	Diary Of A Young Girl	$14.95
	Dirty Money	$14.95
	Dirty To The Grave	$14.95

Shipping and handling-add $3.50 for 1st book, then $1.75 for each additional book.
Please send a check payable to:
Urban Books, LLC
Please allow 4-6 weeks for delivery

ORDER FORM
URBAN BOOKS, LLC
78 E. Industry Ct
Deer Park, NY 11729

Name:(please print):_____

Address: _____

City/State: _____

Zip: _____

QTY	TITLES	PRICE
	Gunz And Roses	$14.95
	Happily Ever Now	$14.95
	Hell Has No Fury	$14.95
	Hush	$14.95
	If It Isn't love	$14.95
	Kiss Kiss Bang Bang	$14.95
	Last Breath	$14.95
	Little Black Girl Lost	$14.95
	Little Black Girl Lost 2	$14.95
	Little Black Girl Lost 3	$14.95
	Little Black Girl Lost 4	$14.95
	Little Black Girl Lost 5	$14.95

Shipping and handling-add $3.50 for 1st book, then $1.75 for each additional book.
Please send a check payable to:
Urban Books, LLC
Please allow 4–6 weeks for delivery

ORDER FORM
URBAN BOOKS, LLC
78 E. Industry Ct
Deer Park, NY 11729

Name:(please print):_____

Address: _____

City/State: _____

Zip: _____

QTY	TITLES	PRICE

Shipping and handling-add $3.50 for 1st book, then $1.75 for each additional book.

Please send a check payable to:

Urban Books, LLC

Please allow 4–6 weeks for delivery